MW01125998

ERIN'S HERO

Book One

A REAPER Security Novel

Copyright © 2019 by Mary Kennedy

All rights reserved.

This book is a work of fiction. The names, characters, places, and incidents are products of the writer's imagination or have been used fictitiously and are not to be constructed as real. Any resemblance to persons, living or dead, actual events, locales, or organizations is entirely coincidental.

No part of this book may be reproduced in any form or by any electronic or mechanical means, including information storage and retrieval systems, without written permission form the author, except for the use of brief quotations in a book review.

Contents

CHAPTER ONE

Joe Dougall, better known to his teammates as *Nine* for his purported nine lives, always relied on the hardcore Midwestern values his father taught him. A Vietnam veteran and farmer, Joe Sr. believed that hard work would always get you where you wanted to be.

Keep your head down, work hard, don't back talk your elders, and don't start a fight with your betters.

His words still echoed in Joe's head.

His father's beliefs were probably true, thought Joe, although he'd started a fight on more than one occasion that he shouldn't have. Hell…he might just be in a fight he shouldn't be in right now. In a country he had no ties to, didn't give two shits about, and with friends he didn't want to lose. Yea…this might have been a dumb fucking move.

Joe's mother died when he was only three, his dad raised him with the spirit of mother and father; to be honest, loyal, hardworking, God-fearing, and country loving. As long as you respect the flag and you respect the men and women in uniform, all would work out well with Joe Sr. His father was still working the family farm in Iowa that had been worked by three generations of Dougalls'.

Sometimes, no matter how much preparation you put in beforehand, hard work didn't always prepare you for missions like this one.

He hated these contracts. Some stupid corporate fuck had gone into a war zone, without the proper protection, and gotten in trouble and couldn't get out. Probably came into this God-forsaken country to take over some natural resource and found out the locals didn't appreciate good ole American industriousness.

These missions were exactly the kind that his team was known for taking on and conquering. All of his team was handpicked – former SEALS, Delta, SWAT, Firefighters, Bomb Squad, hackers and computer geeks. If you could pass the background, intense training, multiple interviews and the litany of tests that you were put through, then you could become a part of REAPER Security...AFTER...you proved yourself.

Joe and his former SEAL teammate Wilson – Dan William Anderson – started the company, with a few other trusted men. Joe and Dan bonded during training over the fact that everyone always tried to make their first names formal – *Joseph and Daniel* – when it was plain old Joe and Dan.

As each new team member joined, they received the option to buy into the company. Joe wanted everyone to feel ownership and leadership in the organization. He was essentially the CEO, but his teammates were equal partners. He trained all of them to take on that leadership role and get shit done when it needed to get done. He didn't have time to be a kindergarten teacher. Know your shit, do your shit, and accomplish the mission – if you could do that, then you were good with Joe.

He trusted each one of his men like a brother. Hell, they were his brothers in every sense of the word that counted. They were well trained, armed to the teeth, and had absolutely no qualms about shooting the bad guys if needed. They had sworn an oath to protect against all enemies, foreign and domestic, and in their eyes – despite retirement – they had not been relieved of that duty.

Dryden Corporation, a major contractor for the US military contacted Joe with the information that one Dr. EG Richards had been kidnapped. No ransom requested from the captors, not surprising thought Joe. Dr. Richards, however, was a value to the organization and they needed the good doctor back. Dryden's request had gone all the way to General Murray and he, in turn, had become Joe's reluctant contact at base.

The problem for Joe was that the general hadn't been very forthcoming with information. He seemed almost reluctant to give his team any intel on the area, chatter from sources on the potential whereabouts of Dr. Richards, or even what time coffee would be served. In fact, he'd gone to extra efforts to slow them down at every turn. First, it was the inspection of their team's equipment taking two days. Then it was the endless questions from the MPs about why they were on base. Little things that sent the nagging tingling sizzles up Joe's spine.

Joe's only info given on their package was 5'8", American, and could answer the question "What was your first dog's name?" with the appropriate response of Finn.

At six-foot-three and a bulky, yet lean, muscled two hundred and twenty-five pounds, Joe was an intimidating force. His intensive blue eyes made women swoon at his feet and made men back down in a heartbeat. He had his share of women, no doubt, although lately he just didn't seem to be interested in the offerings. Oh, his dick still got hard, but every boy from the age of thirteen on knew how to solve that problem and he wasn't averse to taking matters into his own hand... literally.

His closely cropped hair was a dark brown, although lately he'd noticed a few silver strands peeking through. He wore his beard long – just above his collarbone. He could still outrun men half his age and he didn't back down from any fight. Ever. This is what he was born to do and he would do it until he died.

Ahead, he saw his teammate, Trak, raise his hand to still them all in the night.

Their comms were quiet – intentionally. The team's cover was minimal in this area – rocks, a few small bushes and a lone tree scattered here and there. The village below was full of small huts that looked as though with one good push, they would simply crumble. The activity in the village was minimal – which may or may not be a good sign, he thought.

Trak had been observing the small collection of houses for nearly three hours now. At the center of the village was a small hut where on two different occasions someone had entered with food or water and left with nothing in their hands. That's where their package would be located. Simple extraction – in and out, and get the fuck home.

Then why did Joe have that feeling in the pit of his stomach? The feeling that he always listened to because it was always right?

Signaling his men, they made their way quietly down the side of the sparse hill, careful not to loosen any dirt or rocks in the process. Despite their size and weight – all over six feet and more than 200 pounds - they moved as gracefully as a ninety-pound ballerina.

The plan was simple – eliminate any threats as quietly as possible, disable any vehicles, use lethal force if necessary, minimal collateral damage and no innocents harmed; grab the package and meet their extraction team 4.5 kilometers west.

Two men flanked his left, Miller and Code; and two men his right, Trak, with Wilson immediately to his right. Wilson was his most trusted friend and first partner in their security venture.

Joe watched the men making their way carefully between the huts. It was odd, no noise was heard at all; not even a dog barking. They obviously didn't think much of their guest if there was only one guard at the entrance of the hut. Wilson slowly moved past Joe, the large man casting a shadow over his own six-foot-three frame. His quietness belied his size, but Joe knew the deadly abilities of his friend and teammate better than anyone.

Wilson tapped the guard lightly on the shoulder and with one swift movement slammed the butt of his weapon into the man's face, catching him before he even hit the ground.

Damn that man is scary, thought Joe.

Wilson carefully sat the man against the hut, making it appear as though he had fallen asleep. No one would be the wiser for hours.

Inside the small hut was an open space, single room. That certainly made search easier. Quietly entering the room, they noticed to the left of the entrance sat a soldier who looked more like a teenaged boy. His head was bobbing up and down in an attempt to not fall asleep. He heard the rustling of their fabric and sat up quickly in surprise, before he could make a sound, Joe had punched his throat dead center, and he fell, gasping for air. With another solid hit, he was out cold.

Lying on a dirty pallet in the corner, Joe saw a white robe covering a lumpy figure. The man seemed smaller than he expected, but then again, he was some sort of egghead doctor who probably hadn't seen the inside of a gym since grade school.

Joe knelt beside the pallet and touched the shoulder. "Sir," he said softly, "Sir, we're here to get you out. Can you hear me?" He nudged the body and felt for a pulse on the small wrist.

The pulse was there, but so was something else, chipped red nail polish. "What the fucking hell!" His words were barely audible, but Wilson stepped closer. Fuck – it was a woman. A God damned woman. Rolling her on her back, he looked at her bruised and bloodied face. "Fuck!"

"Please don't hit me again, please," she whimpered softly attempting to lift her hands in protection. Her auburn hair was lying across her face tangled around her neck and chest, dirty and bloody. He brushed the strands so she could see him more clearly.

"I'm not going to hit you," he said softly. His tone changing from frustration to concern. "I'm here to help you. I'm an American. What's your name?"

"Dr. Erin Richards," she replied breathlessly.

"Erin? E.G. Richards?" he stated, grinding his teeth together. There it was again… that feeling.

"Yes, Dr. Erin G. Richards," she said.

"What was your childhood dog's name?" he asked.

"What? My dog? I... my dog... was Finn... why?" she asked confused. She looked into his face for the first time, the dim lighting revealing the rough etching of stress and strain in every line. His beard was long with fine strands of gray, which only enhanced the shining, startling clear blue eyes – clear and sexy.

Sexy? Wait – stop Erin! You're in pain and probably going to die and all you can think about is Mr. Sexy? It's a dream... that must be it... he's a dream.

He looked at her once again and nodded. "Did you say you were DOCTOR Erin G. Richards?"

"Yes, Erin Georgia Richards, but I'm not an MD – I'm a PhD."

"Nine." Joe heard Wilson's voice behind him. "We gotta go. What do we do with her?"

"We fucking rescue her. That's what we were paid for." He hated having to drag a woman through this desert shithole of a country – but she was his responsibility until he could hand her off.

"Can you stand?" he asked her, grasping her elbow to help lift her from the pallet.

"Yes," she replied weakly, sitting beside his kneeling body, her hood from the robe fell and her wavy auburn hair fell down her back. Dirty, tangled, hair that matted at her hairline with blood, caked with mud and God knew what else.

But all Joe could think about was wrapping it around his fist. He felt a stirring in his pants and willed himself to focus. What the fuck was he thinking? This woman was in pain and clearly had zero common sense getting herself involved in whatever this shit was. *Down boy* he thought to himself.

She tried to stand using his arm as leverage and he could see the pain it caused her.

"Let us take a look," he said grasping her chin between his thumb and forefinger a little too hard. She let out a hiss of pain and winced.

Wilson eyed him, "Nine, we have to get her out of here. I'll carry her until we can get to a safe place."

Joe reluctantly nodded and Wilson gathered her in his arms. She let a small moan escape her as the big man wrapped her up easily in his arms. His six-foot-six frame enveloping her in safety for the first time in days, but causing her bruised and battered body to cry for relief. "Sorry, sunshine," he whispered.

As quietly as they entered, they left the small village and worked their way back up the side of the mountain. When they found a small shaded area a few kilometers from the village, Wilson set her down to take a look at her injuries.

The other men surrounded her, watching the night for any signs of movement. Nothing, absolutely nothing. Joe's stomach rolled again. No one waking. No one chasing. What the fuck was going on?

"Let's see what we have," said Wilson in a soft sweet voice that once again belied his size. Taking a sterile wipe from his pack, he gently wiped the wounds on her face clean revealing fine delicate features. Her ivory skin illuminated in the moonlight; her hazel-green eyes glowed. Her lips were swollen and cracked, bleeding from one too many punches, but he could tell they would be beautiful when healed.

Wilson ran some steri-strips along the largest cuts just to close the wounds. He wiped away the blood as best he could, revealing a black eye and several small cuts in her hairline. Her left hand was grotesquely swollen and bruised. He lifted it to look more closely and she winced in pain with a small tear escaping her eyes.

"Sorry, sunshine, I have to check," Wilson's large brown eyes were warm and sympathetic; his touch was gentle and kind. But pain is pain.

"It's broken," she said softly, "I set it myself two days ago. The two men who were torturing me took turns stepping on it." She gave an indifferent shrug and looked away.

Joe was standing over Wilson's shoulder and winced, knowing the pain that must have caused her. "You set it yourself?" Wilson said raising an eyebrow. All of the men in the circle did a slight turn in admiration, raising eyebrows out of respect for the tiny woman.

"I had to. It was starting to go numb." She gave a slight nod as if it were no big deal. "I think I have a rib or two broken as well. They seemed to enjoy practicing their soccer kicks on me." *Good*, he thought, *she hasn't lost her sense of humor.*

"I'm going to touch your rib cage," he said before laying his large hands on her sides. She winced but said nothing. "I think they're severely bruised, but I don't think they're broken."

Joe stepped forward, "We have to go," he said looking from Wilson to her large eyes. He placed his hand below her elbow, helping her to stand and she let out a small cry, whimpering silently. "Can you make it?" he said more harshly than he had intended.

Not saying another word, she moved quietly behind Wilson and followed his footsteps. She heard other men around her, felt their presence, even though she couldn't see them clearly, she knew they must be welcome if her two heroes were not alarmed.

Without a word, they made their way back up the mountain. She knew her injuries were slowing them down, but they had no choice. They couldn't carry her and their packs.

In the distance, they could see that all hell broke loose in the village below, screaming, lights illuminating the small homes, men running from every hut like cockroaches scurrying to their next meal.

"I think they know I'm gone," she said, her voice shaking slightly. She turned back up toward the mountain and moved again, slowly, pushing herself, one foot, then the other. Her white canvas tennis shoes were not ideal for mountain climbing and the pain in her feet was excruciating. But she wasn't about to stop and let her saviors know. They had to move.

"Yep – double time," said Joe. They moved with efficiency, willing her, pulling her, forcing her up the mountain with them. At the top, a young blonde man sat down on the rocks and Joe gave him the signal to turn their comms back on and call for extraction. Erin leaned against a large boulder to catch her breath, every inhale and exhale causing her pain.

"Whiskey One, this is Whiskey Two, we are a go for extraction." There was no sound at first. Dead air only. Then a strained voice.

"Whiskey Two this is Whiskey One – negative on extraction. We have a large sandstorm headed to your area. Extraction will now be 7.4 kilometers west... sending coordinates now. Find cover. We can't risk an extraction tonight. Be ready and able at 0400 tomorrow."

Joe grabbed the sat phone and through gritted teeth.

"Whiskey One this is Whiskey Two, command, say again?"

"Simple Whiskey Two – change of extraction location due to sandstorm rolling in."

"Fuck!" he said aloud.

She stood quietly in the dark, leaning against the only tree on the wretched mountain. She watched each of the men carefully. She was the cause of this. She shouldn't have been here. Her driver was dead. Her interpreter was dead. Her colleagues were dead. But they had kept her alive. And now these men might have to pay the price. She stepped out of the darkness as they were whispering to one another.

"Take me back," she said calmly. They all stopped and looked up. Confusion filled their faces. "Take me back," she said again.

"I don't think so, sweetheart. We were paid to extract you and that's what we're going to do." Joe's words came out hard and without emotion, and he immediately regretted the tone.

What the fuck? When have I ever regretted the tone of my words?

"Paid? By whom?" she asked tilting her head to the side.

"Your employer," he said matter-of-factly.

"Look, ummm sorry, you have me at a disadvantage. You all know my name, but I don't know your names."

"I'm Nine, that's Wilson, Code, Miller, and Trak."

"Cute," she said under her breath. "Listen, my employer wouldn't pay for you to get me back. They wouldn't do that. They don't care. They told me they wouldn't help if anything happened."

"Well, they did care, sweetheart, and we're getting you out." He placed emphasis on the word *sweetheart* somehow knowing it would annoy her, and again his tone was harsh, but this time he meant it. Who the fuck did she think she was questioning his mission to save her ass?

"Listen to me," she pulled his arm with a force that surprised him, and she hissed in pain at the movement. "First – I'm not your sweetheart. My name is Erin. And second, they WOULD NOT because I wasn't sent by my employer. I was sent by yours – the U.S. military."

They looked at one another. It didn't matter that Erin thought they were regular military at this point, but her words did matter. Not a lot shocked Joe any longer, but this one did. What the fuck was happening and why was this woman in the middle of this hellhole?

"We have to move," said Wilson glancing down the mountain side at the amassing group of villagers.

Quickly moving through the short trees, the rocks under her feet painful, she continued to move obediently. Two men were behind her – the man named Wilson and sexy blue eyes – Nine.

Shit! Stop it, Erin.

In front were the men named Code and Miller, and the other she assumed was Trak, but she couldn't see or hear him.

After what seemed like hours, they stopped, resting on a grouping of large boulders. The night sky was still dark, filled with stars, but she knew that dawn was approaching fast and that would put them in more danger – in the daylight and visible to all.

The one in charge handed her a bottle of water.

"We need to get you out of those robes," he said quietly.

Her eyebrows lifted, immediately causing her pain and she winced.

"I didn't mean like that," he chuckled in the darkness, "I meant they're slowing you down and it's too obvious. We need to get you in civilian clothes. We brought extra thinking you were a man, so they may be big." He tossed her the tan t-shirt, fleece jacket, and matching camo-tan pants with a belt.

Waiting, he stood watching her as she lifted the heavy robes over her head, pain streaking up her side as she nearly cried out. The thin white t-shirt that she had worn under the robes was covered in blood but didn't do much for covering up her massive breasts. He could see her large nipples poking through in the cool mountain air. Her tiny pink thong barely covered her front apex and he could only dream of what lay beneath. She stopped, staring at him, staring at her.

Frustrated that he had been caught, he turned and walked away only to discover his four men doing the same.

"Turn around," he ordered, "give her some fucking privacy. You've all seen a woman before."

"Not like that," said Wilson under his breath smiling.

Taking advantage of the momentary respite, they grabbed a few nutrition bars from their packs, and then carefully wrapped up any evidence, ensuring that the boulder looked exactly as when they arrived.

She walked toward the grouping of men, the t-shirt hugging every curve of her full breasts. The pants were baggy and cinched tight with the belt, but couldn't hide the subtle line of curvy hips and a round hard ass. Everything in him stirred and his cock instantly sprang to attention.

"Shit." He muttered under his breath. *Fucking shit. This is all I need.*

Her face, in the waning moonlight, was tinged with purple, yellow, and green bruises. The varying colors giving away the age of each one. Her lips, split and bloodied, couldn't hide her beauty. Her mass of auburn hair hung wildly down her back as she stood in silence.

"Shit!" said Code suddenly. "Shit, Shit! You're her! You're that fucking genius scientist that figured out how to stop chemical weapons once they're initiated! Fucking hell – that's her!" His excitement was like a kid who had just met his favorite superhero.

She stared at them all, suddenly unsure what she should say or admit.

"Say what?" said Joe – looking from Code to her. "Explain, sweeth... Erin."

She gave a small painful smile at his use of her given name.

"I tried to tell you earlier. That's why I was brought here. We suspected that the Taliban will be using chemical weapons on their own, as well as our people. I found a way to neutralize the major chemical component they will supposedly use. I was here to test my design. I was on the way to a secure lab when my driver, colleagues, and interpreter were all killed and I was taken. I was told if I was taken, they would not come for me."

"Well, surprise, surprise – they sent us for you." His sarcasm vaguely masked his anger and Erin knew the big man was pissed.

"I'm not happy that you're in danger either Mr... sorry you didn't tell me your name."

"No." he said harshly, "No I didn't. Just call me Nine. Let's move. If we have a sandstorm coming, we need shelter."

Setting a course west, they moved through the rocky terrain – Wilson and Code in the lead, Miller at the rear, and Joe, right behind her perfect, wiggling ass. Fuck.

CHAPTER TWO

He watched her ass move back and forth in front of him, the soft sway of a woman's hips, and the curve from the small of her back to those beautiful round ass cheeks. His groin was on fire and he couldn't even control it. Her legs were long and the cinched waist of the trousers that were too big only emphasized every damn curve.

How long had it been? A year? No wait, he fucked that cute blonde in Virginia the day before their last mission – she was early 20s, eager, and wanted to fuck a SEAL – albeit a retired one. But before that – nothing worth note for a long time.

Thinking of this woman lying beneath him, he completely lost focus and tripped on a large stone. Catching himself before he hit, he cursed under his breath and looked up to see her tiny hand extended to him. Her long, pretty, chipped red nails reaching for his rough bear paws. She stood so close he could smell the remnants of her perfume, a mixture of some sort of flower and vanilla, mixed with sweat and dust. He didn't take her hand, but stood and held himself at his full height looking down at her.

She swallowed hard. This man was imposing and scary, very scary. He wasn't as tall as the gentle giant Wilson, but he was probably only shy a few inches. Yet there was something that screamed to her and she wanted to push back, but couldn't.

He suddenly realized four sets of eyes were boring into him. Everyone else had stopped as well. Wilson cleared his throat.

"Nine, we need to take a break."

"We don't need a fucking break," he growled.

"Maybe you don't," Wilson said, then slowly pointed at Erin's feet, "but she does." Looking down he saw the blood-soaked canvas on her cheap shoes.

"Sit down," he said, almost pushing her to the dirt floor. She mouthed a small "ouch" and he immediately regretted his roughness.

"Why didn't you say something?" he scolded her.

"Because we can't stop," she said softly. He heard the pain and exhaustion in her voice and felt like a complete ass.

Wilson was already at her feet, gently removing her shoes, but also removing most of her skin with it. She sucked in a breath, tears silently falling down her cheeks. She learned to cry in silence. Quiet was good.

"Wholly fuck – what did they do?" Wilson swallowed hard, knowing that he was hurting her. The bottoms of her feet were like one huge busted blister, skin peeling away, red and raw. They were bleeding in spots and Wilson shook his head in disbelief that this woman had kept up as long as she had.

She gave a gentle shrug the tears flowing freely down her face.

"It was their way of making sure I didn't run. At least once a day someone would come and beat the bottoms of my feet. I think they used a cane, but honestly I couldn't tell."

Wilson's bear paw hands gently held her feet in his lap.

"Nine, I need a space to work." He looked at his team leader and then back at the adorable woman in front of him. "This is gonna hurt like fuck, sunshine."

"Cave," came the low baritone voice.

"Fuck!" Nine breathed jumping slightly, "Trak, could you give a guy a warning?"

"Nope. That makes me less effective. Cave," he repeated, "eight hundred meters."

Erin looked up at the tall man behind the man named Wilson. Trak. That was an interesting name. He gave a slight smile to her, barely perceptible, but something about him made Erin feel instantly calm and safe.

Wilson moved to pick Erin up in his arms, but Joe was there pushing him gently.

"I'll carry her, you go set up." He lifted her against his chest and held her as if she would break. She barely weighed more than his pack, but his pack didn't have voluptuous curves and damned if his cock didn't take notice.

She watched his face, the etched lines, hard and soft at the same time. She saw the worry that was coming from his near-glowing blue eyes and the questions he didn't want to ask. The power coming from him was so overwhelming Erin half expected a spark of electricity to occur between their bodies.

Entering the cave, he gently laid her next to Wilson's equipment and moved his body to sit behind her so that she could lean against him as Wilson worked.

Wilson looked at Erin with his huge brown eyes, looking as though he was telling his childhood dog, he was going to have to put him down.

"I have to clean them and wrap them, sunshine. It's going to be painful, but I need for you to try not to scream. Can you do that?"

She nodded at him knowing that the cleaning would be painful. She knew enough medicine to understand that her wounds, although not life-threatening, would be extremely sensitive and certainly could become infected. Any antibacterial cleanser would feel like fire on her feet.

Nine held one arm across her chest securing her arms to her side, resting his tree trunk-sized legs on either side of her curvy frame, cradling her back against his massive chest. He whispered in her ear.

"It's going to hurt, I'm going to cover your mouth with my scarf, don't be afraid."

Chills ran down her spine, but she nodded and waited. Wilson was trying to be as gentle as possible. Code and Miller stood at the cave opening – half watching her – half watching the terrain. In the distance, she saw the one they called Trak.

Wilson washed her feet with water first, gently wiping away the dirt and using his surgical scissors cutting away the flesh that had fallen from them. He then soaked the cloth and gently placed the antiseptic on her feet. Her body tensed in pain and she held in her screams, breathing heavily into Nine's scarf, trying to concentrate on his smell – sweat, testosterone and something far more dangerous.

Tears rolled down her dirty, sweat-stained cheeks and her shoulders shuddered – once, twice. Nine rubbed his cheek along the side of her head, his whiskers making a strange scratching sound against her hair – but it was oddly comforting.

"The worst is over," said Wilson, patting her calf. "I'm just going to place some antibiotic ointment on them and wrap them up. The ointment has lidocaine, so it should numb them somewhat. We brought boots for you – well for the man we thought you were – they'll be big, but each of us can give you a pair of socks and with the bandages, they should fit. I can give you something for the pain, Erin. Something to help you sleep."

She shook her head and he could see the pain in her eyes.

"No, I would rather stay awake. Thank you." Her voice was barely audible. The utter exhaustion from having pushed herself to the limit.

She had guts; Wilson would give her that. But what Wilson noticed even more, was his hard-assed boss cradling her in his arms, rocking her like a baby. She hadn't even noticed and he doubted Nine did either. The men were grinning at each other and they all turned outward, giving them this moment.

"We can't keep pushing her like this," he said to Nine. "She's in pain and bleeding. We need to stay here at least until the storm is blown over – that is, if it ever hits."

Nine looked at him and nodded. Silently giving him instructions.

"I'm so sorry," she said, her voice frail and soft. She had been tough and non-complaining to this point, but it was as if she were giving up.

I don't think so, sweetheart, he thought, *not on my watch.*

"Joe," he said in her ear.

"What?" she turned her head up to see him, leaning further into his chest, all muscles and hardness. She felt his heartbeat – the rhythmic tap against her shoulder.

"My real name is Joe – not Nine," he smiled, "for real."

"Joe," she nodded, repeating the name, the sound of it soft and sweet coming from her lips. "Thank you, Joe," she said her eyes sleepy, she inched closer and placed a soft kiss against his lips and then she was out.

"Wilson!" he barked. Kneeling beside her, he felt for her pulse.

"She's fine, Nine," he said smiling at him, "she's exhausted that's all. I would imagine the local village people kept her up all night and it wasn't to sing YMCA."

Code knelt beside the two men – Miller still standing in the entry of the cave.

"Nine, Wilson," he said sounding winded, "we have an issue. I just spoke to a connection at base camp – there isn't a sandstorm within a thousand miles of this fucking place."

Wilson looked at Code and back to Nine.

"What the fuck, boss?"

"Someone didn't want us to get to the extraction point." He said flat and plain. No emotion.

He gently moved from behind Erin, laying her carefully down, her head resting on his pack. He watched her head roll to the side and he saw the vicious bruise in full light on her cheek and neck. He swore under his breath and gently pushed back a lock of hair.

"She'll sleep, Nine," said Wilson, "when she wakes, she'll be sore, but she's one tough woman. I know men that wouldn't have been able to hobble on those feet and that fucking woman did it for miles."

"You sound like you admire her," Joe said in a voice mixed with admiration and jealousy.

"Yep," he grinned. His big friend smiled at him, his brown eyes shining in the dim light of the cave. "And so do you. That woman has been through hell and that's only what we see."

He stopped and Joe looked up at him quickly, realizing that his friend was right and he had behaved like a jackass. He had no idea what those men had done to her. Shit! They didn't even ask if she had been violated. He glanced down at her sleeping and he knew that if it killed him, he would get her out of this fucking mess.

⋅ ⋅≫⋅⁚‾‾‾‾‾‾═◄╪►═ ‾⁚⋅≪⋅ ⋅

She opened her eyes and saw the dim purple light of dawn creeping into the cave.

Cave. She remembered laying down, but how? *Think*, she told herself. The one named Nine, no, he had said his name was Joe. He carried her. Laid her here. Her feet – she stretched her toes and immediately wished she hadn't.

It was painful, but honestly, she could feel the difference just with them having been cleaned and bandaged. The big one with the soft brown eyes, Wilson. Yea that was him, he had been so gentle and caring. She pushed herself up on her elbow.

"Hello, sunshine," said Wilson in a way too chipper voice.

"Coffee," she grinned, "where's my coffee, good man?" He smiled at her and gave a soft chuckle, happy that she felt normal enough to joke with him.

"Sorry, sunshine, MRE of the day is all you get."

"The service here isn't much better than where I left," she attempted to wink at him and immediately regretted it, her face sore and bruised.

"Slow down, sunshine. That face is healing nicely and I'd hate for you to ruin my good work." She gently ran her fingers over the steri-strips he had artfully placed on her cuts. She nodded and he handed her a ration.

"Shouldn't we get moving?" she said, knowing the longer they stayed put the worse things could get for them.

"Not yet." She jumped at the sound of the voice that sent shivers down her spine, and warmth to areas she shouldn't be thinking about right now.

He had been sitting behind her and she didn't even know it. Was he a cat or something?

"We have no sandstorm, but we do have thunderstorms and that will make it dangerous and being daylight, we're sitting ducks. We wait until tonight and if the rain has stopped, we may leave. Trak is scouting now. Code called base. We wait."

Trak, she wracked her brain, right, the quiet one with the dark hair that you could barely see or hear. Okay – five men – Wilson – big guy, medic, sweet brown eyes; Code – communications guy – looked like a young Robert Redford; Miller – shortest of them but still tall, solid like a defensive lineman, but looked meaner than a bag of snakes; and Mr. big, strong, sexy blue eyes and lips... *what the hell*... she chided herself. Oh shit! She had kissed him. Last night she kissed him. Her eyes widened as she looked at him and he gave a sexy sinful grin as if telling her he remembered as well.

"You okay, Erin?" he said in a sideways grin to her. She nodded and turned away, curling her legs beneath her. They continued to talk and she scribbled in the sand, formulas stuck in her head. Why? She continued to ask herself. Why?

"Penny for your thoughts?" Wilson lowered his towering frame to sit next to her.

"It's all wrong. All wrong," she said.

"Yea, I hear ya, sunshine. It's definitely fucked up, but these things happen. That's why we don't like civilians in war zones; it's not healthy for any of us." He flashed her a winning smile, which she was sure had melted the panties off many a woman, but it wasn't quite having that effect for her. Oh, he was definitely gorgeous and had a body that she knew would knock a girl's socks off, but there wasn't a spark or a sizzle.

"Yes that I know. But did any of you ever wonder why they didn't tell you I was a woman? Why they told you this was private industry, not government?"

Wilson looked from her face to the face of the others. They had all wondered, but hadn't discussed it yet. He could see their wheels turning. Joe sat on the side of her, staring into her face.

"They sent me here intentionally. By. Request. Actually, by order. Oh, it was in agreement and cooperation with Dryden alright. But my father, General Murray was the one that sent me here." That raised a few eyebrows and Erin had a sinking feeling these men knew something of her father. "They told me no one would come if I were in trouble. This was supposed to be easy and I would be serving my country." *And Daddy's sick twisted plans*, she thought.

"Routine is the word they used. Get in, inspect the lab, leave. But those men that took me? They were waiting for me. They knew I was there and they knew where and how to find me. They sent for someone who was supposed to pick me up today. I don't speak much Farsi, but they called him Orion."

Joe's eyebrows raised and the hair on his arms stood up. He knew the name, everyone did. Known for his torture techniques and his gruesome results. No one ever lived to tell of their time with Orion. He had connections in drugs, human trafficking, weapons, and more. He was not someone that you wanted to fuck. Orion was on the top five list of every agency in the world. The only problem was no one even knew what the motherfucker looked like.

"We leave tonight," he said standing. She looked from one man to the next. "Get some rest," he ordered. She stood, gingerly placing weight on her feet, as he glared at her.

"I need to pee," she said shyly.

His frustration wasn't meant to be slung at her, but he couldn't help it.

"Further in the cave, sweetheart, just pull your pants down and hover that pretty ass of yours over the hole in the ground and go," he said laughing but immediately realizing it was a nervous laughter.

Wilson winced at his attempt at humor and he thought he heard Miller groan.

Normally the quiet obedient type, her anger bubbled to the surface and she finally reached her limit of testosterone that took delight in belittling and demeaning her.

"Hey!" She shouted at him as he started to walk away. He didn't stop, just kept walking. "Hey, asshat!" That made him stop and turn, giving her a look that sent chills through her body.

"What did you call me?" he said squinting at her. His men chuckled but his look quieted them instantly.

"I called you asshat. All I asked for was a place to pee. I realize that I have greatly inconvenienced you. I realize I'm slowing you down. But in the last seven days I've been beaten, repeatedly, starved, questioned until I didn't have a voice anymore, deprived of sleep, and nearly raped, twice. So how about you cut me some fucking slack!"

She turned, with great effort moving her feet, and walked to the back of the cave with the small light Wilson had handed her. She found the hole and let the darkness envelop her.

He cursed himself for his insensitive comment. Wisely, his men made no comment at all.

Erin finished her business and belted the pants, which were easily three sizes too big. She was no stick figure. She had curves for days. Her father always called her plump. But she knew that some men liked her curves. She could tell by their looks, the way they eyed her up and down as if she was their last meal. But even these pants swallowed her curvy frame.

Her feet were throbbing and every step had her sweating profusely. She stopped short of her resting place, her hand on the cold jagged rock. She felt it coming, but couldn't control it. Her hand immediately went to her mouth, trying desperately to quiet her sobs, her emotions completely overwhelming her.

They all heard the soft cries, the sounds carrying in the cave. She held it together for so long, and his one insensitive comment sent her emotions on a landslide. They looked from one man to the next, wondering who would go to her.

Wilson made the first move, leaning his weapon against the cave wall. He felt Joe's large hand press against his chest.

"No. I made her cry. I'll fix this." Wilson looked at his friend.

"She doesn't need fixing, Joe – she needs comforting." Wilson grabbed his weapon and let his friend pass.

She hadn't heard him approach, hadn't felt his presence until he laid a hand on her shoulder.

"I'm sorry, Doc. I didn't mean to make you cry."

"Don't call me doc," she sniffled shrugging off his hand, "I told you I'm… "

"I know, I know," he chuckled, "you're not that kind of doc. I was just trying to be respectful." His hand stilled once more on her shoulder, he nudged her closer and wrapped both of his arms around her, pulling her into his warmth.

She laid her head against his chest, rubbing her face against the concrete that was him, and let the tears flow. He smelled so good and felt so hard and safe. Safe. That was a word she hadn't used in a long time.

"You've been through more than most men could handle. It's okay to cry." She only nodded against his chest as he slid his hands up and down her back, making small massaging circles.

"I'm alright now," she whispered, looking up at him. She attempted to push back from him, but he held her firmly against him.

"Is there a mister doc back home?" he said with a sly grin.

"What?" she asked confused, "Oh, no, ummm, no one."

"Good," he said quickly. He couldn't take his eyes off her. Her eyes turned a mossy green with flecks of yellow that were almost glowing in the cave light. Her lips, swollen, were still red and inviting. He was struggling with his control. He shouldn't take advantage of her. She was scared and injured.

But when she moved ever so slightly toward his face, he couldn't resist any longer. He lowered his head, placing his warm lips gently against her bruised ones, careful not to open her wounds again. Once, twice, three times he touched her lips, pushing a stray mass of hair behind her ear.

"What was that for?" she said breathless, her heart beating wildly now.

"That was because you're beautiful and I'm an asshat," he grinned down at her. "And, I wanted to." He kissed the tip of her nose as if to emphasize his point.

She couldn't allow herself to think about this man in this way. Not now. She would place him in more danger. She knew what it was. He was her rescuer. This stuff happens. Right?

Who are you trying to convince Erin? Yourself?

Still, she couldn't resist. With the distance only inches between them, she pressed her body harder against him and received her confirmation. He was rock hard and wanted her as badly as she wanted him.

CHAPTER THREE

He held her hips tight against his groin and looked in her eyes, hungry, scared, lusting eyes. His instincts knew she wasn't the type of woman to do something so impulsively. Somehow, he knew that to his core.

Her left hand was slowly coming up around his neck and with a gentle tug, she pulled his mouth to hers. Softly touching, while her lips stayed on his, he explored with his tongue.

He felt her leg creep up his thigh and he grabbed her ass cheeks pulling her against him, her legs wrapping around his waist. The heat of her pussy through her trousers, against his bulging cock made him groan, grinding harder against her core. He allowed her to feel his size – she could no doubt feel it through her pants. He slid his hands down the back of her loose-fitting pants, needing to feel her skin, and his eyes flew wide.

She pulled away breathless, smiling a shy smile.

"The panties were dirty. I couldn't put them back on so I stuffed them in my pocket."

He gave her a sexy, approving smile, lustful and admiring. She had the common sense not to leave something so western where their followers could find it.

He pushed her harder against the cold cave wall and thrust his now pulsing cock against her heat. She whimpered, gyrating her hips, rolling against him, feeling the rigid beast against her sex. She couldn't think, couldn't breathe. She only knew that she needed this release or she would surely die. And if she were going to die, at least she would have one final orgasm.

It had been so long all it took was one hard push and her body shuddered in satisfaction. She lowered her head against his shoulder and he stroked her hair, breathing in the remnants of her shampoo. Erin reached between them, sliding her hand down his still rigid cock, feeling the impressive length beneath. He grabbed her wrist gently and held her there.

"Not now. I can wait," he said his voice rough and raw. It was as if he'd slapped Erin across the face.

"But I couldn't?" she said, sounding offended. He smiled and pushed a strand of stray hair behind her ear.

"That's not what I meant, Erin. But I have to keep a clear head. I like you; I really do. But I shouldn't have done that. That's not part of my job."

He knew the moment he said those words they were wrong. *Typical*, he thought. *You fucked up again.*

"Job?" she said a little too loudly. He held up his fingers to his own lips to shush her. "Fuck quiet! That's what that was? Your job? Well news flash dickhead, I didn't need you to calm me down or keep me rational. I was doing fine without you." She started to walk away and turned, seeing his hard, pinched face.

"Do me a favor, *Nine*, just do your *job* and stay away from me." The use of his team name meant she was seriously pissed at him.

She wobbled on aching feet and sat down against the wall near the front of the cave. Wilson stared down through the cave darkness seeking his friend's eyes, giving him a look that Nine understood – he had fucked up.

Miller knelt next to her, his bulky, hard, and tattooed body seemingly straining to do so. He handed her an MRE and some water and not even knowing it was there, he brushed a tear away from her cheek.

"He's not always such a prick," he said in a quiet voice. "It just seems that you've gotten under his skin. And that pretty lady is not normal at all." With that he stood and walked outside, standing next to Wilson.

"Get some sleep." She jumped at the sound of his voice. "We leave at sundown." She didn't respond, instead she rolled over and lay her head against Joe's pack again, shutting her eyes, willing the last week out of her mind.

He stood on the ridge overlooking the valley below. He looked over his shoulder briefly, ensuring she hadn't followed him. Miller and Wilson stood next to him. They both had the common sense not to question him about Erin. He would have to figure this shit out, but not here, not now.

"Orion," he said flatly.

"Yea, fucking Orion," said Miller, almost spitting the name from his lips.

"Do you know what would have happened to her if he had gotten his hands on her?" said Wilson, the concern in him genuine.

"Yea, dip wad, I know, I fucking know." He stepped back dragging his hand over his close-cropped hair. "Sorry, man." Wilson nodded.

"All of this stinks like shit, man. We're hired to pick up an EG Richards for Dryden Corporation, via Mr. Dryden himself – no word that it's a female. We get a descriptor from the good General – who we now know is 'Daddy,' which by the way was pretty accurate – five-foot-eight, auburn hair, green eyes – they just didn't mention she had a pussy, instead of a dick. According to Mr. Dryden she's critical to their organization. So, we get the orders and General Murray at base takes it from there.

"Then Code boy over there recognizes Miss America as some fucking super scientist that could help put a stop to all the shit Orion is doing. She claims she's working for good old Uncle Sam. So, who the fuck hired us and who the fuck is she really working for?" That was the most any of them had ever heard Miller say at one time, in all their years of working together. He finished his speech and walked over the ridge, squatting, watching, and waiting.

Wilson eyed his friend, watching him take in all that Miller had said.

"Well?"

"Well what?" he snarled. "We have a fucking job to do. I'll get my answers."

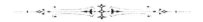

They were hitting her again. Beating her. It was the same two men, but they were forcing the villagers to beat her as well. They even forced the women to hit her. She didn't understand their statements, didn't understand what they were asking her. She brought her arms up to block the blows to her face.

"Wake up. Erin, it's Joe, honey, wake up." He pulled her to him and she let out the most pitiful sobs. His heart was fucking breaking. What had they done to her? If he could get his hands on those motherfuckers, he would cut them into pieces and leave them for goat food.

She looked up at him and sniffed.

"I'm sorry. I was having a nightmare." She tried to push away, but he held her tight.

"Erin, please let me hold you. I'm so fucking sorry. I'm an idiot. I didn't handle this very well. I didn't expect you – I didn't expect us - and I've just never been in this situation before. Please forgive me. I'm sorry."

"You mean you don't kiss all your rescues?" She gave him a weak smile and placed her hand on the side of his face, kissing him softly.

He heard the soft clearing of a throat behind him.

"It's time, Nine," Code was standing with the others at the cave entrance.

She grabbed the boots that had been laid next to her and the multiple pairs of socks. Wilson had been right, with the bandages and the five pairs of socks, the boots fit fairly well. She stood with some pain, but it was night and day compared to just twenty-four hours ago. Wilson really knew what he was doing.

With the sunset, the gods were in their favor, with heavy clouds blocking the moon. The night was pitch black, but the path was relatively straight.

The men moved with such stillness and precision; Erin knew that she must have sounded like a drunk in an alley the way she was shuffling her feet. But not one of them said anything to her.

When they hit the next ridge, Code brought up comms and called for their extraction.

"Wait, weren't you worried that something was wrong last time since there really wasn't a sandstorm?" she asked.

"We were, sweetheart, but this time we called in a favor of an old friend."

She didn't correct him this time when he called her sweetheart, so he smiled inwardly. Damn, how was he going to let this woman go? He wanted to spend more time with her. Quality time, not 'patch her up and fix her' time. He wanted to take her to dinner.

What the fuck was that?

Within 20 minutes, the sound of the chopper blades hovered above them and slowly sat down. Joe picked her up in his arms, holding her tightly, he placed a soft kiss at her temple and moved toward the chopper.

"I can walk," she yelled in his ear. He said nothing, but handed her to the waiting medic. She watched as Joe and the men boarded.

"Ma'am?" She looked at the young Army medic beside her. "Ma'am? Are you okay? Are you in pain?" He was touching her arms, her legs, running his hands up her body. Joe walked forward grabbing his arm.

"She's fine. Our medic bandaged her up. Stop touching her."

"Sir, I have to do my job. Let me do my job." The young man's eyes grew wide with surprise, but he knew enough not to piss off the big man seated across from him. Joe stalked back to his seat eyeing the young medic. She gave the poor young man a tired, thankful smile.

"I'm okay," she mouthed to him over the rotors.

She laid her head back against the seat and closed her eyes. She wasn't even aware of how long it had been, but she felt the thud of the chopper landing and strong arms wrapped around her again. When she opened her eyes, he was laying her on the gurney, staring into her eyes, and then he was moving away. He was leaving. Panic rose in her chest and she felt as if she couldn't breathe.

"No!" she screamed. "NO! Don't leave me! Please don't leave me!" Her cries tore through him and he reached for her hand again.

"I'm not going anywhere, baby," he said calmly, "I'll be here once they've finished looking at you. Let them take care of you. They're gonna clean you up and make sure Wilson did good. I'm going to shower. It's going to be okay."

He let her hand fall from his and he turned to face the group of men staring at their fearless leader who had just shown his hand. The mighty can fall, and mighty Joe had fallen for the auburn-haired doctor.

When the medical team finished their litany of tests on her and re-bandaged her feet, Joe sent Wilson to get her and take her to her hut.

"You the medic that bandaged her?" said an older doctor who had certainly seen his fair share of war.

"Yes, sir," said Wilson.

"Damn fine job, son. She'll have full use of those feet in no time. Smart thinking on your part. And just so you know, all her damage was on the outside." And he walked away.

Wilson knew what that meant. She hadn't been raped. Nine would be happy to hear that. Hell, he thought, the whole team would be relieved to hear that. He carried Erin to her building and waited while she was finally able to shower and change.

They allowed her to bunk in a small visitor hut alone. It wasn't exactly a hut, more like a metal shed or an empty rail car, but it was warm and safe. She wasn't about to complain. She had clean clothes; she was showered and her hair was clean; her nails were now free of the chipped red polish, filed neat, and clean. Her ribs weren't as sore. Her face was fading to its normal color in places and her feet, still swollen, were less painful. So why was she so miserable? She heard a small knock and the pace of her heart quickened.

"Come in." She stood forgetting the pain in her feet and she gave a small groan.

"Sit," said the man in uniform. "Please sit. I know you've been through a tremendous ordeal."

"Ordeal?" she said sarcastically. "Is that what you call it? An ordeal? I was almost killed out there for something you guaranteed was an easy in, easy out. All I had to do was visit the infamous lab that was supposedly in our hands. I was nearly fucking killed!"

"Watch your language, young lady," he scowled shaking his finger at her. "I'm an officer in the United States Army and you will show me some respect." This little bit of courage was unlike his usually docile mouse. *Interesting*, he thought.

"I'm not one of your fucking soldiers, Daddy, dear." And with that, she stalked past him and out of the room into the cool late afternoon air.

"Stop right there!" he commanded, the echo of his deep voice filling the bustling air of the base.

Knowing that voice, she stopped, but so did about a hundred and twenty other soldiers and marines who were within his voice command. When they saw that they were not the target of his anger, they quietly and quickly moved on. Except one. One who stood at the far end of the common space and watched as the General hovered over the woman he had rescued. He listened and watched.

"It was supposed to be easy. You were supposed to be able to get in and out. Something went wrong. These things happen." He said shrugging his shoulder, the tone callous and nonchalant, she nearly cried.

"Dad, I'm your daughter. You lied to me. You lied to those men you sent in for me. You told them I worked for a private company. Everything you've said is a lie. Everything!"

"You do work for a private company and THEY hired those men – not me." Hate filled his eyes as he stared down at her, his cheeks flaring red with anger.

She winced as the reality of those words hit her. Her own father didn't send men in – her company did. Joe had been right.

"They were so fucking worried about you and their liability; they didn't listen to my instructions and instead made the call to REAPER themselves. I was only the contact here. I had to lie. Those men are expendable – my soldiers are not. We need to get inside that lab to inspect what's there. You need to finish the job you were hired to do. You have to go back. You have to be able to get your countermeasures to work and to do that, we have to know exactly what they have."

She looked up at him in horror. She had always known her father was a cold heartless bastard, but she never expected him to sacrifice his only child.

"Tell me, Dad, what would you have done had Orion gotten his hands on me? Hmmm? Tell me, daddy dear."

"I would have prayed for your soul and prayed that they killed you before you talked."

Nine couldn't listen anymore. He started moving toward her, his fists clenched at his sides. Before he knew what was happening, Code, Miller, Trak and Wilson were in step with him. Out of the corner of his eye, the General saw the five men.

Placing himself between Erin and her father, Joe stood eye-to-eye with the man, the others circling her.

"You lied to me. You lied to my men. And worst of all, you lied to your own daughter. What kind of man does that?" said Joe through clenched teeth.

"The kind of man who puts country first." His words were so cold and hard, Joe could hardly believe what he was hearing. His old man had been tough as they come, Marine Corps all the way, but not this.

"We're all about God and Country first, General. You sent her in knowing she could die. Knowing Orion was in the area and would look for her; you're a disgrace."

"Watch your tone, young man. I can, and will remove you and your men from this base. Besides, why are you worried," he sneered, "you'll get your money either way."

His fist clenched and started to rise, but he felt her small hand on his forearm.

"It's not worth it, Joe," she said softly.

The General eyed her for a moment and looked back at the muscled mountain of men standing in front of his daughter. He let a vicious belly laugh escape.

"Well, well, well look who has fallen for her rescuer. Ain't that a bitch? Well don't get too attached to the plump little mouse. She has to finish the job she started." Erin winced at his words, but she was used to them.

"I won't, Dad, I won't go back there."

He started to walk away and turned over his shoulder, giving her an evil smile that she knew all too well.

"Oh yes you will," he said, "and you know why." With that he walked off.

Her body was visibly shaking.

"You don't have to do this, Erin. You don't have to go back." He held her shoulders firmly, face-to-face, nose-to-nose. He noticed a single tear rolling down her cheek.

"But I do," she said with absolute certainty.

CHAPTER FOUR

He looked at her, stunned by her response. Joe wasn't often speechless, but her response had rendered his thoughts muddled. This woman, who had been through hell and made it back alive, was willing to test fates and do it again. She was either stupid or had a death wish. Her father clearly didn't give a damn about her and yet she was willing to give her life to do this for him.

"You're not the woman I thought you were," he said coldly, turning on his heels and stalking away.

She openly wept, her face in her hands as she leaned against the first person she saw, resting her head against Trak's chest. His eyes went wide and his hands stayed by his side for a moment, not sure what to do. The men looked at him and then at her. She was completely oblivious to the strangeness of this situation and the awkwardness that Trak felt. He let out a sigh and raised one hand to her back, lightly, simply holding her in place in a brotherly hug.

"Nine!" Wilson shouted at his friend. "Nine! Fucking stop!" He turned around facing his friend. Wilson was easily three inches taller than him. He never used his size to intimidate his friend, but he was pissed. He knew there had to be a reason for Erin's insistence.

"Hear her out, Nine. There must be a reason. She's a logical, intelligent, strong woman. She wouldn't risk her life if she didn't think it was necessary."

"That may be, but I'm not willing to risk our lives." He started to turn and walk away again and Wilson yelled after him.

"Is this mission over?" He looked at the big man, squinting, trying to read his thoughts.

"Yes." He said flatly. "We got her out. It's done."

"Okay," said Wilson calmly, "then I'm requesting time off. I have something I need to help a friend with."

Joe's mouth gaped open as the big man walked away. What the fuck was he doing? Did he have feelings for Erin? He was willing to risk his life for this woman, who so foolishly believed she should go back into that hellhole.

The men all watched Joe stalk away and surrounding Erin, they walked toward her quarters. Wilson handed her a tissue and she not so delicately blew her nose and grinned at them.

"Thank you all, but Joe is right. Your mission is over. He's going to be very angry if you do this with me."

"He'll get over it, sunshine," said Miller standing with massive arms folded across his chest. "But just for my own peace of mind, why Erin? Why do you have to go back? Why do you have to do this?"

"Yea," said Code, his boyish smile lighting up the room, "I mean I'm all for helping a damsel in distress but why risk your life for this? For your father, who, pardon me, Erin, is a grade-A prick."

"Yes, Erin, tell us." Joe stood in her doorway and slowly entered. All eyes looking at him as he stalked toward her and sat next to her on her bunk. His heavy weight making the bed creak. With all the men in the small space it felt even smaller than before. These buildings were made for a few people max – but people this size – maybe one.

She felt the suffocating air and wanted to start crying again, but they deserved an answer. She had never trusted anyone before. But it was time to start.

She eyed them all and knew she had to tell these men. They would be the only people she had ever told, but they deserved to know why she was risking their lives.

"This stays here right?" she said softly. They all nodded, waiting to hear her response. She had never trusted anyone with this secret. Never. *So why now*, she thought to herself. *Because for some crazy reason I trust these men with my life, and either way my life, this life, is over*. She took a deep breath and looked at them.

Joe sat stoically beside her. Miller, with his massive tattooed arms folded across his chest gave an encouraging smile. Wilson stood next to him, his large frame seemingly sucking the air from the small space. Code sat like a child, cross-legged, in front of her. And Trak? She couldn't see him, but knew he was in the shadows listening.

"My father has always controlled my life. Every aspect. Every movement. Every meal. Every breath. My mom died when I was six. I had already been sent to a school for advanced children at the age of four."

"Four?" Code said, "Isn't four a little young for that? Is that legal?" His innocent face looked from one man to another.

"Yes, Code it is too young," she said, smiling at his sweetness. "But what the General wants, the General gets, and he wanted me out from under his feet. I always tested high in every academic testing they did. But I was especially high in math and science. My father convinced my mother that I should go to this special school. One day he called the school and told the headmistress a driver would be picking me up to bring me home for a few days.

"I was so excited. I rarely got to go home, so I thought this was a special treat. The driver grabbed my suitcase and I was asking questions, wondering what my surprise was. He never said anything, he just drove me home and when I walked in, I knew something was wrong. My father looked at me and said, 'Your mother is dying – go say goodbye.' I was SIX – fucking six!" She wiped a tear away and Joe grasped her hand in one of his larger ones, linking his fingers with hers. She wanted to pull away from him. He had been such an ass, yet she knew that without his strength flowing through her, she would never be able to finish her story.

"After that, I was pretty much in boarding schools constantly; no spring breaks, no holidays home, only school. I graduated from high school at sixteen and headed to college – one of my father's choosing. I had my undergrad at 19, and my master's at 21. Again – grad school was my father's choice. I never had a say in it.

"While I was in grad school, I was dating a young man, Michael, who was in medical school. My father's perfect idea of a husband for me. Except he wasn't so perfect. It started out small at first, a shove here, a push there. And then it escalated. I wasn't ready for, for sex. I kept telling him I wanted to wait, but he took that decision from me. He raped me and beat me that night, and I knew I had to leave." She swallowed the cries wanting to seep from her body.

The men all with clenched fists mimicked her swallow, only for them it was bile and anger. Killing or fighting another man – not an issue. But harming women, children, or animals was not gonna give you a long life around this group.

"When I told my father, he said all men get upset now and then. He said I was probably pushing him. That I had probably done something to anger him. If I had just been a good girl, none of this would have happened. He said I should be grateful! Grateful! Because who else was going to want my geeky fat ass. Those were his words, geeky fat ass." She let out a nervous laugh, searching the faces of the men seated in front of her.

"I tried to stop seeing him, I switched schools, against Daddy's suggestion by the way. I moved to another state. I thought my life was back on track. I even started dating again. I had a few dates with a guy named Christopher, Chris. He was kind, handsome, and smart. I wasn't in love with him. Our relationship never got physical, but he was fun and a good distraction.

"Anyway, one night we went to this party and I saw Michael across the room. I couldn't believe he had found me. When I told Chris, we immediately left. Back in my apartment, I remember kissing Chris goodnight and he wanted to stay, but I told him to leave. I was feeling sick, my head was spinning, I was nauseated, I knew something wasn't right. I opened the door and that's the last thing I remember. When I woke up Michael and Chris were both dead on the floor. Their throats slit ear to ear. I did what I thought I should… "

"You called your father," came the baritone of Trak.

"When he showed up, he lectured me about how careless I had been and that I would be sent away for life, two murders, and two crimes of passion. I had killed my lovers in a rage of passion or anger, ménage à trois that had gotten out of hand. Geez, it made me sick. I shook my head, but I couldn't remember anything. I mean I lose my temper just like everyone else, but lose it enough to kill? I don't know."

She shook her head and Joe remembered her temper flaring at him in the cave. No, this woman couldn't kill. Get angry? Hell yes. But not kill. Especially two grown men in the fashion they were found.

"In the end, some men from what I assume was his unit showed up, cleaned my apartment, took the two men away in body bags and told me to go on with my life. That's when it got worse." She took a breath and Joe squeezed her hand, giving her courage.

"I was studying microbiology at the time. A few weeks later, Dad called and 'encouraged' me to switch majors to chemistry, specializing in weapons chemistry. It would be the future, he said. When I refused anything, he would say, 'It would be unfortunate if someone knew what happened to those young men.' Then, sure enough a few days after my refusal, the police would show up, ask a few questions about when I last saw them both and then leave. Every time. Just enough to put fear in me again. I'm not even sure now that they were the police, only that they would scare me half to death and I would agree with whatever dear old daddy needed."

Once again, she searched the faces of her rescuers, but their well-practiced masks gave nothing away.

"So, you see, if I don't do what he wants, I'm dead anyway. He'll go to the authorities and turn me in and I'll spend the rest of my days in a prison cell."

"And you believe his bullshit?" Joe said. He didn't mean for his tone to be so harsh and he immediately squeezed her hand in assurance that the tone wasn't directed at her.

"I don't know what to believe any more, Joe. I don't believe I could kill two men with my bare hands. They were large. Not as big as any of you, but much bigger and stronger than me. But what alternative do I have, Joe? Tell me?"

The large tears escaped her eyes and a quiet grief overtook her. She had held this in for so long, not telling anyone, not having anyone to tell it to! Her heart was so heavy and she felt as though her life was no longer hers to control.

"I think Joe may have a point, Erin," Trak's voice was almost foreign to her. He barely spoke and when he did, you really needed to listen. "I don't believe you have the ability to kill two men. And I certainly don't think you could slit their throats without a good fight and a lot of training."

"What am I supposed to do?" She searched their faces. "His men took care of everything. The evidence, the bodies, everything. I was so scared, so alone I had no one else to turn to."

"You have no siblings?" asked Joe.

"No. I'm an only child. My mother was sick for as long as I can remember. I don't even know what from. My father would never tell me. I spent all my time in boarding schools and made very few friends. You don't make friends when you have an IQ of 168 and large breasts."

She winced at her own words feeling the immediate rush of heat and crimson on her neck and

cheeks. She looked around the room. The guys all had one eyebrow raised and sly grins on

their faces. "Sorry, that was crude of me."

"Don't be sorry for telling the truth, baby," Joe held her hand in his lap now, rubbing his

thumb along hers. "I'd be friends with you for having those qualities."

He smiled and the men in room, lightening the mood all agreed, nodding and winking at

her. These were good men. Quality men with morals and a belief system that matched hers.

She might have found her light in this very dark tunnel.

Joe looked from one man to the next, dragging his hand over his head. He was

frustrated and finally in exasperation spoke.

"Well ain't this some fucked up shit?"

"I understand if you can't come back with me, but if I don't agree to do this, within the

week, my father will turn me in. Of that, I have no doubt. You all saw him. He's heartless,

completely and utterly without remorse. It's what makes him good at his job."

"Being heartless doesn't make a soldier good at his job, Erin," said Miller softly. "Having

a heart makes us good at what we do; compassion, knowing when to take a life or spare a life.

My sense is your father never distinguished between the two."

Joe looked at her swollen red eyes, those lips he had touched with such intimacy and his

heart melted. He knew he couldn't walk away from this woman even if he wanted to.

"If we do this, we do it my way, Erin. You follow directions, you take orders, and you do as you're told when you're told. No arguments." The sigh of relief that she exhaled from her body told him that a weight was lifted from her. She lay her head against his shoulder and nodded, barely perceptible. "I need to hear you say 'yes,' Erin."

"Yes," she said through cloudy eyes, "I will do as you say."

"Okay," he said looking at his men, "are you all in? This will be unpaid, you know that right?" They all nodded in agreement.

"I have money. I can pay you whatever your regular fee is, no problem," said Erin quickly.

"Nope. Not happening," he said looking around at the other men, knowing they would be in agreement.

"Alright then," he kissed her forehead and stood, "I'll be right back, I'm going to give the team their assignments and then I'll come back in to talk to you."

Stepping into the cool night air, they gathered around the big man. Joe paced around the team a few times, running his hand over his head and stroking his beard, scratching at it nervously. This smelled of shit, through and through.

He didn't trust the General any further than he could throw him. He knew his history. Career man, thirty-plus years; hell, he should have retired a long time ago, but wouldn't leave, from what Joe heard. Bad news followed this man around like flies on horse manure. He never had to work under him personally, but he knew more than a few people who had, and nearly lost their lives because of his decisions. He stopped, looking at the men in the tight circle.

"Do any of you honestly believe that woman could have killed two men with a knife? Even enraged? Even if she were high on drugs?"

"Not in a million fucking years," said Trak. Being the resident expert on knives, Trak would know.

"Yea, that's what I thought," he said sarcastically. "Miller, call the home office. See if we can get Tailor and Angel to do a little detective work for us. Find out everything you can about those two men, Michael and Chris or Christopher. Were they reported missing? Obituaries? Family? Let's see if we can find out what Daddy is really up to." Miller nodded and with big strides, walked away from the circle.

"Code," he said turning to the young man, "see if you can find intel on where Orion is and if there is any chatter on what the hell he wants with Erin. Also, see what you can pull up on our favorite General."

"Trak, Wilson, find out where the fuck this lab is she has to get to. Figure out a way in and a way out. Once you do that, figure out a second way, and a third. We are going to keep everyone in the dark about this. No one will know when or how we move. We are not going to lose anyone in this shithole of a place." They both nodded and strode off.

He blew out an exasperated breath and reentered her room. Erin was still sitting in the same spot; the tears had stopped but her puffy eyes gave away her fatigue.

"Hey," he said, "we're in this together. You should probably get some rest."

"Wait, Joe!" she stood and reached for his hand.

Damn! he thought, as her touch set him on fire. Her fingers sent sparks and little electric currents up his arm and it was all he could do not to strip her right there. He could smell her freshly washed hair – some sort of flower and vanilla reminding him of spring days on the farm. Her curves were killer. Her large breasts, so full and perfect, straining through the t-shirt. But the sexiest thing was she didn't have a clue how fucking gorgeous she was. She sat there all innocence and insecurity and it fucking turned him on big time.

"Please don't leave me yet." Her voice brought him back to their linked fingers.

"Listen, Erin," he said squeezing her hand, "right now I can't think of anywhere I want to be more than right here with you. Beside you, inside of you, but this will not keep my focus. I don't regret what happened in that cave. Not for one fucking minute, so don't even think that. But I have to keep you safe and you deserve better than being made love to in a shithole military quarters building in the middle of fucking Afghanistan."

Her breath was forcing her breasts up and down and he saw her swallow, drawing her tongue across her bruised lips. She looked down at her lap and nodded and he did what he knew he should not. He kissed her.

The taste of her lip balm filled his senses. Such a simple, silly thing, strawberry, but he could feel every nerve ending come to life and begging him to take this woman. The taste of her, the smell of her, and God help him, the feel of her body against him would be his end.

She touched his zipper and felt his rigid cock below.

"You said you couldn't touch me, be inside me," she smiled at him, "but you didn't say I couldn't touch you."

He let out a loud groan and wanted so desperately to stop her, but forgive his rotten soul, he couldn't.

She unzipped his pants and freed his swollen cock, throbbing, bouncing in her hand. He had begged for release for three days. She needed to feel him, to touch him. She needed something to let her know that her life had meaning and that she wasn't the woman her father said she was. It had been so long for her. The fear of being near another man, or touching him made her live as a recluse. But this man, this man made her feel safe, desired in a way she hadn't experienced before. All the pain. All the emotions of the last few days suddenly lifted from her.

The heat that was radiating off his body to her, would have kept a small village warm during a harsh winter. She smelled his desire on him and as she stroked his huge cock, she felt the warm pre-cum at the slit. She once would have felt fear, but now only peace and desire and heat. The heat this man was putting off. He was like his own bit of global warming and she planned on getting warm fast.

CHAPTER FIVE

His cock was larger than she expected and certainly larger than anything she had ever experienced. When she felt it in her hand, she knew he was big, but glancing down at the swollen purple head, the veins popping out along his rigid mass, she nearly backed away.

How will he ever fit inside me?

Of course, Michael had been her one and only. She could only describe him as mechanical. She hadn't paid attention to whether or not he was large or small, only that it was painful.

With the feel of Joe's hard, long cock in her hand, a sudden pleasure crept up her spine as she searched his eyes for any emotion; desire, pain, disgust, but he was a master at covering them; hiding his thoughts from all that sought them. Then, just for a moment, his blues changed a shade and the lust and need he felt bled into her very soul. He needed her as much as she needed him and that was the only clue she needed to continue.

She let her fingers slide over the rigid steel rod, feeling his need, his desire, his heat. The drops of warm liquid at the tip telling her that he needed this and wanted this as much as she did.

"Erin," he said with a heavy breath, "I don't want to...,"

"You don't want to what?" she said in a seductive, pleading tone. "Have sex with me? I know this isn't love, Joe, you've made that clear, but this is saying something very different about your need. I need this, Joe. I need you. Please. If only for tonight." She slid her tongue across his lips and he groaned, moaning with sweet need and agony.

"I don't want to lose you and if we do this, I can't guarantee I will be able to focus in the field." He tried to move back but his feet felt like they were encased in cement. "And this, will NOT be just sex. Understand? I can fuck anywhere. You and me? I don't know what it is yet, but it's not just fucking."

"Maybe," she said between kisses down the base of his throat, "maybe this will keep you more focused. Maybe this will make us both more focused."

She trailed down his neck on either side of his beard, to his chest, and releasing her hand from his cock, she pulled his t-shirt over his head and ran her tongue from one side of his massive chest to the other, tracing the tattoo over his pec. Down, further, sliding down his body until her mouth found what it was looking for. He thrust his hands in her hair, holding her there; watching her lips move over him; her eyes gazing up at him in a knowing smile. She had him. He knew it. She knew it.

Fuck... he thought... *I'm totally fucked.*

She had only just started when he lifted her off the floor, his cock bobbing from her mouth, he pulled her shirt over her head, the black bra revealing what he had dreamt of – large full breasts spilling over, begging for his attention. He quickly released the hook and the weight of her filled his palms. Gently kneading each one, he rolled her erect nipples between his finger and thumb.

"Fuck baby, you are so gorgeous!" He was breathless and the need to be buried inside her was overwhelming. If possible, he got even harder. The strain of his erection making him lightheaded.

She undid her own pants and kicking off her tennis shoes, she wiggled her beautiful round ass out of the pants, letting them pool at her feet. She stepped out of them, then slid her panties off as well. Lying back slowly on the bed, her breasts spilled before him, she shyly opened her legs in an invitation he could not have refused even if he tried.

His fingers found her soft flesh surrounded by the beautiful auburn curls shaved to a gorgeous landing strip. He eased one finger inside.

"Fuck, baby, you're so wet," he kissed down her neck and took one nipple in his mouth. Then he slid a second finger in.

She was so fucking tight he thought he might burst. Her juices were literally running down his fingers. He was losing his fucking mind. Her soft mewling sounds, telling him of the pleasure she was experiencing at his hand.

"I'm gonna make you cum, baby. Then you'll be ready for me. Come on Erin, cum for me, baby." With two fingers insider her warmth and wetness, he rubbed his thumb over her hard bud. It had been so long since she even pleasured herself, she knew it would only be a matter of moments before she shattered. She arched her back and moaned as he leaned down and kissed her, swallowing her scream of delight. Her body shook with satisfaction and he placed himself over her.

"Are you ready for me?"

"Please, Joe, please… I need…" her breath caught as the tip of his cock entered her wet pussy.

"Is that what you need, baby?" She nodded and bit her lower lip and he slid in further. "Are you okay? Did I hurt you?"

"No," she said, shaking her head, "you're just so big. I'll adjust." She brought her knees higher and wrapped her legs around his waist.

"Fuck baby, just what every man wants to hear. Easy baby, I've got you. How long, baby?" She looked at him confused. "How long has it been?"

"Six years." She said definitively.

"Six years? Fuck you need to cum again."

"I did twice," she said with satisfaction, "just now and once in the cave," she said with a seductive smile. "I think it's your turn."

"How about us both, baby?" He stopped mid-stroke, the sex fog ringing a bell in his brain. "Fuck."

"What? What? Please don't stop, Joe."

"I don't have a condom, honey."

"It's okay. I'm on the shot and I've been tested recently. I'm clean, Joe."

"Me too, baby. We get tested regularly. Are you sure?"

She nodded and he started to move again and knew that her warm, wet pussy was exactly where he wanted to be. She was driving her hips hard against him and sending his head back in a low growl. His beard tickled her breasts and he saw when he whisked it over her nipples, they hardened and goose bumps rose from their brown circles.

He wanted to last for her, but shit, this was not going to happen. He was so hot for her body. He ran his hands up her thigh, the firmness of her sending him into a tailspin. He reached the plump hips and then the narrowing of her waist, his hands fitting perfectly in its curve.

When she pulled her leg higher, he nearly came. Pumping harder and faster, he rubbed his thumb over her swelling clit and her breath caught in her throat. Before she could even think, she released on him, her cum dripping on his waiting cock.

When he knew she had let herself go; her body quivering beneath him, he pumped faster and released inside her, shuddering with a low, animalistic growl, he held her tightly against him. He didn't want to move; he didn't ever want to move. He kissed her temples, then her nose, and then softly kissed her waiting lips.

Mine. Fuck! What was that about? No man will ever touch her again. Shit!

They lie quietly in the darkness, their breath synchronizing, even and calm.

"Fuck baby, I wanted that to last a little longer. You deserved better than that." He kissed her forehead.

"It was perfect, Joe. Perfect." She ran her hands over his face, stroking his beard and giving a playful tug to pull him to her. She let her tongue slide along his lips, tasting him.

"Why six years, Erin?" he finally asked.

"I just couldn't after what had happened. I knew my father would find another reason to hold something over my head." She stared at the roof of the dingy metal building. "So I, basically, just removed myself from society. At first, it was just school, grocery store, and then home. Then I immersed myself in work."

He nodded, knowing he had done that on occasion himself. Oh, the blonde in Virginia had been a sweet little piece of ass, but that's all she had been, and she knew it. A diversion from reality. Until her, it had been more than a year.

"Why is your last name Richards and the good General is Murray?"

"You caught that huh?" she said sarcastically. "I use my mother's maiden name. I always have for some reason. It's even on my birth certificate, I think. My father said it was so that I would be safe from any of his enemies. I didn't care. I didn't want to be associated with him anyway. But somehow I think it was safer to not be attached to him at all."

He nodded, kissing the top of her head, breathing in the smell of her shampoo again, stroking her hair as she lay against his chest. The bed was definitely not made for two people and certainly not when one of the two people was the size of Joe.

"You need to sleep," he said rising from the bed and pulling on his clothes. "I need to find the guys."

She sat up, her breasts falling heavy against her body and he instantly got hard again. He muttered under his breath and turned away while he dressed. She smiled to herself, sensing what had happened and pulled her t-shirt on, making it worse with her nipples now poking through the thin fabric.

"I'm scared, Joe," she said in a soft meek voice. She hated admitting that to him. They were all so brave and didn't ever seem to be scared of anything. She had worried every day of her life since that incident and she wasn't sure she even knew how to cope without that kind of stress in her life. *How fucked up could you possibly be?*

"What? My little warrior is afraid now? The woman who gave me the only dressing down I've had since the SEALs?" She gave a half-smile. "I promise I won't let anything happen to you, baby. I can't let anything happen to you. Someone will be watching at all times, believe me. My team seems to have taken a liking to my warrior. I'll have to make sure they know the boundaries."

She smiled at him as heat flushed her cheeks.

"I'm not worried for me." She said almost confused by his statement. "I'm worried about you and the guys. What about your families? What are they risking for me?"

He shook his head at the beauty and courage of his woman.

His woman – shit – where did that come from!? She was worried about his battle-hardened warriors, not herself.

"They know what they're risking, baby." He could tell that his answer didn't satisfy her.

"Okay, here's the deal. Code isn't married, hell I'm not sure he isn't still a virgin. But he's one of the best tech and comms guys I've ever known and seems to be able to understand any program, any piece of software within minutes. He served in the Marines for eight years. He's written some programs for us because he's great with writing and breaking code without a sweat, hence the name. And he's one helluva shot, the Marine's taught him that. His real name is Will Erickson."

"Miller has been married," he stopped and grinned at her, "I think twice – but he doesn't talk about it. He has more women hanging around than you can shake a stick at, but no one permanent. He's the deadliest sniper I've ever worked with and pretty handy with explosives. His name isn't Miller but it's his favorite beer. His real name is Peter Robicheaux." He smiled sweetly at her and she grinned at the handsome man beside her.

"Trak is, well Trak is Trak. He's Native American or something but you can't get more than five words out of him usually. I've known him a long time and he has an interesting history. He can sense danger a mile away, he's wicked with a knife, and he can find a road out of any situation. Delta taught him well. His real name is Oscar Smith, go figure. No wife. No girlfriend."

"He's the one that's always way in front of us?" Joe nodded. "There's something about him. I mean he's scary and all that, but it's like I know him, but I know I don't." She shook her head.

"And Wilson?" she said.

His stomach did a backflip and he wasn't sure why. Did she have feelings for Wilson?

"Wilson is a trained medic. Actually, he's an RN, but doesn't let anyone know that. He and I were in SEAL training together. We call him Wilson because of the character on *Cast Away* with Tom Hanks. You know the volleyball. Wilson?" She nodded. "He was a beach volleyball player in college. His real name is Dan Anderson."

"Married?" She asked.

"No. Why?" he said harshly. She smiled up at him.

"You're jealous."

He didn't respond with words, but held her tight against his still rigid body and kissed her with a fever and hunger she never felt before.

"I don't get jealous, Erin, and I don't play games. I also don't share. If you plan on playing games with Wilson, that's a dangerous game to play, sweetheart."

She eyed him insulted at first and then suddenly felt in her heart that perhaps someone had done that to these two men once before. She held his forearm as he started to leave.

"Joe," she said pulling him back to her, "this is not a game for me. Wilson was just so amazingly kind to me when I was hurt and scared. I can tell he's loyal and a great friend. I hope to earn that friendship and loyalty from him as well. I've never felt this way about someone so quickly. You must know that about me already. I've had two boyfriends my entire life and both are dead, according to my father, because of me. And this is not me falling for my rescuer, and it's not some game with Wilson. He's sweet, that's all.

You're," she hesitated, "you're dangerous, and sexy, and scary, and…" He planted his mouth over hers before she could continue, tasting her, running his tongue through her mouth, taking her almost violently. He grabbed her bare ass, the t-shirt barely covering her cheeks. If he didn't leave now, he wouldn't be able to walk out.

"Sleep," he said setting her back down. "Sleep well, and tomorrow we'll meet up for breakfast."

"Joe, what about you? Your name? Any one at home?" She felt the blush creep up her cheeks and she looked down at her still bandaged feet. He lifted her chin, forcing her to look into his eyes.

"My name is Joe Dougall. Actually Joe Andrew Dougall. No Joseph. I'm thirty-six years old, I've never been married, not even close, and I have never," he slowed and looked down at her, "never, baby, felt this way about someone so quickly and so deeply. I'm hooked."

She rewarded him with a bright smile and seductive kiss.

"And your name? Nine?" He grinned back at her as he headed toward the door.

"Nine lives of course."

She gave him a wary smile, watched him leave, but wondered just how many lives he had used already.

She smelled of him, his manhood, his sweat, his soap. She loved the smell and felt oddly comforted by it, as if he were there with her in the empty room.

She locked and secured the door and then pulled the key from her shoe in her locker. She opened the briefcase she had carried with her, still safely tucked in her duffel bag. Inside the folder were the documents on the lab. She wanted to look at them one more time; something was still bothering her.

The list of the cache of chemicals allegedly stockpiled was impressive, but they made no sense. Some of them were ordinary food or medical preservatives – propylene glycol, sulphur dioxide, propylparaben. They were used to preserve ordinary foods, pharmaceuticals, and cosmetics. Then a list of others that were deadly alone or when mixed. Ammonia, arsenous chloride, benzyl cyanide, and at least fifty more. If someone were creating chemical weapons, they were going about it the hard way and certainly had a plethora of items at their disposal. It just didn't make any sense at all. The lab perhaps was a first stop for the ingredients, maybe a mixing or testing point, but not the point of full creation.

She glanced at her watch and the glowing dial told her it was already 23:20. She closed the folder and placed it back inside her green bag, hiding the key inside her shoe again. Lying in bed, she could still feel his warmth, his touch, his smell; she ran her fingers down her belly to the apex between her thighs and groaned at the need for satisfaction again.

She was still soaked from his juices and the thought of him dripping from her made her groan with delight. When had she become so bold? So wanton? She didn't really care; she just knew that Joe had unleashed something in her.

She massaged herself, spreading her legs wide, squeezing her breasts, twisting her nipples as he had done. *When did you get so daring and wicked, Erin?* The satisfaction it brought her was almost instantaneous; her orgasm came fast and she grinned to herself, tasting her fingers, the taste of her own sex, mixed with his. Four orgasms in less than seventy-two hours and only one was by her own hand. That was a record for her.

Closing her eyes, the weight of exhaustion blanketed her and she fell asleep, the faint pain of her feet still present. Let me dream tonight, she prayed. No nightmares, let me dream.

He waited in the shadows and watched the four men leave her hut. But where was the fifth? The lead dog stayed behind to rut with his bitch. Nice. He smiled to himself. These men might become more useful than he had originally hoped. The boy scouts were coming to the rescue of the little princess. How sweet he thought and how utterly disgusting.

He turned on his heels and headed toward his waiting CTV. He had a midnight meeting with an old friend and he couldn't be late.

CHAPTER SIX

She woke as dawn broke over the nearby mountains, the sunlight streaming through the cracks in her hut. She pulled on her own cargo pants fitting her generous curves perfectly, cinching her waist, only to emphasize the size of her breasts. She pulled on a lavender vee necked, long-sleeved t-shirt and found her own hiking boots.

Her feet, still bandaged, felt much better and she pulled on her thickest pair of socks and laced the boots snugly so her feet didn't move too much. Pulling her thick, nearly waist-length hair back in a ponytail, she secured it with a rubber tie and tucked the long tail through a baseball cap trying to hide the fading bruises on her face.

Erin had never really bothered with makeup. She didn't have time, and what was the point? She didn't date, so who was she trying to impress. At the last minute, she dabbed on some concealer over the worst of the bruises, a light coating of mascara and just a little lip balm. Grabbing a light jacket, she stepped outside and headed toward the mess hall.

Erin noticed her father was across the common speaking with four soldiers, intense in conversation. She ignored him, her stomach flipping over at the sight of him and rushed hoping that he wouldn't see her either.

When she entered the mess area, she immediately saw Wilson, a head taller than all the others, waving at her to come over to where they were seated. She graced the men with a shy smile and nodded, indicating she would grab her food and be right over.

Finding herself famished after last night's lovemaking, she filled her tray with eggs, bacon, toast and potatoes and then sat next to Joe. His leg nudged hers, rubbing it, and letting her know that he was there to support her. A silent signal that last night was not a mistake. She smiled and bid everyone good morning. He smiled down at her and looked at the tray full of food.

"Hungry, baby?" She only blushed but didn't respond.

"So, where are we?" she said quietly. "Do we go today?"

"Negative," said Joe. "We have a few more things to work out. We're not quite ready."

She nodded, grateful for the reprieve if only for a day. She knew that this was a death sentence for her, but she didn't want it to be a death sentence for all of them. And if she were going to die, Lord please let them all survive.

Joe nodded across the table at Miller, giving him a silent message to start.

"Erin, I need to ask you some questions and they might be difficult," said Miller softly.

She nodded staring at the man who only a few days ago terrified her. Now when she looked at him, all she saw was a big cuddly teddy bear. His dark brown hair was shaggy and looked like it desperately needed a comb. His whiskey-colored eyes were piercing, and the variety of green and yellow in them was really beautiful. She could see how women would fall for this man.

But what truly stood out was that he honestly looked as though he had been carved from a whole block of granite. His shoulders were wider than even Wilson's and his arms bulged from the sleeves of his shirt, yet his waist nipped in tight. She stared at him intently, taking him in and wishing she knew him better. He was beautiful, but she didn't doubt his skills. She didn't doubt that he would kill if he had to.

"Erin, part of our team back home did some investigating into Michael and Chris or Christopher. How long did you know them?"

"Michael, I met in grad school as I said. We dated, oh, I guess four months or so before, before the hitting started. Part of it I'm sure was that I didn't..." She looked down at her lap, her hands shredding the napkin in a nervous gesture she could not control. "I didn't want to have sex yet. I wasn't sure he was 'the one' and so I kept putting him off. My father claimed that was probably why he had started hitting me. I was making him frustrated. He said I should be grateful that he wanted my body."

"No man hits a woman because she says no." said Trak definitively.

For the first time in full light, Erin looked at the quiet, big man. He was about the same size as Joe only leaner, more runner than full-blown muscle-bound. He had high cheekbones and dark brown eyes, somewhere between dark chocolate and black that gave him an unintentional scary look. His jet-black hair fell longer than the others, barely touching the tops of his shoulders. The top was pulled back in a tight bun that just oozed sexy. He had no facial hair and straight white teeth. But even when he smiled, she realized that it didn't reach his eyes. This man was hiding a pain and it was as if she could feel it in her soul. She understood that.

"Christopher I only knew for about two months."

"Think carefully, Erin, where, exactly, did you meet both men?" Miller's eyes stared at her face.

"Michael approached me at the campus Starbucks while I was studying. He said he was a resident at New York Presbyterian. I was attending NYU. He said he noticed me from across the room and wanted to buy me a cup of coffee. At first, I said 'no' that I needed to study, but I appreciated it. But, I'm embarrassed to say, that no one had ever really approached me before and I was flattered, so I said yes."

"You have no reason to be embarrassed, baby. Any man would want to spend time with you and you're a desirable woman who should say yes. Not anymore, but previously." He gave her a quick wink and she blushed while the other men let their soft chuckles float over her.

"So, you never actually went to school with him?" asked Miller.

"No. No, we didn't." she searched his face and continued. "Chris, well oddly Chris approached me in a coffee shop as well. Obviously, I have an addiction to coffee."

She raised her empty mug as if in salute, and instantly Code grabbed the cup and refilled it. She smiled at him when he returned with a hot, fresh cup. Mouthing a soft "thank you," she was graced with his beautiful golden boy smile.

"Now, this is really important. Was there an obituary for either man? Were their bodies found?" Her forehead wrinkled and she felt the beginnings of a headache. She shook her head slowly.

"No, no there wasn't. I never saw anything about the bodies being found. I didn't want to look really. My father said the families wanted privacy. I wanted to reach out to them. I didn't know them personally but I still felt like I should give my condolences. Michael said his parents lived in Boston and Chris and I hadn't talked much, but he mentioned a little brother, so I assumed he had parents somewhere. My father said it wouldn't look good for me to reach out to the family. He said it would make me look suspicious, not caring."

"What about a funeral? Anyone you know talk about the funerals?"

"No, but I didn't know any of their friends." She stopped suddenly realizing her statement. Her stomach wavered and she felt as though she might lose her breakfast. "Oh God, I didn't know any of their friends. I never met anyone associated with either man. No friends, no classmates, no family.

"My father said they had hidden everything. He said no one would know," her breathing became more rapid and she felt the bile rising in her throat. Christ! What was happening? What had happened?

"Erin, look at me," Miller reached his large paw across the table and held her hand as if he were cradling a baby bird in the palm of his larger one. "Erin, you're a brilliant woman. From what your number one fan, Code, here tells me, you have an IQ of a million or something. That's pretty impressive, but didn't it seem odd that no one at school, no one in town, the news, nothing, no one spoke of two murders, two disappearances? Even in a city like New York, two murders make the news."

Joe knew that he had made the right decision in choosing Miller to talk to her about this. He would have lost his patience, but Miller, he was patience times a thousand. His former skills as an interrogator were unparalleled. He had also been SWAT at one time working hostage negotiation. Top that with the fact that he had six sisters and eight brothers, the man was made for negotiation and discussion.

She searched their faces, glancing from one man to the next. She shook her head, pressing her fingers against her temples. No, no this couldn't be. How could she have been so naïve and trusting?

"What are you saying? I saw the blood. I saw the bodies. They had no pulse." Her breathing was becoming dangerously rapid and Joe feared she would hyperventilate. He leaned in, whispering softly to her.

"It's okay, baby. Calm down. Breathe. Breathe. Look at me." She turned and stared into his eyes. "It's me. You're okay." She searched his eyes for answers. Something, anything that would help her center herself. The blue of his eyes was so warm she focused on that and willed herself to calm her breathing. She nodded and looked at Miller.

"Miller, how could this be? How could I have not known? Was I so willing to allow my father to control my life that I didn't question any of this? Doesn't that make me the most pathetic woman in the world? Are you telling me that those men might be alive?"

"You're not pathetic, Erin. Your father is, well, I'm saying, Erin, that your father has a very interesting past. I'm saying that there are drugs, and you're probably aware of a few, that can lower a man's heart rate to the point where people think they're dead when they're not.

He's had more than a few missions involving top-secret extractions, and he did it by making it look as though they were dead. It's one of his many skills." She noted the venom in the last sentence. "Erin, from the time that you called your father, how long before someone was at your door?"

She thought carefully for a moment and realized how quickly it had all happened.

"I called him and he, he didn't even sound surprised. Why didn't I remember that before?" She almost said it to herself, not the others.

"He said, and I quote, 'Oh, Erin, we both knew you would get yourself into a mess sooner or later.' He said I was fortunate he had men in the area. It couldn't have been more than 20 minutes later that they arrived." She looked up at Miller who showed no expression whatsoever.

"So, if these men aren't dead, then I can walk away, right?" She suddenly saw a light at the end of her death tunnel.

"Not so fast, sweetheart," Joe said grabbing her hand, "if you decide to walk away, I'm gonna bet that Daddy will find two bodies, two graves, and a whole bunch of evidence. We have to prove what he's doing."

"Jesus," she blew the word out with a whisper. "I've always known he was a ruthless cold-hearted bastard, but this one would be one for the ages. You set up your only child with fake murders and hold it over her head for years?"

The men all looked at each other. Having seen files that were supposedly sealed, they knew secrets about General Murray that would certainly put them all high on his hit list if he knew they had viewed them.

Trak moved in closer to the table and sat in front of Erin. He was a man of few words and the men knew that whatever he was going to say would be important.

"Erin, forgive me, but you don't seem distraught by the fact that your own father might have set you up?"

She eyed the big man with whom her soul seemed to connect in a different way than with Joe's. He was right and it was odd that he noticed that before even she did.

"You're right. I'm angry, and hurt, and confused. But distraught? No. My father is capable of absolute chaos, anarchy, and maelstrom. So, this? This doesn't surprise me at all." He nodded at her and stood again. "So, what now?" her tone was one of defeat and it broke Joe's heart.

"Now," Wilson stated, "now we wait until we have our plan in place. We wait until Code can find something for us on Orion – a photo, a location, anything. We're gathering weapons and information now to get you to that lab. Trak has a buddy here that's guaranteed us transport in and out, so your father won't know when we leave and when we arrive. We all think that's safer. We need to keep the information close to our chest on this one. Trust no one except those here at the table."

She nodded.

"Baby, we need to know what you know about this lab. What's in it? What's supposed to be there?" Joe squeezed her hand and pulled her closer to him.

She looked around the room and realized that most of the men and women had left. They were alone, save for a few, huddled at their table.

"Every chemical has a good and bad component. Sort of a positive and negative if you will," she started.

"Like an alter ego," said Code smiling, his childlike face lit up with a smile. Wilson punched him in the arm. She chuckled at the brotherhood and affection between the two men.

"Actually, Code, that's pretty accurate. It's like an alter ego. I can take an innocent chemical, something you eat every day or something in your shampoo, and if I add the right additional ingredients, I can make it deadly."

"Shit, dude," said Miller looking at Joe, "don't let her cook for you."

"Actually, that's probably a good idea," she said smiling, "but only because I don't cook. Anyway, it occurred to me that if we can create an alter ego, using Code's words, for these chemicals, we could create something that could neutralize those same chemicals. It's been attempted before, but never fully vetted and successful.

"Anyway, chemicals are either organic or inorganic, so are their counters. Even better is if I could put the neutralizer in a sort of mister if you will, a vapor or spray, so that no matter how the chemical was introduced into the environment, the neutralizer could either be delivered via air or absorbed into the soil, or skin, and so on."

"Okay, I get all that," said Joe, "but what about the lab."

"I'm getting there. I've done nothing but read the reports on this lab for weeks. Reports, I should say, provided by General Murray. The primary purpose seems to be basic. Formulations for foods, cosmetics and some OTC drugs. Which, by the way, makes no sense in the middle of Afghanistan. I mean who would manufacture those items here.

"Then they started delivering these odd chemicals that alone were fine, but if combined with other things could create something horrific. But the strange thing is, the things they need to combine them with, were not in that lab. Again, all information provided by daddy dear. I think there is a second lab somewhere. I think they brought the chemicals into this mainstream lab to cover it up from the UN and just slip on by."

"Back up a minute," Trak's deep voice rumbled in her chest. "What do you mean something horrific?" She let out a breath and stared from one man to the next.

"I mean complete annihilation within a five-hundred-mile radius if delivered via the right vehicle. He could commit genocide of an entire small country."

"Fucking hell," Code breathed the words and ran his fingers through his messy blonde hair.

"Yes, definitely hell, Code," she said looking at the boy. She noticed that in the very bright light of day, Code appeared a bit older than she originally thought. Still young, but not a boy.

"I think maybe they're going to try and create a more 'refined' version of anthrax. It could be absorbed into the skin or inhaled and it wouldn't need to be in close contact. It could be dropped from say a balloon over a small village. You would think it's innocent, kids running – 'look at the pretty balloon' – the balloon bursts and this fine dust or mist falls. Within eight to nine hours, everyone would be dead. And not a peaceful, go to sleep and die. It would be excruciatingly painful. Internal organs exploding."

"And you have a way to stop this?" said Joe.

"In theory," she said. He raised his eyebrows at her. "Listen, Joe, it's not as simple as testing a new car engine. I can't test this on a massive scale without endangering people. I have tested it on a small scale."

"How small?" asked Wilson.

"White mice. To be more specific, albino white mice. They have very similar skin to humans. We released 100 in a sealed acrylic cube. We released the chemical agent and then twenty minutes later the neutralizer."

"And?" said the men in unison, except for Trak who offered his question with a raised eyebrow.

"They all lived but one."

"Those are pretty damn good odds I would say," said Miller.

"They are, but remember nothing has been tested on a massive scale. Think about all the variables. A shift in the wind could blow it away, or out to sea or against a mountain. Or it could blow it back at the deliverer. Should this mystery chemical agent be released, I would need at least seven hours to create the neutralizer on a massive scale and then we would need something to drop it. Remember this has been tried before. It all seems very simple; very easy, but it's really not. The timing of everything would have to be so perfect it would be highly unlikely we would ever be that lucky."

"Any ideas on how we could deliver an antidote?" Joe said looking at the group.

"How about a crop duster?" asked Code.

They all smiled and looked at the young man, who knew he had hit the right answer. He grinned wide and a slight blush fell across his cheeks.

"Perfect," said Erin, "where do we find a crop duster in this place?" Joe smiled, looking at his men.

"Don't worry, we can always find what we need."

"Great, but I have to get to this lab first to verify the information. I'm telling you, it all seems too easy, too perfect. Not having the chemicals, but the information all seems too buttoned-up. And then, I have to find the second lab that I know is out there, to figure out what's there."

She laid her hands flat on the table and took a deep breath, relieved to have discussed her burden with someone after all this time. Her left hand was snuggly encased in an air cast, her fading bruised fingers wiggling for air.

"Wait," said Joe, "you want to find both labs?"

"I have to, Joe. You know that. After what I just told you, if I don't find both I will only be working with half the information. You would never do a mission with half the information."

She held his hand and laced his fingers through hers. He glanced at her good right hand noticing that she had removed her chipped red nail polish. Somehow, that made him smile and hard all at the same time.

Joe nodded knowing that she was right, but also knowing that it placed her and his men in more danger. Two labs. Two locations. Twice the danger.

"Okay," said Miller, "I'm still waiting for more intel from Tailor and Angel. Once we have that, we should be able to move forward. Code is working on the last of the equipment and the rest of you know what you need to do." Joe looked at Miller and nodded.

Joe was the team leader of this group, but he had always told his men to take on leadership roles. He wanted every man to be able to lead at any given moment. They were all in such sync that their thoughts and ideas usually gelled perfectly.

"What do I do?" she said wanting to help, wanting to be a part of what she knew was a foolish mission. Deep in her soul, she knew this was not going to end well.

"Nothing you can do, babe," Joe kissed her forehead and the men all lowered their heads, grinning at the softness their grizzly boss showed.

"I don't think she should be alone," said Trak softly.

Joe's eyebrows raised. He always listened to his old friend. He and Trak met on a joint mission with Delta. The man was absolutely, terrifyingly fucking deadly. No sound. No visual of him at any time, until it was too late. You wanted that man on your side. During that mission, they all walked away having made a few kills. But Trak? He left eight men in his wake, without one shot fired.

"What do you mean, Trak?"

"She's being watched. Non-stop. Twenty-four seven."

"What?" she said looking around the room.

"Don't make it obvious, Sister," said Trak, his voice even and calm. "I noticed two men when we left her room last night. I noticed one more after Joe left." Erin's cheeks flushed, the others paid no attention, having the decency not to bring up the obvious.

"This morning, the same two walked in behind her. There are two in the kitchen that keep checking out here."

Sister? Joe would ask about that later. Joe nodded.

"Alright, Erin is never to be alone. Someone will be with her until this shit is done. You are moving in with our team. You stay with us. You don't leave our side even to piss," he smiled at her recalling their argument in the cave and she graced him with a beautiful, bright smile that melted his heart.

He would not let harm come to this woman. He would not lose her.

Oh shit! He thought, *I'm done. I'm cooked.*

Somehow, he had fallen in love with this woman in just seventy-two hours. Fuck!

CHAPTER SEVEN

Erin knew that these men would protect her at all costs. She knew it with every bone in her body. She just wasn't sure she was prepared to *let* them protect her at all costs. She looked at the faces of each one. Hardened warriors. Even sweet Code looked older than his years in many ways. But her alternative was dim. Her father would stop at nothing to get what he wanted. He was ruthless in everything he did. Doubt continued to plague her however, that nagging, niggling feeling that things were not as they seemed.

"Erin? Earth to Erin?" she turned and Joe was smiling at her, but his eyes were cautious and curious.

"I'm sorry," she said shaking her head. "I was just thinking about my father. It's really eating at me."

"Don't feel bad, Erin, even my sweet old man could be a real asshat too," Miller winked, using the term she had used on Joe, attempting to lessen her concern. She let out a small laugh and smiled at him.

"Yes, he's definitely that and much more. But it's something else," she said quietly. They all looked at her waiting for her thoughts.

"What do you mean, baby?" asked Joe. "Anything could be helpful."

"Okay, here's the reader's digest version of this. My father asked Dryden to put me to work on this project of neutralizing chemicals. They were happy to do it for the good General, plus it would mean huge military and government contracts if we succeeded. Initially I was thrilled. I felt as though finally my father believed in me, believed in my work.

"But here's the thing guys, and I don't mean to sound condescending to anyone, but any of you could have figured out what I did. I was building off work done before me. With your background, Wilson, knowing how chemicals react with the body and Miller, with your knowledge of explosive chemicals, given time you guys could have figured this out. It's been attempted before but never fully vetted out.

"Then daddy dear sends me on the wild goose chase, which was clearly not what it seemed and he doesn't come and get me. In fact it's obvious he never had any intention of coming to get me. But Dryden calls you guys. I'll tell you what I think.

"I think. I think this was all some big diversion of some sort. I don't think I was supposed to do any of this. I think Daddy thought Dryden would just roll over. But I think when old man Dryden discovered I was missing, they called you to protect themselves legally, not realizing that my father would not have cared either way. I think once they made that call to all of you, the good General couldn't look away." She stopped and looked down at her hands, and then searched the faces of each one of the men at her table.

"I think you may be right, Erin, and if that's the case, Jesus, this is one fucked up situation," Miller grumbled. Wilson looked at her, his face etched with lines of worry and frustration.

"So what do you think is really going on here, Erin?"

"I'm not sure, Wilson. But I do think I wasn't supposed to survive the trip to the first lab, let alone have an opportunity to get to the second one."

"Let's talk this out," said Joe, "but not here." They all nodded recognizing that they were being watched.

Heading toward the door, the men easily identified the General's men who had watched their every move. *Where the fuck did he get these guys*, thought Joe. They were so obvious it wasn't even funny. Which worried him even more. Trak brought up the rear as always and squeezed his hand into a fist as he walked by the first two men.

Walking back to her room, they all chatted casually, cautious of what and who might be around them. Making their way through the common area, Erin spotted her father at the edge of the fence line speaking to a man. Easily two hundred yards away, she squinted in the sunlight and suddenly froze, her entire body stiffened and she stopped so suddenly Trak ran into her, an unheard-of incident for Trak.

"Erin, I'm so sorry," he said grabbing her shoulders. "Are you okay?"

She turned abruptly, looking up at Trak, seeking comfort and safety in his dark eyes, fear etched in her face. Joe stood beside her, his arm hugging her waist, pulling her beneath his shoulder.

"Erin?" Joe looked at her pale face, looking around the area and spotted the General on the far side, his back to the team. "Erin, who is that man talking to your father? Erin?"

Erin continued to look up at Trak as if praying for protection, cover. She couldn't move. Frozen in fear. She cowered in the circle of the men. Trak held her gaze, his eyes solid brown, his calm was helping her to breathe, and he gave her the slightest nod, as if to tell her all would be well.

"It's Chris," she said so quietly they weren't sure they heard her correctly. Trak's eagle eyes peered above her head.

"Chris? As in dead Chris?" asked Code.

"Yes. I mean, no. No. I mean he's obviously not dead. It's been six years, but that's him. I would know him anywhere. See the purple mark on his neck?" They all nodded casually. "That's a port-wine stain or birthmark. He hated it. It was visible no matter what he wore and made him very self-conscious."

She continued to remain as she was, back to her father, tucked under Joe's arm and staring straight up at Trak, who had the good sense to take a half-step back when he realized just how close he and Erin were.

"Son of a bitch! You were all right. I'm going to fucking kill my father and then him. Again. How could he do this?" She started to move from under Joe's arm and he pulled her tight against his body. Joe held her back against him.

"Wait, bruiser," he said with a half-smile, "it's two hundred yards away. We have to be sure. It could be anyone."

As if sensing their presence, her father turned and saw the group, immediately placing his body between their vision and the man he was speaking with. Pulling a scarf over his head, the other man turned and he and the General walked away.

"Trak," Joe said.

"Got it," and with that Trak disappeared, but not before looking into Erin's eyes and giving a small smile that somehow made her feel that everything would be okay.

"Into our room now," Joe said pushing toward the team's quarters. Their quarters were similar to hers, only slightly larger and smelling of men. Sweat, testosterone, and she thought she even smelled whiskey and cigars. Joe led her to his bed and looked at the others around the room. She pulled her baseball cap off and removed the elastic that had been holding her hair back, running her fingers through her hair and twisting it nervously.

"I don't understand," she said trying to remain strong, but barely holding her composure. "How could he do this? How could he let me think Chris was dead? WHY let me think Chris was dead? I'm sure Michael is probably alive as well. Shit, if Michael's alive I'm really in danger! And if all this was only to get me to a lab seven years later in the middle of some God-forsaken country. That's crazy! Right?!" She searched their faces, her voice breaking.

"Erin," Wilson sat his big body next to hers and the bed groaned under his weight. "This is why we asked about the incident before. We, none of us, believes that you killed those men. It's just not possible. Your father wants something from you, but I don't think it's about chemical weapons. He continues to put you in harm's way and that isn't going to happen anymore. Not with all of us here."

Joe stepped forward and knelt in front Erin, taking her face between his hands, he placed a small kiss across her forehead. She was so beautiful, so strong, and yet at this moment, seemed so frail. Her world was turning upside down and she couldn't stop it.

"Erin, we need to back up even further than the alleged murders. We need you to go back to your earliest childhood memories. Everything is important."

She nodded and sat quietly as they all found a place in the close quarters to sit.

"I'm not sure where to begin. I think I was happy as a little girl; I mean a really little girl. I don't really remember. I was always good at school. I remember that, even pre-school. My mom was a teacher." She smiled at that memory. A distant memory of her mother teaching her ABCs and addition and subtraction.

"She started to get sick when I was around four, I think. That's when Dad said I had to go away to 'big' school. I still remember that. He told a four-year-old she would have to go to big school." She smiled and held Joe's calloused hand in her smaller, softer hand.

"It wasn't a traditional school. It was a school for exceptional students with exceptional academic skills. I had round-the-clock care, my own room, everything I could ever need except my parents. My skills were particularly good in math and science. Don't ask me to quote literature, I can't. But no matter how well I did, the General kept telling me I had to do better. In the meantime, my mother was getting sicker and sicker. He rarely let me in her room to see her and when I was allowed in, there was always someone else with me. Either him, a nurse, or..." She stopped for a moment and rubbed her head as if willing a memory to come forward.

"There was another man in the house all the time. He wore a uniform. I don't know why I didn't remember that."

The others looked at one another, but Joe just kept stroking her hand.

"Then one day I get called home from school and he said I needed to go upstairs and say goodbye to my mother. I asked if she was going on a trip and he looked at me and said 'no she's dying.' Just like that. Can you imagine saying that to a six-year-old?" She took a deep breath willing herself to continue.

"I remember my mother looking so frail, so sick. She was gray. I didn't even know why she was dying. For years I've tried to find out. Tried to get the death certificate and somehow, he blocked me every time. He said it would bring up painful memories for me. I didn't question him because I trusted him.

"I know this now. No one is that color just from being sick. I think she was poisoned. Anyway, I remember kissing her cheek and her eyes got big and she smiled at me. I think she was happy in that moment. She died later that night and immediately after the funeral, I was sent off to boarding school. Six years old and sent away.

"If I didn't ace an exam, I received a stern note from the General. Nothing was ever good enough. When I finished high school early, I wanted to attend Stanford. But he wouldn't allow it. I had two choices. Georgetown or NYU. No reason given except he wouldn't pay a cent for school unless I chose one of his picks. I was so frightened of him and yet wanted his approval so desperately. I chose NYU because I felt like it was far enough away from the Virginia/DC area where he lived. The rest you know."

"An obedient daughter who knew nothing else," said Miller quietly, his massive arms folded across his chest. Erin noticed the full sleeve of tattoos on both arms that were now peeking out beneath his pushed-up shirtsleeves.

"You said your father basically told you to change majors," said Miller, "did he give you a reason?"

"No. He just said it would be best for me and that he would be terribly disappointed if I didn't take his advice. I was scared of him. I know that now. I did whatever he said because I was frightened and I thought as long as he held the murders, well, I guess I can say alleged murders now, I just figured I didn't have a choice." She closed her eyes for a moment and let out a long slow breath.

"I was telling you guys that none of this fit. It all seems too convenient." They nodded, waiting for her to continue.

"This lab visit makes no sense whatsoever. I mean there are always stories of WMDs being in the Middle East. But the UN generally sends in a team to investigate, not private contractors. So why send me to this little nothing of a lab in the middle of nowhere, with no evidence whatsoever that they are actually producing this toxic chemical agent? Why risk all of this knowing that Orion is out there and for some reason wants me? It's just feeling to me as if my father is trying terribly hard to place me in danger." She searched their faces waiting for some sign of agreement or disagreement.

"You're not off, Erin," said Wilson, "I feel the same way. Erin, what are you working on at Dryden outside of this project?"

"I have a few smaller projects. Just looking at different drugs on a contractual basis. Something we do all the time. Pharmaceutical companies or biotech companies come up with things all the time but don't always have the resources to look at things completely. We also look at new street drugs."

"Street drugs?" Miller's brow raised.

"Yes. A police department discovers a new street drug and wants to know what the chemical makeup is. Sometimes it's simple but lately there are a lot of designer drugs on the streets. I look at them to help determine what the chemicals are, and if possible, their sources. I have three such cases now with DC Metro."

Joe stood to his full height in front of her.

"Okay we're going to figure this out. We're going to get to that lab and find out what's so fucking important about it. We're going to finish this mission and then we're going to have a long chat with General Murray. Code?"

"Yes, sir," said Code standing from his spot on the floor.

"Any word from Tailor or Angel yet?"

"Tailor said Sly had a little trouble getting into the database with the General's records, but finally got in. With thirty-seven years of service, there's a lot to go through. They're compiling everything now and will send it over as soon as they can."

"Okay, Miller? Do we have a plan, a backup plan and backup for our backup?"

"Yep." Joe nodded knowing that it was all he needed to hear from the big man.

"Alright then, we leave at 0130. I don't want anyone to see us or hear us when we leave. Understood?" Everyone nodded. "Erin, you're staying with us. Code will go back to your room and get your things."

"All I need is my own clothes and the small green pack in my locker, Code. It has the testing vials I need and my files on the lab." Code nodded and graced her with a big beautiful surfer boy smile. She couldn't help but grin back at him as he headed out into the waning evening light.

"Are you hungry yet?" asked Joe. She looked at her watch and couldn't believe it was already dinner time. They had missed lunch completely.

"I am a bit," she smiled shyly.

"How are the feet?" he asked, moving closer to her, the other men already backing out of the room.

"I can barely tell now. They feel great actually. I promise I won't slow you down."

"Erin," he closed his eyes and let out an exhausted breath, "I didn't ask out of concern that you would hold us back. I asked because I care. Because I'm worried." He tucked a wild strand of her auburn hair behind her ear and kissed her softly.

"Because I'm crazy about you."

She looked into his beautiful blue eyes and lost herself. She buried her head beneath his chin and breathed in his strong masculine scent, the smell of his soap and deodorant. His arms wrapped around her and squeezed.

"I'm crazy about you too, Joe." She felt his smile, with his chin resting on the top of her head. "Joe, I don't think anything my father is doing is for the good of mankind or the Afghan people or peace or anyone but him. I don't think he wants to stop chemical weapons at all. I think he wants them in his hands."

He nodded, still holding her against his warm body, amazed that this brave woman was so rational at a moment when everyone would have expected her to lose all rationale. Orion had known too much about Erin. Someone was leaking information and her father was the obvious choice. He could only hope that the team back home would have information for them tonight before they left. And if this Chris, if that was his real name, was alive and well, then he would just have to kill him all over again.

"Baby, can you handle a weapon?" She nodded.

"I'm still the General's daughter, Joe. He taught me to use a weapon and forced me to take part in some hand-to-hand combat training." Her sarcastic tone belied pain hidden deep within her and Joe was determined to get to the man responsible for it.

He reached into his locker and pulled out a sleek black Walther P99. She took it from him and easily disengaged the clip, checking for ammunition, and replacing it. She carefully slid it beneath her belt, hidden under her jacket.

"We all carry the same weapons so that we can easily share ammo if needed. If you need to, you shoot and don't worry about who or what it is until later." She nodded slowly, knowing that she might actually have to shoot someone. "Just make sure it's not one of us." He said with a smile.

"And Erin," he said softly, "if by some fucked up reason the worst happens, if I'm dead or injured, if the guys are all down, if you know Orion is coming for you and there is no way out, don't let him take you." She looked into Joe's eyes and for the first time saw something she never thought she would see in him. Fear.

He grabbed her close to him and held her again, breathing in her clean scent, the vanilla of her perfume, the floral scent of her shampoo.

God, please don't take this woman from me. Not now. Not when I've just found her.

"But, baby," he said raising her chin to look at him, "if you think for one minute that we're going to let anything happen to you, never in a million fucking years, baby, a million fucking years." He kissed her long and deep finally raising his head for air. He gently pushed her toward the door, knowing his men were still waiting outside. He adjusted his pants, feeling the outline of his rigid cock and that it would be visible to everyone and honestly not giving a fuck. As they walked out of the room, sure enough the team waited patiently in the fading evening light.

"Joe?" she said quietly.

"Yea, baby?"

"None of you will die. You're all too good. Too stubborn. I won't let it happen." He laughed a nervous laugh and his teammates smiled at her as they walked.

From your lips to God's ears, baby.

CHAPTER EIGHT

They ate in silence at their table. The chow hall was buzzing with the loud conversations and laughter of men and women grateful for a respite from this miserable place. No one at their table said a word. When they finished, they walked as a group back to the room. Waiting inside was Trak, who had disappeared after the Chris sighting.

"He was good," he said in his soft voice, "but I was better."

Joe smiled at the lean, dark man. His midnight-black hair laced with dust, dirt on his clothes.

"I followed him along the fence line until he got in a CTV and took off with three other men. I borrowed a truck and followed." Wilson raised an eyebrow at the man.

"Borrowed?"

"Yea, borrowed." He said plainly. "They have a small camp about five miles out. They were all in uniform but I doubt that any are actually active duty. Nothing was right about the uniform. The big guy who was in the kitchen earlier? The redhead with the tattoos? The name on his blouse was Vasquez. How many red-headed Vasquezes do you know? I couldn't get close enough to hear any conversations but I can tell you that they have enough weapons to have their own private little war."

"What about Chris?" she asked. "Or the man I think is Chris?" Trak pulled out his phone and showed her two photographs he took.

"They're not the best, but they're clear enough." She nodded and looked at them all.

"That's him. I'm one hundred and ten percent sure. That's him."

"Okay," said Joe, "Trak send those pics home. See if our facial recognition software can give us any clues. After that, everyone sleeps. We get up in four hours and head out. We'll be taking a truck out of the base, but we're going as cargo." He smiled at his men and gave Erin a reassuring smile. She thought it best not to ask questions.

"Erin, you take my cot. I'll sleep on the floor." She nodded and lay her head down on his pillow, smelling his scent. Soap and sweat and man. She breathed in deeply and closed her eyes.

Code nodded to him to step outside and he quietly walked outside their quarters with the young man.

"What's up?"

"Tailor sent something on General Murray."

"Well? Do I have to fucking beg for it?" he was tired and hadn't meant to jump at the young man. "Sorry, Code. I didn't mean that."

Code nodded and flashed his boyish grin.

"S'okay. Seems General Murray has more than a few secrets. Number one is he had a near-deadly case of scarlet fever as a child."

"Scarlet fever? But I thought that could make a man sterile." Joe was confused.

"It does and it did. According to his physicals, all of them, at West Point and every single fucking one after that, he was, is sterile. He is not Erin's father. It's not possible."

"Fucking hell," Joe raked his hand over his head. "What else?"

"The General has never been married. Never. There is no record that he has ever had a wife or a child. Now, if he actually wiped out a record of a marriage and a daughter, we're dealing with one very sick son-of-a-bitch. But I'm telling you, boss, Tailor and Sly, are never wrong. Erin is not his daughter and he was never married to her mother. Her mother, Eleanor Grace Howell, was married, however, to one Master Sergeant William Richards. That's right, Richards. Erin's last name isn't her mother's maiden name. It's her biological father's name."

"What the fuck are you up to old man?" Joe shook his head and looked out into the night sky. "Okay Code, thanks man. And thank Tailor and Sly for me. See if they can find birth records for Erin and a death record for her mother."

"Already on it, boss. They said it will take a few days but they're working on it. What about Erin? Do we say anything to her?"

"No," he said quietly, "we say nothing right now. We don't have all the facts yet. Let's figure out this cluster-fuck and then we'll clue her in."

Code nodded and went inside their quarters. As he was entering Trak was coming out, a towel draped across his shoulder.

"I'm gonna hit the showers so I can get all dirty again in four hours." Joe nodded and watched his friend stalk off so quietly he wondered if the man was half-elf. He stood in the cool night air for a moment to clear his head. The sounds of the base were quieting and he hoped it would stay that way.

⋅⋅⋅◇⋅▬▬▬◆✦◆▬▬▬⋅◇⋅⋅⋅

0130 was way too early to be woken up from a hard sleep. Joe held his hand lightly over her mouth and she immediately sat up. She cleared her eyes and nodded at him, understanding that they couldn't speak. Having slept in her pants, she pulled on two pairs of warm socks and her own hiking boots, her feet barely feeling the effects of a few days ago. She pulled on a long-sleeved t-shirt over her tank top, and on top of that a dark green sweater and then her jacket. She wrapped the scarf around her neck, pulling it up over her auburn hair, hoping it covered the obviously different color. She shoved the small green briefcase into her larger green backpack.

There were energy bars, MRE's, and water shoved in there along with clean socks, clean underwear, and a few medical supplies. She was feeling more prepared this time and a helluva lot more protected. The men were ready and waiting for her at the door. Joe nodded at her, his index finger at his lips indicating silence. She nodded back.

Trak opened the door and indicated for them to follow. Walking slowly through the camp, she followed Joe, who was following Trak. Code, Miller, and Wilson took up the rear. At the edge of the camp was a truck being loaded with supplies to head out to another basecamp. Trak walked confidently toward the guy at the truck and the driver slapped his shoulder and then turned and walked away. Trak waved at them and they all climbed into the back of the covered vehicle. There were several large crates, with canvas tarps over each one. They hid behind the crates, covering each other with the tarps, crunched into the small space. Joe pulled Erin tightly against his body.

Joe looked at her and with his two fingers just barely over his eyes; he indicated that she could sleep if she felt the need. Was he fucking kidding? Sleep? She had so much adrenaline pumping through her she hoped her heart wouldn't explode. She shook her head and he smiled at her, winking.

They felt the truck move from its spot and head out of the base. The roads were bumpy, dusty, and had more potholes than I94 in May. Her ass would never be the same.

In what seemed like only minutes, she heard a banging on the back of the truck and the man opened the flaps and let them out.

Trak thanked the man and pointed to the trail up the mountainside. No one spoke. No one stopped. To her, it felt as if no one was breathing. The trail up was difficult and clearly meant for goats and not men. She was grateful for her hiking boots, and for the fact that she could place her hand on Joe's rear-end and feel her way up the trail. The night sky was clear, filled with more stars than Erin thought she had ever seen before.

In another place, another time this could be a beautifully romantic moment to be with Joe. But nothing about this place made her think romance right now. She felt herself blush at the memory of her own forwardness with Joe. How she had been the aggressor. She had no idea what possessed her to be so daring. All she knew was that with everything in her body, she craved this man and wanted to be in his safekeeping, but more than that, she wanted to be in his heart.

After more than three hours of climbing, they stopped on a rocky ledge and Joe handed her a water bottle. The night was at its darkest hour. She looked at her watch. 0522. The late autumn sun would rise in a little while.

Joe looked at the group and they huddled close to him.

"We have about another hour. Over that ridge," he said pointing to the northeast "should be the lab. We get in; we get out before Daddy knows we're gone from base." Everyone nodded and began moving again.

Just as Joe had predicted in almost exactly an hour, they were overlooking the ridge at several metal buildings in a small valley below. Nothing else seen for miles around. Mountains. Dirt. Rocks. And this tiny grouping of buildings. There was no movement. No people. No guards. Nothing but dark metal buildings.

"This can't be it," said Erin breathlessly. "There would be guards, people, twenty-four-seven protection." They all nodded, but motioned for her to continue.

They made their way carefully down the side of the mountain. Trak marched ahead scoping out the terrain and finally stopping them so he could search around the buildings himself. They looked larger from above, but close up they seemed small and completely uninhabited.

Trak sent the signal that there was no one on site and gave the all clear.

Joe tried the door on the first building and it easily opened. They searched the room. Various desks and chairs were stacked against the walls, file cabinets; drawers opened littered the room. Searching each room, each building they found the same. Finally, Joe gave the all clear to speak.

"Something is so fucking rotten in Denmark," said Miller.

"And here," said Code sarcastically.

"Look at the dust," she said swiping a finger along the top of one of the file cabinets.

"Baby, I don't think they worry about dust here," he smiled at her.

"I know, Joe, but this was supposed to be a lab. Dust is the enemy in a laboratory environment. They would have kept it immaculate. This place hasn't been cleaned, or used, in months, maybe years. This is nothing."

"We need to leave now," said Trak suddenly feeling the hairs on the back of his neck stand up. Exiting the building, Trak stopped them. He pointed to the opposite side of the valley. "Go that way."

They jogged to the other side of the complex and worked their way through the trail on the opposite mountainside.

Suddenly they all heard what Trak had heard. Helicopter. The familiar whump, whump, whump and whir of the blades. The helicopter landed in the flats outside the buildings and as if anyone would have bet against it, General Murray and the not-so-dead Chris stepped from the chopper.

Four other men exited the two choppers, heavily armed, all with masks, and all in black. They entered the buildings moving swiftly from one building to the next. As Miller watched them leaving each building, carefully placing wire around the doorway, he knew in an instant what they were doing.

"They're setting a trap," he said low, to Joe.

"Yep," said Joe, "for us."

Trak pulled them back and they headed further up the trail where there were large boulders for them to hide behind.

"When they find out we beat them here, Daddy is going to be very angry," said Wilson.

"We can't go back the way we came," said Joe, "they'll see us."

"We don't want to go back that way," said Erin looking from one man to the next.

They all looked at her in the darkness and saw her face harden in a way they never thought they would. She took out a folded piece of paper and laid it on the rocky trail.

"I found this shoved into one of the desk drawers. Those buildings did have chemicals at one time. But they were closed about eight months ago. Everything was moved to this facility here," she pointed to a name and address on the paper. "I know this facility. It's a known factory for producing hazardous chemicals."

"Fuck," Joe said under his breath. "So the good General was going to kill us here and make it look like Orion did us in. We have to get to that facility." He checked his GPS and the coordinates on the paper.

"We should be about 35 kliks from there. Wilson," he said over his shoulder, "take Erin back."

"No," she said sternly. "No. I'm not going back and waiting. You need me to see what's there. Besides, if I go back without you guys, he'll just think you left and didn't do your job and send me out again. I won't be safe without you."

"She's right, Nine," said Miller.

"Yea, yea, I know she's right." He looked at his team. "Okay. We move after they've left the buildings. Once they're gone, we'll make sure that it looks as though the buildings blew and we were in them. Then let's find one of those infamous fucking caves and get some sleep. We move again tonight, only in darkness. We have to move fast and get in a lot of ground. Understood?" Everyone nodded their head in the affirmative.

The group of men in the compound stood close speaking to one another, but nothing could be heard above the rotors of the helicopter. As quickly as they arrived, they loaded back into the chopper and headed off.

When the sounds of the machine could no longer be heard in the valley, Joe gave a nod to Miller and Wilson and they expertly slipped back into the complex. With precision only capable by these two men, they moved quickly and efficiently adding their own wiring and detonation devices to the buildings. Backing out of the complex and up the mountainside again, Miller set the timer for twenty minutes. Enough time to get himself and Wilson out of the way. They met up with the team and began moving.

Precisely twenty minutes later, the mountain rattled with the explosions on the valley floor. The buildings were shredded to pieces, leaving only a small crater where they all had once stood. Erin looked back in shock and her stomach flipped.

"My God!" she whispered. "That could have been us."

"But it wasn't, babe. And it won't be." Joe grabbed her hand, moving her back up the mountain.

They trekked quietly through the rocky terrain for hours, and as the sun made its way high over the first peak, Trak pointed ahead to a small covering. Not quite a cave, but enough of a rocky overhang they could sleep and get out of sight.

"I'll take first watch," said Trak.

Everyone nodded and tucked into the space. Joe lay back against his pack and Erin sat next to him. Not caring anymore if the others saw, she rolled into his arms and immediately fell asleep. He closed his eyes as her soft breathing indicated that she was already sleeping. Sensing the smiles and eyes on him, without ever opening his eyes, he spoke.

"One fucking word and I'll kill you all myself."

"General," said the man standing next to him, "call." He handed the man the phone and watched his face turn that familiar shade of purple when things weren't going exactly his way.

"It looks like they've left, sir. They are headed toward the buildings." The voice on the other end of the phone got quieter.

"When did they leave? How?" he demanded.

"I'm not sure, sir, but their rooms are empty and they are nowhere on base."

"Well that doesn't tell me a whole fucking lot does it?" The man had the good sense not to respond to the rhetorical question. "No matter, when they arrive this will be a tragic end for our heroine and her band of merry men."

He handed the phone back to the man standing next to him.

"Do you think she made me?" said the tall man, his large purple birthmark evident on his neck.

"No, she was too far away. Beside she's so disgustingly obedient and frightened she would never question."

The other man just stood there, not saying anything. He admired the General and, in some respects, even agreed with this psychotic plan. He wanted to end this war and get the hell out – alive – and with as much money as he could. But he disagreed with the General on this one thing, his daughter was not frightened, or weak, or even obedient. She was smart. Very smart. And in his world, smart was dangerous.

CHAPTER NINE

They slept and ate during the day not wasting the much-needed energy for the evening journey.

At night, they walked until they couldn't walk any longer. With the onset of winter coming, the nights were longer, which played in their favor and allowed them to make their destination quicker.

On the third night as they came around a narrow ledge, they saw the group of buildings in the distance. It was similar in construct to the first location, but definite activity happening in the compound. Surrounded by a fence, lit well, and guarded, this group of buildings was vastly different than the last.

"Let's find a place to rest. We'll take a look and make a plan." Joe pointed to a small cluster of boulders and trees against the western ridge and they settled in for the night, huddled together against the cold.

Looking at the complex through night vision goggles, more commonly known as NVGs, he could see at least four armed guards on the outside. But it wasn't as heavily guarded as he would have expected. The difference was that there was activity. A lot of it.

Trucks were moving in and out of the complex almost every hour on the hour. People wandered from one building to the next. They certainly weren't hiding their presence from anyone, but would anyone even know they were here? Surrounded on all sides by mountain ranges, they were perfectly hidden in this little pocket of a valley.

He leaned back against his pack, with Erin lying next to him. He watched her breathe softly and he kissed her cheek, feeling the warmth. She had been so brave. They had marched hard and not once had she complained or asked to stop. She ate when they ate; she slept when they slept. Each time Wilson would check her feet and clean or rebandage them.

Trak signaled that he was going down to take a closer look. His silent hand signals easily understood by Joe. He signaled for the man to be cautious and in true brother fashion, Trak flipped him the bird.

"Sir," Chris stood in front of the General, "there is no trace of any of them. No body parts, no clothing, nothing. They all seem to be gone."

"Well, they didn't just fucking turn to dust you idiot. Are you telling me there are no bodies at all?!"

The man had the decency to blush and look down.

"Are you all incompetent fucks? Find them. Start searching the area around the base. Look up into the mountains. Search again for bodies. But find them!"

In the late afternoon, Trak crawled under the rocky ledge and ate his first bite of food in more than twenty-four hours. He easily loses time when he's working and often forgets to eat, something he is reminded of only by his growling stomach.

"Anything?" said Joe, not moving from his spot.

"Lots of activity, lots of people, but it doesn't look like it's some super-secret chemical weapons factory. It looks like any other business in the modern world. Computers. Phones. But there is a pattern in the guards' rotation. Four men on the perimeter, four men on the inside. They rotate every two hours."

"Thanks, brother. Get some sleep."

Trak was down and out before the last words left his lips. They all possessed the strange ability. When you needed to sleep, you slept; no matter where, no matter how.

She heard the men whispering and turned to see Joe and Trak speaking softly. She rose from her spot and walked carefully behind the tree line to where they indicated everyone could relieve themselves. It was the only part that she was not okay with. She wanted a real toilet and a real bathtub. By the time she got back to Joe, Trak was fast asleep and the others were moving quietly packing their things and eating.

"Do you think he's down there? Orion?" she asked quietly.

"Maybe," said Joe, not wanting to hide anything from her. "Maybe not. We won't know until we're there. We go in tonight." She nodded and looked at him, her head tilted knowing he was keeping something from her.

"What is it, Joe? What aren't you telling me?"

Code and Miller looked his way, and Wilson cleared his throat. She looked at all of them and back at Joe.

"Joe?"

"Baby, listen to me. I need for you to stay calm and no outbursts okay?" She nodded. "Erin, the General isn't your father."

"What? That's absurd, of course he's my father. I'm not happy about it, but he's my father nevertheless." She said it almost in the tone of a question. Her stomach lurched and she wasn't sure if it was out of delight or disgust.

"Erin, he can't have children. He could never have children and there is no record of him ever having been married. Your father was Master Sergeant William Richards."

Breathing heavily, she sat on a large rock near the men.

"That's not possible. Surely my mother would have said something." Her voice was so quiet she wasn't sure any of them had actually heard her.

"Baby, he had scarlet fever as a young boy." He stroked her hair, grabbing her into his embrace. She knew what that meant. She was well aware of the medical implications of scarlet fever.

"I don't understand. Why? Why not tell me? Was he even my legal guardian?" She wasn't crying. He was glad for that, but sooner or later her emotions would bubble to the surface and they needed that moment to not be tonight.

"We're not sure, Erin. Tailor and Angel are looking into it." She was quiet and her thoughtful expression gave nothing away. She stared off into the distance, her thoughts millions of miles away. The silence filled the night air and Joe finally intruded. "Erin?"

"Why are they called Tailor and Angel?" she said matter-of-factly.

"What?" He looked at the other men confused.

"You all have meanings to your names. Why Tailor and Angel." Wilson looked at her recognizing the diversion tactic.

"Tailor's name is Billy Joe Bongard. He's a great kid from Arkansas who also happens to be about six-foot-seven, so clothes were hard to come by when he was a kid. He can sew or fix anything. He was pretty poor growing up, so had to learn to constantly remake his clothes. He was a soldier and firefighter and actually repaired a leaking hose in the middle of a massive structure fire and was able to put the fire out." He took a breath and she nodded.

"And Angel?"

"Angel, well we all believe Angel has an Angel sitting on his shoulder. He's been shot more times than all of us put together and he's still alive and kicking and it seems whenever he's with us, we all survive despite all odds. His real name is Luke Jordan."

"Thank you for telling me that."

They watched her and waited for something, anything that would indicate where her mind was.

"It makes sense now you know," she finally said in a soft voice. "The way he's always treated me, like I was a commodity, not a child. He didn't love me. He wanted to own me. I think he wanted my money." She stared out over the valley.

"Your money?" Miller questioned.

"Yea. I didn't think it was a big deal to mention before. I mean if he were my father, then he would have had a huge amount as well. But now, now I get it. My mother's family was dirty filthy rich. Old money. She became a teacher so she could help people. She taught in one of the poorest areas in all of Virginia. She didn't need the money.

"My grandparents made their money from smart investments. In fact, they were some of the original investors for Dryden. When my mother died, I received fifty-three point six million dollars in a trust. I can't touch the bulk until I'm thirty. Which is in about five weeks.

"I think he killed my mother thinking the money would go directly to him as my guardian. But she outsmarted him by putting the thirty-year-old clause in there. I think she knew that even if he was my guardian the money wouldn't go to him. I know for sure there was a clause in there that if anything happened to me prior to my thirtieth birthday the money would go to charities. I checked it myself when I thought Michael might kill me. But after thirty? My fath... General Murray is my beneficiary. The problem is that the stocks for Dryden would go to him as well. I guess she didn't get around to sorting that out."

"Baby, you don't know anything for sure." He wanted to agree. Hell, he did agree with her. But he wanted to be sure. He needed facts.

"You won't find proof. I've tried for years. Oh, he gave me a death certificate, but I know it was a fake. Knowing now, what I know, that gray coloring she had lying against those stark white sheets. I know she was poisoned. He killed my mother and I'm going to kill him." She said it without emotion. Flat, even and not even a flinch in her voice.

He was worried more now than before. His beautiful, sweet Erin was turning into a woman driven by vengeance. And that was a very dangerous place to be.

"You won't have to," came Trak's deep rich baritone. "I'm going to kill him."

She smiled to herself. She loved that man. Oh, not like Joe, but in a brotherly way.

 Oh shit! She loved Joe. Shit! Shit! Shit!

She heard the chorus of responses.

"You'll have to beat me to it," said Code.

"And me," said Miller.

"Ditto," said Wilson. "See, baby sis, we're in this together."

"Baby sis?" she laughed at the big man.

"Yep," said Miller. "Trak named you that a few days ago. You might as well be our sister. We can't touch you because your personal bodyguard is a dick and would kill us if we did. But we all think you're amazing, Erin. You need a family and we're it. The dysfunctional, fucked up lot of us."

She laughed softly not wanting her voice to carry down the valley. Her family. Yes indeed, they were more family to her than she had her entire life. She couldn't ask for more.

"Okay," she held up her hands, "okay, we all want the good General dead. At least we all agree on that. I need to change the beneficiary on my will. My attorney will let me do it via electronic signature if I explain the situation. That needs to happen soon."

Joe found himself once more amazed by her strength and resilience. She had been handed a piece of information that would have made anyone else crumble, but she had held up and moved forward. Perhaps because somewhere in her deepest memories, she had known all along.

All these years she had a sense of not belonging and now there was a very clear reason for that. He wondered what the younger Erin had been like. The studious Erin who always did what she was told. Had she ever broken the rules? Because she was about to break some big ones today.

He pulled her close and held her to his warm body. Her hands moved up and down his arms, feeling the ripple of muscle beneath his shirt.

"We move in at 0200," said Wilson, "that's the next guard change."

Joe nodded and told everyone to get some sleep. This mission had turned into an absolute cluster. A simple extraction. Simple. Except nothing is that simple and he should have known it wouldn't be. He saw a large garage door slide up on the main building and several workers started walking out, all in clean suits and breathing apparatus. The others sensing something as well, all turned.

"We have a visitor."

Erin looked down and grabbed the NVG binoculars. One of the workers was carrying a small plastic bag.

A black car with tinted windows drove casually through the gates. The worker slowly walked to the car door and the passenger rolled the window down and slit the bag open, dipping his finger in. Cocaine. It's cocaine!

"Cocaine," she whispered.

"What?" Joe looked around at her and grabbed another pair of the night vision goggles. "Son-of-a-bitch! They're not making chemical weapons, they're distributing cocaine."

"I don't understand this at all. Here in this place? I mean I thought cocaine was made in South America or Mexico, but not here." Erin looked at the men she now called brothers waiting for some response.

"It's actually more common than you think," said Wilson. "Soldiers get hooked on the shit all the time and it's a way for them to make money in this place. They can transport it back home and make a killing. It's not just cocaine, but heroin too."

"Change of plans," said Joe. "Trak, you and Code will go down tonight and see if you can get your hands on something to prove what's going on. Files, documents, e-mails, anything."

"Wait!" Erin raised her hand.

"No," said Joe too quickly, "You're not going with them."

"Well, thank you for that Father Joe, but I wasn't going to ask that." He gave a slight smirk at her sarcastic tone. "Code, did you remember to bring my laptop?" He nodded and pulled it from the pack for her.

"Then that's all I need. If I can hook into their network, I have an encryption program of my own invention. I can hack into their e-mail system and see what's going on."

They all looked at one another and smiled, their baby sis was full of surprises.

"I like her," said Trak lying back down and covering his face with his ball cap. Joe just smiled.

"Okay, let's see just how smart my baby girl is."

CHAPTER TEN

"Well done," said the man inside the car. "It's premium quality. Get ready to ship it tomorrow."

"Yes, sir," replied the man in the white suit. His hands were sweaty and shaking. He knew how dangerous the man in the car was. He hated these moments; he was ruthless and without conscience and if he didn't like you, you were dead. Orion was a name that they all feared.

He had watched almost all of the men in his remote village die at the hands of this man. Not just die, but they were tortured, mutilated and forced to have their families watch. All he wanted was the money to be able to get his family out of the country. Yet deep down he knew this man would never allow that to happen. If he could just get the money to his wife and children, at least he could die knowing they were safe.

"Ajib? Have you noticed anything unusual? Anyone snooping around?"

"No, sir, the guards are on duty all night," he eyed the man in the car, careful not to look directly into his eyes. "If anyone were around, they would have noticed, sir."

He nodded his head and indicated for the driver to move. They had one other stop to make and then he would board his helicopter and be back where he belonged.

Ajib walked away, joining his fellow workers in their white suits.

"What did he say, Ajib? Can we leave soon?" asked an older man.

"He was pleased," Ajib tried to keep a smile on his face, knowing they would all die. "We will be done soon my friends and then we can all leave this place." But Ajib knew Orion would never allow for any of them to leave this place. He had to find a way out for all of them.

———◦⟶ ———⟨⟩——— ⟵◦———

The darkness enveloped them and Erin pulled the dark poncho over her head and over the laptop to block the light. Her encryption program had been working for more than an hour and suddenly it clicked.

"I'm in." she said quietly. She heard the shuffle of feet around her and knew the men were near.

"Anything, baby sis?" Miller said. She smiled under the poncho at the term of endearment.

"Lots of messages back and forth saying 'he's coming' or 'he will be here soon.' They seem frightened by 'him.' They're pushing one another to make things perfect. Wait. This one is from a worker to a family member or friend. He's saying he just wants to come home and he hopes they can make the boss happy enough that he will let them go. I don't think these workers are here because they want to be."

"It makes sense, Nine. These people have nothing. They're innocent villagers. If Orion got to them, I'm sure he's threatening their families." Miller sat next to Trak. Joe ran a hand over his long beard.

"Christ, is anything easy anymore?"

"Geez, this system doesn't really have any securities beyond the first set. Once I was in, I'm seeing files galore. You guys aren't going to like this. They're delivering those drugs locally, but also to military bases, both in-country and out."

They all looked from one man to the next. Drugs were commonplace on bases, although much harder today than twenty or thirty years ago. Still, where there were soldiers, marines, airmen, and sailors, there was inevitable boredom and the need for recreational drugs. Orion had found his perfect direct sale. If they weren't using the drugs, they were selling them and returning them somehow to the U.S.

Suddenly Trak lifted his hand to silence the others, but Erin was still under the poncho. Code silently knelt down beside her and leaned in.

"Do not speak. Do not make a sound." Code's voice was barely audible, but Erin heard "do not" and "speak" and she froze in place. She didn't touch the keys, didn't move for fear of making a sound.

Trak pointed to the spot below their ridge where a man was walking up the mountainside. A cell phone was glued to his ear as he spoke quickly. Trak was the most proficient at the language and he listened carefully.

As the man moved closer, he suddenly stopped and looked back down at the valley. He sat on his heels and started to cry, repeating to the person on the other end of the phone that he loved them and would see them one day again soon. He closed the phone and stayed where he was, hunched over, crying like a lost toddler.

Joe gave signals to everyone and they carefully moved from their positions to flank the man. His crying helped to cover the sounds of their movement. Code laid his hand on the back of Erin and whispered again, "no." She understood and again, did not move.

The man suddenly felt as if someone were watching him and he stood abruptly only to be greeted by a giant of a man. His trousers and his weapons indicated that he was American and the man suddenly knew that his life was over.

Speaking rapidly in his own language, Wilson knew the man was pleading for his life. As Joe and Trak crept up beside the man, Miller stood behind him. They frisked him for weapons, finding nothing except the cell phone.

"Do you speak English?" asked Joe. The man nodded.

"Please," he cried, "I was only saying goodbye to my family. I know Orion will kill us all tomorrow, but please send my earnings to them. I wish only that they are safe."

"Good news, friend," said Wilson. "We're not with Orion."

The man's face squinted and he looked confused and then frightened again. This was worse. If Orion knew he had been caught, he would be murdered in a most horrific way. He would be made to suffer and so would his family.

"Tell us what's happening down there," asked Joe.

"We can help you," Erin's soft voice carried in the breeze and the man turned wide-eyed and even more fear passing across his face.

"You!" he said pointing at Erin. "You are supposed to be dead or will be dead. And if you show up here, we were supposed to notify Orion immediately."

"Why?" she asked.

"We don't know. We only know that when you arrive, they were going to take everything and we were to wait in the buildings with you." He looked from one giant man to the next and silently wondered if Americans drank something to make them so large. "I believe Orion will kill us all and that he was going to kill you as well."

"But why?" asked Joe moving toward the man in a most unsettling and threatening way. The man cowered again and sat low on his heels. Wilson lowered his large body so that he was kneeling in front of the man.

"We're not here to hurt you. We are here to help you if we can."

"You cannot help," he said in a voice that indicated he had given up. The helplessness that was palpable around the man was oppressing. "We are all dead. He has killed most of my village and the men down there now, will be dead tomorrow."

He searched the faces of the Americans again looking for some sign that would help decide what he needed to do next.

"When you arrive," he pointed to Erin, "the drugs will be loaded on the helicopters in crates that will go back to the American bases for sale and to my own people. They will tell your customs people that it was all con... con..."

"Confiscated?" Erin helped the struggling man.

"Yes, yes. No one will know what's in them."

"What do you mean what's in them? It's cocaine, right?" she said softly. He looked at her and then at the ground.

"The lady asked you a question," said Trak. The poor man looked as though he would wet himself.

"Yes, it is cocaine, but they have us mix other things in it. It is not designed for pleasure. It is designed for death. We will all become useless. You," he pointed at Erin again, "were expected by tomorrow afternoon with soldiers. We were given your picture and told to treat you with respect, but we were also told you were a liability that he could afford no more."

"It's not your fault," she said. "What's your name?" He looked at the woman, the kindness in her eyes.

"I am called Ajib."

"I'm Erin, Ajib. And we're not going to let you and your families die."

"Erin," Joe said in a sharp tone that made Ajib jump, "you can't promise something like that."

"I can and here's why. We're going to give Orion what he wants."

"What the fuck are you talking about? If you think I'm going to let you get blown up you can forget it."

"I'm not going to get blown up. No one is." She laid the palm of her hand against his cheek, kissing his lips softly. She looked at all the men sitting on the rocky slope.

"Ajib? Are all the men down there from your village?"

"Yes, except the guards. They were hired by Orion. They are evil men and believe me, I know evil men."

"Alright then," she said nodding. "Joe, don't you think you guys can take out the guards?"

Joe nodded eyeing her suspiciously. Eight guards total, and his five men. Great odds in his mind.

"Well then, while you guys do that, Ajib, Trak, and I will talk to the men. We're going to act like business as usual. While we're walking around, I'm going to get photos, samples, anything else on the drugs that I can find. Code and I will download any files we can from the system, anything. We're going to make this look like an accident alright, only Orion's not going to get his drugs. They expected me tomorrow afternoon. Well I'm going to arrive much earlier."

"I like her," Trak repeated his earlier statement and flashed her a rare, perfect smile. Joe looked at his teammate.

"You like her because she's fucking crazy and she's going to blow shit up!" He took a breath. "Okay, okay, Ajib tell us where everything and everyone is. How many men are there total? Where are the drugs located now?"

Ajib nodded and in the dirt, drew a perfect map of the camp. He indicated the sleeping quarters of the workers, the dock where the drugs were being held, office space, and the guards. These men were his only hope. If he could get to his family then he would walk them out of the country. They would find somewhere safe to live. There had to be one place on earth left safe.

"Miller, once we take out the guards, you find the explosives. Make sure they're not on a timer and if they are, change the time. And if there aren't enough, place more, more is better."

"More as in how much more?" Miller smiled at his friend.

"I want that fucking place to be a moon-sized crater. I want that hole so big he won't have a speck left."

"Roger that."

"Erin, you will be seen going into the building, but not coming out. We're going to make sure one guard survives to tell the tale."

"Ajib, you wake your friends and take them out this back entrance. We will cut a place in the fence so you can make your way up the mountainside. Hide wherever you can. Once this place is blown, you will be on your own. You'll have to make it back the best you can."

"That is more than we could hope for yesterday."

Erin closed the laptop and handed it to Code. She then started to place her things inside her backpack. The folder she had been carrying with the lab information slipped from her hands and fell to the ground, the contents strewn across the dirt, including a photo she carried with her of her father, well no longer father, but General Murphy. Ajib knelt and carefully dusted off each piece of paper and handed it to her. He held the photograph she carried.

"Why do you carry a photograph of Orion?" he asked, his hands visibly shaking.

"That's not Orion, Ajib. His name is General Murray." She said quietly. The men all stopped, cold hard stares pointed at Ajib.

"No miss, this is Orion. Believe me. I have had to deal with this man for many months. Two times a week he terrorized me and my friends. I've watched him torture my friends, beat them, and kill them with no mercy. You tell me this man is an American General? Then I am more frightened than I was yesterday."

She shook her head. The man who had pretended to be her father was Orion. She searched Joe's face and the clarity and concern made her shiver.

"The fucking old man has been playing all of us," said Wilson through gritted teeth.

"He was going to kill me from the beginning," she said sitting on the cold ground, wrapping her arms around her knees. Joe looked at his team.

"We're going to help these men get out, blow those drugs sky high, and lay low for a while. We have to figure out all the working parts to this and I'll be damned if we can do it in this shithole."

CHAPTER ELEVEN

Erin and Trak walked up to the front gate and showed their identification. The guard glanced up at them and then down at their identification again.

"Why are you walking?" the man asked in broken English. It wasn't a Middle East accent they heard, rather an Eastern European accent, perhaps Russian or Slavic.

"Our truck broke down about four miles back. We decided to walk in while they stayed with the vehicle. I'm hoping you can give us a ride back and help start the truck." She said with a huge smile. Damn thought Trak, she's pretty good.

"I can give you a ride anywhere," the man looked her up and down, licking his lips and Erin immediately wished she hadn't smiled.

Trak's strong hand was on her back and moving her forward. The guard opened the main gate letting them through the first outer gate. The security was pretty dim at this place, but being that it was in the middle of fucking nowhere, and run by Orion, Trak figured it would be doubtful anyone would bother them. And Orion's name alone would pose enough of a threat that no one would come near.

Ajib approached from inside the gates, where he had made his way back only moments before. Ajib spoke to the guard in his native language, and Trak listened intently making sure the man did not say anything that would put them in danger. The guard looked around Trak at Erin, with disgust in his expression. It might have affected a lesser woman, but Erin was not such a woman.

"We expected more than one soldier with you," the guard said. Trak's ears instantly perked up.

"Like I said, the other men are back with the truck, they will wait with the vehicle until we can get it fixed." The guard nodded and smiled a malicious, vicious smile that made her skin crawl.

"No problem pretty lady, like I said, I can give you a ride," he smirked.

Trak wanted to move on this man, but knew his time would come. The guard opened the inner gates and Ajib began speaking as if giving a tour. Without even turning around, Erin knew that the now familiar thump she heard was the guard hitting the ground. Trak propped him up in the guardhouse and slowly moved in behind her and Ajib. As they made their way across the grounds, another guard joined them, not noticing that his buddy at the gate was no longer standing, but sitting.

Wilson and Miller made quick work of the other guards around the perimeter and without drawing a heavy breath, began the elimination of the guards on the inside.

Code searched each of the offices for files he thought could be important and slipped a thumb drive into the USB port of one of the computers, downloading all that he could from the slow system.

Joe moved quietly from building to building waking the men and telling them to leave through the now open chain link fence. The men all looked at him wary at first, but in his broken Farsi, Joe explained that he was there to help and was working with Ajib.

Miller worked to reset the explosives and added a few extra blocks of C4 – just in case. He needed to make sure any chemicals inside the drugs would burn before they could become airborne.

Walking around the complex, Ajib finally brought her to the main lab building. The guard opened the door for her, allowing her, Ajib and Trak to enter. They turned on all the lights, and continued their conversation as if nothing was amiss.

Erin was looking around the room taking in all of the equipment. Everything appeared to be relatively new, yet definitely used on a regular basis. She took note of the folders at each station and testing equipment. While standing at one of the stations, she noticed three white blocks sitting near several microscopes. Casually walking toward the area, Erin appeared to be testing some of the equipment.

The guard, now standing outside the door peered through the small window watching them cautiously. She saw his sly grin and then heard the click of the key in the lock and realized he had just locked them inside the building.

As if sensing her panic, Trak moved behind her, gently touching her back and whispered.

"Business as usual, sister."

She simply smiled and continued, making it appear she held interest or fascination by each of the items on the table in the lab. Once the guard was no longer at the door, she slipped one of the blocks of white powder into her bag.

When Trak received the all clear from Wilson, they moved to the back of the building and without a sound, made their way to one of the windows. Trak, being much larger than Ajib and Erin, had to maneuver one shoulder at a time through the small window. He landed on his hands, almost in a handstand.

Erin thought it looked graceful, his long body easily held up by his arms. They made their way along the fence line until they found the opening cut for them. Once through they worked their way to the easiest route up the mountainside.

At the rendezvous point, Joe sat with Miller, Wilson, and Code.

"Everything okay?" he said rising to hug Erin. She nodded, but held onto him, breathing in the safety of his scent. Looking at Ajib, Joe stretched out his hand.

"Thank you, my friend. The rest of the men are just up above those boulders. Make your way home. We can't help you from here. You'll have to disappear."

"Will they not be suspicious when they find no bodies?"

"They will find bodies," said Joe, "but it will be the bodies of the guards outside the buildings. The buildings themselves will be decimated. Nothing but ash."

Ajib nodded and looking at Erin he gave a small, respectful smile.

"I wish many blessings and I will pray for your safety."

She nodded back at Ajib recognizing the gift he had given her. The gift of respect. He started to make his way up the mountainside.

"One more thing, my friend," he said looking at Joe, "there is another factory somewhere. I've never been but I know I overheard him saying things about a location where other things are made." Joe nodded and thanked him once again.

"Ready," asked Miller.

"Ready," said Joe.

With a flip of a switch, the buildings became massive clouds of fire and smoke, leaving in their place only crater-like holes of debris. The rumble and impact of the amount of explosives sent rock and debris sliding down the mountainside and they all huddled behind a boulder waiting for the tremors to stop. Just outside the gates were two guards, placed carefully so they would survive. They would remember nothing, believing that they had blacked out by the explosion.

"That should be seen a few miles away," smiled Wilson.

"Yep," said Miller, "some of my finest work."

"What about us?" said Erin looking at the men around her, "What now? If we go back to base, he'll want to know where we've been and how we survived. If we don't go back, I will have to live hidden for the rest of my life."

"For now," said Joe, "we'll keep it as missing. With this blast, they'll think we went with it, at least for now. We need time to figure out what it was he wanted with all of this. We also need time to prove that he's been dealing drugs through U.S. military personnel and equipment."

The sounds of a helicopter from above were heard and Erin immediately began to feel panic rise in her throat.

"That's our ride," said Trak.

"Ride where?" said Erin.

"Somewhere safe," said Joe kissing her forehead. They continued to climb the mountainside until they reached the small plateau where the helicopter had landed.

"Hey asshole, nice to see you," said the man in the chopper. Erin could only assume they were friends since they were both smiling and Joe didn't take his head off. "I see you've caused chaos again."

"You know that's my specialty," Joe smiled at the man, helping Erin into her seat. When everyone was strapped in, headsets on, the pilot moved the chopper swiftly from the mountaintop. The early morning hours were approaching and they wanted to be in their temporary location before sunrise. It seemed as though they had only just gotten up, when they were making their way down again on another plateau.

Lifting their gear out of the chopper, the pilot handed Joe two large duffels.

"There's extra food, water, clothes and ammo in there; also, a little something from the team back home," he winked at Joe and waved, "See you soon, asshole."

"Who was that masked man?" asked Erin sarcastically. Wilson laughed at her.

"Just a friend of ours who works with the Delta teams. He helps us out on occasion on a contract basis."

Joe opened the bags inspecting the items and inside the second bag, as he had indicated, was a present from home. Twenty thousand dollars in cash.

Pointing toward a barely visible trail, the team moved toward what appeared to Erin as a granite wall, but upon closer inspection was a gray door in the side of the mountain. Trak entered first, inspecting the space and turning on the battery-powered lights in the small space.

The dark cave transformed into a small cabin-like feel. Six cots lined the wall, a small gas stove on a table in the center of the room, worn Persian rugs spread across the floor, and four small chairs filled the space.

"Home sweet home," said Joe, "for a while anyway. Code, get comms up and see what Tailor and Angel have found."

"Comms?" questioned Erin, "You're telling me that you get Wi-Fi in this cave?"

Joe smiled at her and without a firm yes or no, she knew that somehow, they had the equipment that would link them with the rest of the world. He kissed her forehead and with his hand at the small of her back, pushed her toward the rear of the cave and one of the cots.

"Sleep, baby, it's been a long night." She didn't have the energy to argue and couldn't even think of anything except rest. Laying out on her blanket, she stretched and within minutes was completely gone to the world. He watched her sleep and thanked God that they had been able to get out alive. But he knew that the General or Orion, wouldn't stop trying to find her.

Walking toward the front of cave, Code sat at the small table pecking away at the laptop.

"Check it out, Nine," he said pointing to the screen.

Joe sat at the table and turned the laptop so he could read more easily. The e-mail from Tailor and Angel was filled with information. The good General had moved in on Erin's mom immediately after the death of her father, who suspiciously died in a training accident with his unit. Everyone assumed they would marry, but it seems the grieving widow refused to commit.

And then she became mysteriously ill. No records of hospitals, specialists or doctors, other than an Army doctor, ironically a classmate at West Point with Murray. He was the only one to see Mrs. Richards on a regular basis. When she died, with no family left to care for Erin, the General pulled as many strings as he could, and graciously took on the responsibilities of caring for Erin.

Except the pattern was clear, the General chose every school, every path, every aspect of Erin's life. Erin was correct, she had been left a hefty inheritance that she couldn't touch until her thirtieth birthday. The General was her beneficiary after her death. But if she died before then, the dear General would never receive the money. He was going to have to keep her alive until her thirtieth birthday.

Except it appeared that Murray created what was surely a false will for Erin, filed and signed in the courts of the Commonwealth of Virginia. In the will, it stated that despite the trust requirements, the money would be left to her grieving father upon her demise. There was no doubt he expected to have that money.

As for the General, eight times, he had come under suspicion by the Army for inappropriate conduct and eight times, cleared. It all seemed too easy.

His current duty station was considered the worst possible place to be, by anyone sane. But he had volunteered to stay long after they encouraged him to not only leave, but to retire. It seems the General had senatorial, and private contacts that felt his presence in the Middle East was a positive one. The only mission the General failed on? Capturing Orion. Nothing referred to the fact that Erin was his daughter, only that he had an unofficial guardianship.

Joe stood and blew out a long breath.

"That's not the good part, Nine," said Code. "Look at this. Sly did some extra digging for us. Seems the General, although good, was not as good as Sly. He has four different bank accounts. One in the Caymans, one in Switzerland, one in Columbia, and one in DC. The one in the U.S. has more than $390,000 in it. Hefty, but not something that would draw extreme suspicion. I mean the guy makes a General's salary and lives on a base. So, we could argue that he saves and invests well. The other three though? They are all in the name of parent companies that the General just happens to serve on the 'board' for. The total? $174.4 million. And the largest sum? From Dryden."

All the men stood up straight and looked at the e-mail. $174.4 million is a lot of money. But why kill Erin for more?

"So that's it?" asked Joe. "This is all about the money and more money. This piece of shit is trying to kill U.S. soldiers and the woman I love for more money?"

They all looked at him and Wilson was the first to let the smirk escape his lips. Joe drew his hand over his face.

"Fuck. I'm fucked, aren't I?"

"I like her," was Trak's standard line, but this time he added. "You are fucked. But she's a keeper."

"Joe, it's not all about the money," said Code. "The information I downloaded from the factory was sent to Angel for review. The cocaine was no doubt cocaine, but it was also going to be used as a chemical weapon as well. His intention was to lace the cocaine with a toxin that when released would kill everyone it touched. You didn't even have to snort it. You could just touch it. And I don't think it's one chemical, I think he had a rainbow of chemicals to use depending on his twisted fucked up plan of the day. He didn't want Erin's antidote, he wanted to make sure it wouldn't work. In theory, his plan was most likely to play it off as drugs being transported were accidentally released and killed those in harm's way. Just an accident. Clumsy drug mules, something along those lines."

"What now?" asked Wilson.

"It's time to turn the tables," Joe said. "We find the other lab Ajib told us about and then we bring that fucking son-of-a-bitch down."

CHAPTER TWELVE

Erin was dreaming. It was a good dream, not one of the nightmares that had been plaguing her for the past few days. She dreamt that she and Joe were lying on a beach somewhere, the water lapping against the shore, the birds flying overhead. She could feel the warmth of the sun on her bikini-clad body.

She looked over at Joe and his muscles rippled, the six-pack abs that really looked like an eight-pack, shone from suntan oil and sweat. His tattoos seemed to glow in the light of day and she licked her lips wanting desperately to run her tongue down his body. She squirmed in her lounge chair, rubbing her legs together to stop the pulsing of her clit. A small groan escaped her lips and she brought his hand to her lips, kissing the tips of each finger. She started to suck each finger, pulling it into her mouth and out between her teeth. His cock strained against his swim shorts and his smile went wide. Erin? Erin?

"Erin, baby, wake up," he whispered in her ear.

Her eyes flew open, her breathing was heavy and she knew without even checking that her panties were soaked. She held Joe's hand against her mouth, the wetness still there. He was sitting beside her on his cot, staring at her lust-filled green eyes, his own heated and full of desire.

"Baby, all that sucking on my fingers is making me rock hard and the guys are all in here." His lust-filled eyes looked down at her, the grin tugging at the corner of his mouth.

"Oh God," she immediately felt the flush of her skin and humiliation rose in shades of red. She tried to pull her hand free from Joe's. "I'm so sorry. I was dreaming."

His perfect smile beamed down at her.

"It was a helluva dream, baby, and I wanna revisit that once we're in a different place with a little more privacy. But we can't here." She nodded seeing the guys talking and seated around the table behind him. "Come on, we've got some chow ready and a few things we need to discuss."

"Give me a minute." Erin relieved herself and ran a brush though her tangled mess of hair. She looked at herself in her small compact mirror and groaned. She looked tired and the bruises, still present but fading, didn't help. How long had it been since she had put makeup on her face? Geez she wasn't even sure if she had brought any. She did however remember to bring deodorant, sliding a generous amount under both arms and changed her t-shirt. She pulled her hair back in a tie and walked to where the guys were congregated.

"Morning, or afternoon," she said with a smile.

"Morning, baby sis," they said in almost perfect harmony. She grinned at the four men around the table, realizing that Code was missing, probably on watch. "So, what's the plan?"

"There is so much we need to figure out and we can't do it here." said Miller.

"Erin," came Trak's soft baritone voice, reverberating off the walls of the cave, "do you still have the evidence you took from the lab?"

"Yes, it's in my pack. I was going to try to analyze some of the content today. We don't have a sterile environment, but I might be able to tell what they laced the drugs with." She walked back to her cot, grabbing her green backpack and the box of small vials she had brought with her. "This won't give me definitive answers, but it's a start and can help me to understand what is NOT in the drugs."

"Okay, we'll continue to sort through the intel sent from Angel and Tailor, see if we can make heads or tails out of this mess." She nodded and moved to the small ledge nearest the light giving her better visibility to her equipment. She felt someone sidle up beside her and looked up to find her quiet friend, Trak.

"Hi, Trak," she said softly.

"Can I help?" His offer took her by surprise and her eyes grew large and round. "If you need..." Her smile made him relax and the awkwardness that he felt in offering instantly melted away.

"I'd love help, Oscar." She smiled again at him and then went back to pulling things out of her pack.

The use of his name surprised him. He meant what he said to Nine. He liked this woman. Not as anything other than a friend and as Joe's woman. But he didn't like most people. He was a great judge of character. A gift from his grandfather for sure. He could tell within sixty seconds whether you could be trusted, whether you were telling the truth, and whether or not you were hiding things.

His intuition was magnified beyond anyone else's and he knew it was both a gift and a curse. His friends, his family were the men of REAPER. He had no wife, no girlfriend, not even an applicant hoping for the job. He was good-looking, even though he had no ego, he knew enough about what women like to know that most found him attractive in a dark, brooding sort of way.

His body was hard, muscled, lean, and made to pleasure a woman. He just seemed to have a harder time than the others with women. He knew that his quietness, both physically and verbally, unnerved women. He had been raised in an environment where being loud didn't get you any prizes, it only got you noticed which in turn got you beat.

He almost laughed at himself. Oscar Smith was nobody. It was a name he adopted when he left the reservation so that he could forget who he really was. He found someone who would forge his papers and he ran with it. His military records, his time in Delta, hell even his paperwork with REAPER was all in the name of Oscar Smith.

But that wasn't who he was at all. Only a few people knew that while in Delta, he had put himself through school. He had a master's in economics and spoke four languages beyond his native tongue and English. He was fluent in French, Russian, and Spanish, and nearly fluent in Farsi. But no one needed to know that. People knowing things about you only made it easier to hold them over your head.

He smiled down at the top of Erin's head. Her auburn hair was closer to a true red, almost like a dark fire. The smattering of freckles across her nose, mixed with the fading bruises made her look younger than her nearly thirty years. He could definitely see how his hardened friend had fallen for her.

"Okay," she looked up at his smiling face and suddenly felt herself blush. Trak quickly looked away, fidgeting with the small bowls she had pulled from her backpack. "We need to wear these masks so we don't inhale anything. Put these gloves on as well. I don't want to take any chances. We're going to put a small amount of each of these liquids in the vials. Add to that just a tiny bit of product and the colors will help to tell me what could be in the product besides cocaine."

He nodded and donned the gloves and mask. Carefully slicing open the bag of cocaine, he dipped the tip of a knife inside and dropped a tiny amount into each vial of liquid.

"Perfect," said Erin.

He felt a sense of pride, which was silly. His work gave him pride every day. But working next to this woman was satisfying to him. He was glad he could help her and in turn, help his team. The vials each turned different colors.

"What does this mean?" he asked.

"It means we have a very nasty drug here. I'm detecting arsenic and ammonium chloride. One sniff would kill anyone. I don't think there is enough in here to send this out as a bioweapon, but sold on the street and used like any other recreational drug, it would definitely kill you after first time use."

Erin made her notes in the small binder she kept with her and carefully disposed of what was in the test vials.

Joe watched his dark, silent friend watching Erin. Normally he would have gone berserk alpha male on anyone that close to his woman, but he knew that Trak was only helping. He trusted the man like the brother he was.

There weren't a lot of rules on their team, but fucking with another man's woman was probably near the top of the list. He knew that Trak could be trusted completely, and if it came down to it, he would be the one Joe would choose to get her to safety. Trak had his secrets. Joe was smart enough to know that. But some secrets weren't meant to be shared and he knew that if it were going to endanger the team, Trak would divulge it.

He had also seen the man in the shower. Not that he was looking, but some things couldn't be avoided, and whether you wanted to or not, five or six guys in the shower saw shit. Nuff said. He saw the marks on Trak's back and buttocks but never once did he ask the big man about them. In time he would talk to them all if it suited him. Until then he would treat him no differently than anyone else.

"What did ya find, babe?" Joe said moving towards Erin and Trak.

"Pretty much what we expected. It's laced with poisonous chemicals and would definitely kill the user. But this is no bioweapon. It's just a very deadly drug." He nodded, looking at her to continue, knowing she had already formulated her own thoughts.

"I think this drug is exactly what the drug was that I have been working on for DC metro. I don't have my notes and obviously have more equipment at Dryden, but I would bet my career on it. I'd love to get this back there, but that doesn't seem reasonable at this point does it?"

Joe sucked in a deep breath and rubbed his hand over his hair. His once closely cropped hair that was now growing fast and driving him crazy. She smiled up at him, touching the side of his face and his eyes closed briefly, feeling the warmth of her fingers against his whiskered face.

"You're going to go bald if you keep dragging that hand over your hair." She grinned up at him and saw Trak lift one corner of his lip as he attempted not to smile. Joe let out a snort of laughter and turned to pull everyone together again, just as Code was walking through the door.

"I think we need to arrange to get back to the states." Erin looked up in surprise and terror filled her face. He reached for her and pulled her under his arm, holding her tightly to his body.

"I know what you're thinking. But we can't do anything more here. For now, he thinks you, or maybe all of us, are dead or missing. If we can get you back stateside without anyone seeing you, we can keep you safe until we figure this mess out. I need to be able to get a few of my own friends on Capitol Hill to help me with the General Murray situation. We need some power – both political and military – to stop him. We also need to be able to get you access to the equipment you need and with all of us working together in one space; we may be able to get this done fast. We have to be able to end this before your thirtieth."

She felt her eyes begin to water and she willed the tears back, holding her breath.

"I don't know. I just don't know. You've all done so much and I can't keep asking you to help and put your lives at risk." She searched the faces of the men around her.

"I know you know my story. And you know that I didn't have a family. You all have become the closest thing I've ever had to a real family. You've become my three older brothers and my baby brother," she smiled at the large men in the room and winked at Code who blushed and flashed his million-dollar smile.

"And you," she turned to Joe, "I don't care that your men hear but, but, I've fallen so hard for you. I couldn't live if something happened to you. This last week has been the happiest in my life. Despite everything that's happened. Ignoring what I found out about who I thought was my father. No holds barred, this is the best week of my life. That should tell you all what kind of life I've had and what you mean to me." Tears floated down her cheeks and Joe kissed the top of her head and drew her back against his chest, his arm wrapped protectively around her chest.

"We're in this together, Erin," said Miller. "We choose our own path and this is our path." The others all nodded in agreement.

Trak walked around the table and Joe turned Erin in his arms so she could see his friend. He cleared his throat looking at Erin in Joe's arms.

"I like you," he said with his trademark statement for her. "I didn't have family either. At least not any you would want. You have my protection for life. I will be your brother and your protector when Joe is not around. Ayóó ánóshí my sister." He bent and placed a kiss on Erin's forehead.

The men all looked at one another with a raised eyebrow.

"What the fuck was that? What did you just say?" asked Wilson.

Her dark-haired protector gave her a rare hug and the men all thought they were seeing a transformation like none other. She squeezed him and felt his ragged breath flow across the top of her head.

Joe eyed the man but not in a threatening way. Something was changing in Trak and for the life of him, Joe couldn't figure out what or why, but knew in his soul that it would be a good change. He had never heard Trak use the language he just heard. Never. He had just willingly given them all a piece of his history.

"What was that language, Trak?" she asked quietly.

"Navajo." He offered no more and they asked nothing else. But it all seemed to make some sense them. She wanted to ask what he had said. But not now. She knew that it would pain him to say more. So, she nodded at her protector in understanding and thanks.

"But Joe, how do we even get home? And how am I going to be able to carry a kilo of cocaine in my backpack? Even if I get on a transport out of here, when we hit customs in the

U.S. there will be dogs. I'll be recognized by someone. My hair and eyes are definitely a give-away."

He knew she was right, but they had to get that stuff home.

"Coffee," said Code. Erin raised her eyebrows and looked at the men whose faces were giving that 'what the fuck do you know' look.

"He's right," she said. "Coffee can hide the scent of drugs. If we broke this up into smaller packages, we could hide it inside coffee. It may be our only chance."

"And just how the fuck did you know that piece of information?" asked Miller.

"Maybe I'm not so squeaky clean," said Code with a slight shrug of his shoulders.

"Right!" said Miller with a loud snort, "And maybe I like white wine."

"Okay, that's solved," she said looking around the room. "Now how do we get home?"

"Walk in the park, baby," Joe gave her a slight squeeze and kissed the top of her head, walking toward the waiting laptop. He was going to get his team home and protect his woman at all costs. There was a shit ton to do before he could let her be visible to the world again, but there was no way he was allowing whatever calamity the General had planned to rub off on Erin.

He had waited thirty-six years to find the one woman that would make his heart melt. The one woman that he knew he could not only live WITH, but that he could never live without. He was going to make sure that she knew every day how beautiful and how special she was. Even if it killed him.

CHAPTER THIRTEEN

Somehow, Joe and the team had managed to get a transport home. They made their way first by walking, then by a mysterious truck that seemed to appear out of thin air to drive them to a nearby base. No one questioned who they were or why they were there. The General had his connections, but so did these men.

When they arrived at the base, Erin watched as Joe was deep in conversation with a man that had the clear markings of a colonel on his blouse. She was curious as to what they were discussing, but knew that her life was safe with this man, THESE men. He shook Joe's hand and turned his back, as if not wanting to see any of them. Without another word, they were loaded on a plane and headed for Germany first and then the U.S.

By the time they landed in Virginia, Erin was tired, hungry, cold and she knew that she smelled every bit as bad as the men around her did. She desperately wanted to get to her apartment and shower, put on clean clothes and slide into her nice warm bed. She didn't have much. She never splurged on things for herself. Her apartment was sparse to say the least. A small efficiency with a daybed, one small armchair, a small television and her personal things. That was the extent of her life.

Actually, what she really wanted to do was disappear with Joe. Just board a plane to somewhere warm and forget the world. But she knew running would never be the answer and she couldn't outrun the General for long.

As if sensing her nervousness, he reached over and pulled her close.

"It's going to be okay, baby, I promise."

She gave a slight nod and smiled at the men around her. She looked out the window, seeing the gray skies of fall. It looked cold and with the movement of the plane, she knew it was windy.

"I need you to pull up the hood on your jacket and keep your head down. Stay between me, Wilson and Miller at all times. Hopefully, all they'll see is a short guy in the middle of us." Again, she nodded.

"And what if the General sees you and knows you're alive? What then?" she whispered.

"Then we just tell him that you were killed in the explosion and we were all so distraught we came home. Our mission was done." Miller said it as though he were speaking the truth. A cold hard truth.

"I just want to go home," she said in a childlike voice. "I want to get in my own bed and have my own things around me, pathetic as they may be."

"I know you do, baby, but you can't go back there. Not now." She started to protest and he held a finger to her soft lips, the small cuts were healing and in the light of the plane, he noticed that her bruises were nearly gone as well.

"We can't risk someone watching your place. We're going to our compound. It's really more of a small community that we happen to own. We all have our own places there. I've already sent Angel out to buy you clothes, toiletries, and anything else he thought a beautiful woman would need." He smiled down at her, kissing the tip of her nose, and her heart did a little backflip. "If you need anything at all, one of us will go out and get it."

"I can't let you pay for all that. I have money, you know that."

"Baby, it's not about the money. We all have money too. You can't access your money right now. You can't use a credit card or a debit card." He was almost hurt by her statement but he knew her intention and quickly dismissed his feelings.

Jesus this woman was turning him inside out. He felt the stab of pain at the fleeting thought that she might die. How could this have happened to him? How could he have fallen so hard and so fast for this woman?

"Tell me where we're going. Where is this compound?" she asked.

"When we retired, Wilson, Trak and I first," he pointed to all the men, "we bought about a hundred acres outside of Berryville a few years back. It already had a large farmhouse on the property which Wilson and I live in. It needed some love, but we've done a lot of updates and it's pretty modern now, but still looks like a farmhouse from the outside.

"If you're looking from the road, it looks more like a gated community. It's highly secure – fencing, cameras, sensors, the works. No one gets in or out without us knowing about it." He looked at her and saw her intense gaze around the plane.

"The other guys have built their own homes around the property, but in the enclosed area. We also have a small bunkhouse built onto the main house in case we have to lock down or create a secure environment and perhaps guard beautiful green-eyed women." He gave her a sly grin and she chuckled at his ability to ease her nerves even in the worst of circumstances. "Once we leave the plane, we move together directly to the waiting SUV. Angel is here for us."

She only nodded but the pit in her stomach was making her feel very uneasy and she worried about what her father. Damn, not her father. She would have to stop thinking of him like that. She worried what the General would do to them when he found out she wasn't dead.

Just as Joe had instructed, she first pulled her hair up and twisted it in a tight bun, so that no strands could be seen from the hoodie. She left the hood loose around her head, like that of a teen-aged boy instead of a hiding female. She remained between the three larger bodies of Joe, Miller, and Wilson and watched as Trak's eagle eyes looked in every possible direction at once. From the rear, Code was babbling on about needing a beer and a burger and a woman. Just like one would expect from a man returning from a mission.

Joe's friend the Colonel, arranged for expedited security clearance so they found themselves at the front of the line, with no hassles. The only thing that caught suspicion was Erin's injuries. When the customs officer looked at her passport and then her injuries, he eyed her suspiciously.

"Are you alright, miss? Do you need help?" Joe stepped in front of Erin eyeing the name on the officer's chest.

"Dawson is it?" the man nodded eyeing the big man in front of him, "I'd like to speak to your supervisor." Dawson obediently waved over his supervisor and asked what the issue was.

"Name's Dougall, sir. I believe Colonel Webber called you." The man looked the men up and down and immediately motioned for them to pass.

"But, sir," interrupted Dawson, "I haven't scanned their passports. It's policy, sir."

"I'm well aware of policy, Dawson. They have clearance." Joe nodded at the older man and they made their way through the sliding glass doors.

As they exited the doors of the airport, a large black SUV was waiting at the curb. Without a word, the men pushed her inside, loaded the gear, and sped away.

Erin could hear the murmuring voices of the men in the front seats. She leaned her head back against the leather seats with Joe's wide shoulders pushing on one side of her and Wilson's on the other. Hell, she didn't need a seatbelt. If they crashed, she would be sandwiched between the two of them – all safe and sound. The hum of their deep tones made her relax and the gentle rocking of the SUV lulled her to sleep.

She was dreaming of sweet things. Dreaming of being in Joe's arms, and then warmth.

She felt the strong arms wrap around her and she rolled into the crook of his neck, inhaling his scent. She tried to will her eyes open, but every attempt failed and she finally gave in and simply allowed herself to be cocooned by her protector.

Joe lay Erin on his bed as gently as he could. He had several spare rooms, but he couldn't bring himself to put her in one of them. He told himself it was so he could watch her more closely, but he knew that was bullshit. He wanted her, needed her to be near him, beside him.

He gently leaned her forward against his chest and removed her jacket with as little disruption as possible. Lying her back against the pillows, her auburn hair was loose now around the pillow having escaped from its elastic confines.

He untied her shoes and placed them next to the bed. It was late afternoon and the setting late fall sun would soon be gone. He prayed she slept through the night. Pulling the blanket up around her, she rolled to one side and curled into a ball, her still casted hand tucked safely against her body. She looked so damned cute, he smiled to himself and let out a long breath, running his hand over his head again. He stopped mid-way and grinned, remembering her warning about his hair loss. He couldn't lose this woman. But fucking hell, this was a mess for the ages.

He heard the noise first and jumped as Trak stood in the doorway. He nearly barked at the man, but instead stood and moved into the hallway with him.

"I swear I'm going to tie a fucking bell around your neck." He gave a half-grin at his friend.

"She'll sleep, Nine, and she'll be safe. You have my word on that." Joe nodded and as Trak started out the door, Joe called him back.

"Trak? What did you say to her back in that cave? In Navajo?"

Trak looked at his friend a long time and hoped that he would understand his message and the intent.

"I said 'I love you my sister.'" Joe raised an eyebrow and nodded at the receding back of his friend.

"This is some fucked up shit, boss," said Wilson reclining in the large leather chair.

"Yep," said Joe definitively. "You hungry?"

"Always, but I'm gonna shower first and then I'll order." said Wilson with a huge grin on his face. "Pizza?" Joe nodded.

"I'll call it in and text the guys to see if they'll join us. We use the card, boss, and the General knows where we are and that we're safe."

"Yea, I fucking know. Chances are he knows already. I've got cash, no worries." Wilson nodded and started to walk into the kitchen.

"Hey, Wilson?" The big man stopped with the phone in dial mode and turned. "You think I need to worry about Trak's feelings for Erin?"

"Are you fucking kidding me right now?" Wilson almost looked angry at Joe. Almost. "That man would do nothing to hurt you or hurt her. I think it's exactly as he said. He loves her like a sister." Wilson calmed himself and sucked in a breath.

"Look Joe, we don't know a lot about Trak. I mean you and Tailor know the most and that's not a lot. The guys at Delta all said he was one mean son-of-a-bitch. But a friend of mine over there said he had one fucked up life. Abusive, alcoholic mother on the reservation and other shit that we don't know. If you're asking me? I think Trak is protecting her as a sister. Like maybe the one he couldn't protect."

Joe nodded at the big man as he listened to his order of eight large pizzas for seven men and a tiny woman who probably wouldn't wake until the morning. The guys slowly started to trickle in, clean, fresh clothes and some of them even shaved.

Miller and Code walked in together arguing about the front line of the Redskins. Angel and Tailor followed close behind and finally bringing up the rear, Trak walked back through, his hair wet from his shower and pulled tight into a man-bun.

They sat around shooting the shit for several hours, they touched on the situation they had left in the mountains but didn't speak further to it knowing that Erin would want to hear all that was discovered. A few hours later as they sat with full stomachs and more than a few beers, they looked up to see Erin enter the room.

Her hair freshly washed, fell in big damp curls down her back. She had on a pair of snug jeans that outlined every curve. Her dark green t-shirt only highlighted the color of her eyes and her bare feet poked out of the bottoms of her jeans.

"Hi," she said suddenly shy. "Ummm, thanks to my personal shopper. You did good."

"Hey, baby," Joe got up and kissed her soundly, causing an instant pink flush to creep up her neck and cheeks. "Erin, this is Tailor and Angel."

Erin walked to the man named Angel and couldn't help but think that's exactly what he looked like. Like the other men he was over six feet tall, he had soft blonde curls that framed his face and neck and the most angelic blue eyes she had ever seen. She held out her hand and knowing she would get the effect she wanted.

"Hello, Luke."

The guys all burst out laughing, but Angel's eyes got huge and for once, she was not the one in the room burning with embarrassment.

"Angel, ma'am, just Angel. And you're welcome, as your personal shopper I think I did a pretty good job." He winked at her and heard a low growl from Joe. But she nodded and gave him a wink right back.

Tailor stood almost nervously, worried now. He was by far the largest, bigger than even Wilson. She strained to look up at the man with mocha-colored skin. His head was completely shaved, shining in the light of the living room. His eyes were the color of warm hot chocolate and when he smiled down at her, the flash of white teeth was nearly blinding. He had a large dimple on the right side of his face that made him appear almost boyish. Almost – but this man was no boy. He was all huge muscle and intimidation.

"Ma'am," he said in his deep base voice.

"Billy Joe," she returned. And he favored her with deepest belly laugh she had ever heard. It made her giggle like a little girl.

She liked these men. All of them and wondered at how fate had given her a group of brothers she could have never imagined for herself.

"Okay, assholes, stop flirting with my girl." Joe pulled Erin closer and led her to one of the three long leather sofas in the man-sized living room. Actually, it was sized for these men. Not ordinary men.

"Do I smell pizza?" she asked shyly.

Trak stood and grabbed one of the boxes. Pepperoni and mushrooms filled her senses and her stomach growled so loud she heard chuckles behind her. She grabbed a paper plate and placed two slices on it and gave a small smile to Trak.

"What the fuck, dude? He's flirting with your girl!" said Angel.

"No," said Trak straight-faced. "I'm helping my sister."

Joe nodded at all of them and his heart warmed at the brotherhood that was filling the room. He loved these men and he loved his woman.

Fucking hell this was all so fast but be damned if he knew how to, or even wanted to, stop it.

They made Erin instantly feel at ease, telling stories about each of them, making her laugh. He smiled inside at the natural way his team had accepted Erin so quickly into their trusted fold. But he knew that this time of eat, drink, and be merry was about to end. They had to talk about business and it wouldn't be pleasant. He looked at the clock and realized it was nearly midnight.

As if on cue, Erin yawned and hid her embarrassment as they all grinned at her.

"I think we call it a night, boys. We'll meet in the conference room at 0800."

Joe stood and took Erin's hand lifting her from the couch. The men cleared the plates and pizza boxes, leaving no trace of their food fest. As Joe opened the French doors at the rear of the house, with Erin by his side, his men all grinned at him and as each one passed, they shook his hand and give a small kiss to the top of Erin's head.

"Night, baby sis," they each recited and smiled.

Her heart instantly picked up a few beats and she smiled. As Trak stepped forward, he lightly touched the top of her head with his lips.

"Yá'át'ééh hiiłchi'į'." And he stalked into the darkness.

Joe closed and bolted the door, turning to see Wilson standing in front of them.

"You didn't think I was going to be left out of this did you?" He grinned at his boss and knew it would piss him off, but lifted Erin easily off her feet and placed a kiss on her forehead. She squealed and giggled as he placed her back down and before Joe could punch the man in the arm, he backed away toward the stairs and yelled behind him.

"You're slowing down, old man. Goodnight, Nine."

Joe couldn't stop the grin that spread across his face. He took Erin's good hand in his and walked around turning off the lights, making his way down the long hallway back to their bedroom.

Their? Where had that come from? He had never had a woman sleep all night in his bed. Never. He didn't bring them here. This was his sanctuary. His safety. *Well, isn't that all gone to fuck in a handbasket?*

Joe shut the door and turned to see Erin in the darkened room, the only light from the bedside table illuminating her porcelain skin. She gave him a sultry look that immediately made his dick brush against the zipper of his pants.

"You tired, baby?" he asked praying her answer would be no.

She shook her head and slowly unzipped her jeans. Taking her time with every pull of the teeth in what seemed to Joe was a foot-long zipper. She gently tugged on the jeans, shimmying her hips from side to side until they were at her feet. The black lace thong beneath made him swallow so hard he knew she could hear him. It barely covered her and he could smell her sex from where he stood. He'd have to thank Angel for the purchases and then beat the shit out of him.

She grabbed the bottom of her shirt and pulled it over her breasts. The matching black lace bra barely held her large globes, creamy white skin peeking over the top, the nipples poking through, begging for his mouth. She walked slowly, seductively toward Joe and he didn't move. Leaning up on tiptoes, she kissed him sweetly, her now erect nipples brushing against his chest.

"Joe?"

He couldn't answer, he only growled.

"Joe, you have too many clothes on."

He nodded and with movements faster than she thought he possessed, he pulled his shirt over his head and his jeans were instantly gone. She noticed that he had gone commando and wondered how often she would have that pleasurable thought in her mind. Seeing his cock standing at attention, she turned for him to unhook her bra and she let it fall, her heaving breasts falling as well.

Joe couldn't stop himself. He lifted her to the bed and immediately pulled her legs apart, pulling the thong to the side he inhaled, and her scent filled him with such erotica he nearly came against the sheet.

"Fuck, baby, you're so wet, I can see it. I can see it glistening against your pussy hair. You smell so good." He looked up at her wide eyes and realized that this may be something she had never experienced before.

Joe wasn't a gentle man. If he wanted something, he took it and although he could be sweet, in the bedroom, he was generally crude and to the point, with a lot of dirty sex talk. Make no mistake. A woman would know what Joe wanted and what he was thinking.

"Baby, has anyone ever eaten you? Anyone ever pleasured you with their mouth?" She suddenly looked shy and scared and shook her head. "Don't worry, baby, you're gonna love this. I'm gonna eat that pussy until you scream my name. You're gonna feel things you've never felt before."

Joe yanked on the thong and pulled it from her body with little effort. He pushed her thighs further apart and slid one finger into her tight wetness, groaning at the agony that was developing in him. In and out he slowly moved, sliding his tongue up her slit, grabbing her clit with his lips, she gasped. He licked her juices, sucking and tasting every part of her. She was so fucking wet he couldn't believe it.

His baby was ready for him and wanted this. He slid another finger in and let his tongue roll up her beautiful pussy lips again, lapping at the juices that were dripping from her.

"You taste so fucking good, baby. I'm going to make a habit of this."

Taking her clit between his teeth, he pulled gently and then sucked hard, all the while finger fucking her. She started to buck, slowly at first, timid and afraid, then finally in tune with her body, she bucked against his lips and held his head.

"God, Joe... Joe please... " her voice trailed off and she continued to move.

"That's it, baby, fucking cum for me. Let me have it." He grabbed her nub between his teeth again and sucked hard and he knew she was done for. He felt the tremors against his fingers and her body shuddered with satisfaction. He licked her once, twice, and trailed his way between her thighs to her stomach and then finding her breasts. Her beautiful, full, fucking gorgeous tits. He rolled one of her nipples between his lips, nipping at it. Already getting aroused again, he knew she could go for more.

"That was amazing," she said breathless.

"We're not done, baby," he smiled down at her pushing her legs further apart with his knees. He grabbed one of her breasts and twisted the nipple making her squeak with delight.

"You're fucking ready again aren't you, baby?" Joe was an alpha all the way, but Erin suddenly realized he was Mr. Mega Alpha in the bedroom. He liked control and he was going to take it here. That was fine with her. She had a lot to learn and LORD this man was teaching her things she never dreamed about.

"We still good with no condom, baby? I have one, but I gotta be honest I want my cock rubbing against that sweet pussy, not some rubber."

She licked her lips and reached for his cock feeling the wetness dripping from him, she guided it to her opening and she nodded. He was so large. She had felt him before obviously, but here in the light, she noticed he was thick, long, and so sexy. She wondered if he would actually fit all the way.

With small movements, he pushed into her, slowly letting her get used to his size again. He was big, he knew that, but he was also wide and the width was what made most women scream. Erin never screamed, not in their quarters in shithole central and not here. She opened wider, inviting him in.

He pushed – more, more – and as if reading his thoughts, she took his face in her hands.

"Fuck me, Joe – more – all the way," and she slid her tongue deep into his mouth tasting her sex on his tongue, taking his breath from his body, mouth fucking him.

He didn't even nod he simply pounded into her, his balls slapping against her wet ass and pussy. He filled her completely and this woman was the most sexual thing he ever experienced. Her tongue explored his mouth, but when she nibbled at his lip and reached up and twisted his nipple, he lost his shit.

"FUCK! Baby, fuck!" he screamed. "Baby, if you keep doing that it's going to make me come. God baby, do you know how I feel about you? Do you get it?"

She shook her head but looked him in the eyes, showing that she felt the same. She rotated her hips higher, wrapping her legs around his waist, pulling him further in and she twisted his nipples again and slammed her tongue between his lips. He couldn't hold out any longer.

His load released in her and she felt the warmth instantly. The flow of his juices filling her, already leaking out of her, down her crack. He continued to move, slowing with each thrust until completely drained. She held his head against her breast, but they didn't move for what seemed like hours. He finally lifted his head and kissed her passionately. "Don't move, baby."

She watched his tight ass move toward the bathroom and a few minutes later he opened her legs and with a warm cloth cleaned her. She immediately moved to cover herself, but he shook his head.

"No, baby. We've seen too much of each other for you to be embarrassed by this. I take care of you. Period."

She reluctantly opened her legs as he wiped their juices from her and then he bent and placed a kiss on her pussy sending a chill up her spine. He smiled a wicked, knowing smile and her stomach did that backflip thing again.

Joe slid in beside her and curled her body next to his, her sweet round ass rubbing against his cock made him instantly start to go hard again. She started to reach around and grab him, but he held her still.

"Sleep, baby. We have time."

A lifetime, he thought. *Yep. Fucked.*

CHAPTER FOURTEEN

Nine heard the soft knock on the door but wanted to ignore it. Someone knocked harder this time and he heard Erin moan and roll against his warm body. Joe raised her arm from his chest and moved slowly out of the bed. He pulled his boxers on and opened the door to see Wilson standing there, sleepy with a phone in his hand. Nine glanced at the bedside clock – 0430 – he stepped into the hallway and quietly closed the door.

"What's up?" he said hoarsely, still not fully awake.

"It's General Murray. He said he tried calling you but your phone kept going to voicemail. Son-of-a-bitch even asked if you were killed in the explosion. I almost said yes."

Nine nodded to his friend and they made their way to the living room. He unmuted the phone and put it on speaker so Wilson could hear the conversation.

"General." There was no love lost between these two men and Joe was not about to give him any satisfaction at all.

"Son, you were supposed to let me know when this mission was done and you and your fucking team left without even saying goodbye. Now I'm kinda hurt by that but I'll forgive and forget. For now. There seems to have been a massive explosion not far from where you were last seen. I take it your team is okay?" He waited but Nine said nothing. "Where is my daughter?"

"First of all, *General,* don't call me son. My team is licking its wounds. We carried out our mission and delivered your daughter to the lab and as if you didn't know, it was a fucking set-up. While we cased the perimeter that whole thing was blown sky-fucking-high. Now I don't know what you're playing at *General* but I don't appreciate being set-up and I will find out how you were involved in all of this."

"Don't threaten me, *son*. Where is my daughter's body?" There was absolutely no emotion in his voice. Nothing to give away any sense of grief or remorse.

"I told you. Everything was blown to bits. Now forgive me for not picking up her pieces for you. My mission is complete. We are done." He gritted his teeth, seething anger at the phone. Wilson held his arm trying to calm him before he crushed the phone in his grasp.

"We're done, for now. But don't go too far." And with that the General ended the call.

Joe blew out a shaky breath and the pit in his stomach just became a major hole. Wilson stood to his full height and looked out the back windows, the view showing the distant lights of the rest of the team's homes. Most of them were up by 0500 to run or lift weights, so nothing was unusual.

"I'll have the guys check the cameras and sensors on property. We have to make sure that Erin goes nowhere, Nine. If she's seen now, this could end all of us."

"You don't think I know that?" he said. "I don't think he believed a fucking word I said, but it gives us at least a little time. I have to find someone in DC that can help us with this cocksucker." He took a ragged breath and stood beside his friend.

"I can't lose her, Wilson. I can't explain it, man, but I can't lose her." Wilson nodded his head and started for the stairs.

"Where are you going?" asked Nine.

"I'm going to visit an old enemy that I hope will become our friend in this. I'll be back late tonight." Joe nodded and headed back to the bedroom.

Too wound up to sleep, he pulled on a long-sleeved t-shirt and running shorts and donned his running shoes. A nice long run would work. He rarely slept more than four or five hours at a time and running was his way to feel normal again.

When they built the facility, Joe and Wilson made sure they had a state-of-the-art gym, a 12-mile running trail, a ropes course, climbing walls, and much more. They included the highest-end security features, cameras and sensors. No one would get in or out, without them knowing about it.

He made a mental note to introduce Erin to the security tech team, who quite literally lived in the tech space on-site, in the basement. They actually liked living in the dark – computer nerds – go figure. But truth be told, they were as highly trained as anyone on the team. For now, he needed to run, he just needed to expend his energy.

Taking off toward the running trail, he started out slow and then began to pick up a brutal pace. Joe always loved running and carried that love with him even after leaving the teams. He heard soft footsteps behind him but only as they were nearly on top of him, but he knew immediately they weren't unfamiliar. Striding next to him was Trak, not saying anything, only a slight nod.

Damn he wished he knew how the man did it. He was so silent sometimes you really had to look to see if he had teleported in.

The dark man's face was a mask of disinterest and showed no signs of exertion. He barely sweats, barely made a breath appear in the cold morning air, and in some ways, it truly pissed him off.

As if on cue, Tailor's heavy footfalls fell in stride with the two men. Unlike Trak, Tailor could be heard coming a mile away when he was running and not on a mission. In mission mode, he was considerably quieter – but still nothing compared to Trak.

"Damn, Tailor," said Nine, "good thing we weren't trying to sneak up on anyone."

The big man gave a chuckle.

"You try running quietly with a size sixteen shoe."

Tailor had been the butt of many jokes due to his foot size, but the men all knew that the myth was true for Tailor about shoe size and the size of his cock. That man swung a club! Not that anyone of them was actually looking, but some things you just couldn't help but see in close quarters or when showering during a mission or in a locker room. And damned if Tailor wasn't one of those men that you noticed.

As they picked up the pace and made their way back toward the main house, Joe could see the lights in the living area on and knew that Erin was up. When they stopped on the back patio, stretching and grabbing water from the outdoor fridge, he looked at both men.

"The General called this morning. He knows we're back and he wants to know where she is. I told him she was blown to bits, but I don't think he believed me. I need both of you on her at all times if I'm not here." Neither man said a word, but nodded in agreement and turned jogging back to their homes.

Joe looked in the windows and saw Erin making coffee. He realized that being alone had let him feel more confident and he rarely closed the automatic blinds on the back windows. He would rectify that immediately. Using the handprint recognition keypad, he opened the back door and was graced with her beautiful smile.

"Good morning, handsome," she beamed to him from behind the kitchen counter. The large open space allowed anyone in the kitchen to see and hear what was happening in the living room. The enormous fireplace had a very modern feel, but could easily heat the room if power were down. The cathedral ceilings with worn beams added to the homey feel and she thought to herself that this was certainly well done for a man cave.

The large painting above the fireplace appeared to be a landscape of a farm, but she noticed there were no personal photos. No pictures of any of the men, no family, no children, no wives. Nothing.

"Are you hungry?" she asked.

He pushed the button on the blinds and she looked at him at first puzzled and then with an awareness of why he was blocking out the room, a chill ran up her spine and she knew the feeling of panic would overcome her.

"Oh shit! Oh shit! He knows." Her knees buckled and she fell to the floor wrapping her arms around her legs.

Joe scrambled behind the counter and pulled her to him. She sobbed against his chest, shaking with fear. His hands rubbed her back, comforting her, letting her get this out of her system. With each sob, she settled more and he finally pulled his head back and lifted her chin with his hand, lightly kissing her lips.

"Better?"

She nodded with a small, nervous smile.

"What now?"

"Now we keep you safe," said Tailor with a huge grin. Joe actually jumped at the sound.

"Damn!" he said. "You taking lessons from Trak?" The big man just smiled at his boss.

"Yep. Are they working?" He winked at Erin. "I stink, but I grabbed some clothes and I'm gonna shower in the gym."

He moved toward the basement stairs, which Erin assumed was the gym area. Joe knew that it was because of what he had asked the big man. He knew that he would most likely shower with the door open so he could hear if anything went down. He'd have to warn Erin to not go down there if Tailor were showering. She might not recover from that sight.

"Breakfast?" asked Erin. Joe smiled at her.

"Let me shower and I'll cook."

"No," she put her hand up, "I'll cook."

"Um, babe, you said you couldn't cook." His nose wrinkled in feign disgust.

"Ha ha. I can cook, I promise." She pushed him toward the bedroom and she heard the shower turn on.

A few minutes later Trak and Code entered the back door by the patio. Both looked freshly showered and ready for the day. She looked up at both men and flashed her big warm smile, pushing her hair back over her shoulders.

"Morning, guys! Coffee?" They both nodded and accepted the cups that Erin extended to them.

She continued scrambling the three dozen eggs she knew the men would eat, and flipped the pancakes, moving easily through the kitchen. Cooking was her therapy, something that had always made her feel better. Of course, the General had warned her against it. He told her that with hips like hers and all the "extra" weight, she shouldn't cook at all, but only eat raw vegetables. What did he think she was a rabbit? She loved her curves, and it was becoming more and more apparent that so did Joe.

It was very clear that when Joe and Wilson had bought this place, they also made sure they had the most modern conveniences in the way of appliances, electronics and anything else.

Without a word Trak grabbed plates and started to pull out syrup, napkins, hot sauce, and other things that she hadn't even thought about. He laid everything out on the bar giving a silent hint to Erin that buffet style was the way to go for these men. Neither said a word, but moved efficiently in the space.

A few minutes later Miller and Angel walked in, and Tailor reappeared from downstairs. Just behind them, three more men entered that Erin had never met before. She made a slight move to stand behind Trak, but he turned and gave a small nod to her. Because all of the men had welcomed them in, she knew they were friend, not foe.

Joe walked down the hall, his tall frame now snugly encased in faded jeans, boots, and the sexiest blue henley she had ever seen on a man. His eyes glowed with desire when he found her in the kitchen and she knew without a doubt, that if the other men had not been there, he would take her right on the counter. Looking around the room, he grabbed the three unknowns and walked over to her.

"Erin, this is Bull, Grip, and Tommy." Erin's eyebrows lifted questioningly.

"Hmmm, maybe later tell me why 'Bull' and 'Grip', but Tommy, no offense seems pretty unoriginal."

The man looked at her and grinned. He seemed to be the oldest of all the men, probably mid-forties. His salt and pepper hair trimmed close to his head in Marine Corps fashion. He was probably six feet give or take and easily two hundred pounds of solid muscle.

"No nickname needed, ma'am. Tommy says it all." He winked at Erin and walked away sitting at the long table with the rest of the men.

Erin plated up all the food and Trak and Joe carried it to the tables for her. Eggs, pancakes, bacon, hash browns, and even mixed fresh fruit – enough to feed a small army. Which she suddenly realized she had sitting in front of her.

"Where's Wilson?"

"Have a seat, babe. He had a trip to make today. Let's eat."

The men with their gracious manners waited until Erin had food on her plate and then it seemed as though it were a free for all. Mounds of food were placed on each man's plate and they didn't seem to bat an eye. She immediately thought to herself that she would need to make more next time.

Instantly the groans of satisfaction came from around the table.

"Holy shit, baby sis," said Miller, "these pancakes are fucking amazing!"

"Mmmm, I agree, Erin, and I don't know what you did to the eggs, but awesome!" Code's smile was wide and sweet as always.

Their playful banter and teasing started in immediately. It made Erin feel safe and comfortable. Joe sat on her right so that he could grasp her good hand and Trak sat to her left to help place food on her plate. Surrounded by men, whom she knew that somehow, somewhere deep in her soul were now her brothers, she had never felt so protected and so cherished in all her days. The moisture gathered in her eyes as Trak looked at her and with his silent message, let her know all was well.

As the men finished and began pushing their plates away Erin rose to start cleaning the table. Joe grabbed her arm, pushing her back down and cleared his throat.

"We got a call from the General this morning. I'm not sure he really believes Erin was blown to bits." She winced beside him at the term and he instantly regretted his choice of words. He gave a silent sorry to her via his expression and she nodded, settling back down beside him.

"The good news is he doesn't know that we know he's not her biological father. I also don't think he believes we know what's happening, but it won't be long. Once he confirms that Erin is alive, he'll know that she's talked to us. From this moment forward Erin will never be left alone. Someone will always be in this house with her." The men all nodded and Joe continued.

"Erin, you cannot leave the property until we clear this up. Not for anything. Food, clothes, whatever you need we will get. But you cannot leave." She started to speak and he held his hand up. "Non-negotiable, babe."

Then men around the table all grinned at his term of endearment and he bit back a smart-ass comment.

"I know it will be difficult but we're not messing around. I need for you to tell Miller and Code what you need from the lab and they will get it for you."

"But they won't be able to get in. That place is like a fortress." She said looking around the table. There was complete silence for a moment and then loud laughter.

"Baby sis, you should know by now we can get in anywhere we want to get in." Miller gave her a sly wink and began picking up the plates. He looked across the table. "Rules of the house – if you cook someone else cleans." It wasn't a rule, but Joe knew that going forward it would be.

"If the two drugs are the same, from the same source, we have another lead." They all heard a shuffling noise and from a small door underneath the stairwell, two more men appeared.

"Any food left?" said the shorter one. Joe nodded and pointed to the plates in the center of the table.

"Erin, meet Sly and Pigsty." Erin raised her eyebrows, but they all just grinned. The one called Pigsty blushed a deep red. His dark brown hair was long, past his shoulders and his soft blue eyes made him appear very young. Although he was tall, he was extremely thin, at least compared to the other men, and Erin immediately wanted to make him more food. He reached his hand across and she brought up her hands to reveal the encased left one, so shook with her right.

"Morning, ma'am," said Sly. He was easily the youngest in the room. His red hair and freckles made him look as though he should be on a school playground, not around a table of hardened warriors. But even at what she guessed was around six feet, he was muscle bound with tattoos peeking from his shirtsleeves.

"Sly and Pigsty are our tech guys. Along with Code, they can pretty much do anything we ask for or need. They have eyes on the property at all times. They have visuals on the cameras, the sensors, everything from heating and air conditioning to the phone systems. We know your phone was lost when you were taken, but we can't use another in your name now. We'll give you a burner that will be non-traceable. You need to carry that phone with you everywhere. And I do mean everywhere, babe." She nodded and graced them both with an appreciative smile.

"Anything guys?" asked Joe.

"Umm, yea," said Sly with a mouth full pancake. "We have a hit on the two faces you sent us."

Erin let out a small gasp and Sly looked up apologetically.

"It's okay," she said. "I didn't mean to react that way." Joe nodded for him to continue.

"The first one," he pulled out his phone and showed the picture of Christopher, "Wilhelm Christopher Klowitzki, alias Christopher Bennett, alias Chris Brownlee, alias Christian Kruger, and about twenty other aliases. He was born in Poland, but somehow ended up in Germany where he attended Free University in Berlin. He graduated with a business degree and then joined the German militia until they kicked him out for raping a female recruit. Brutally raping I might add. He should have been killed for what he did."

Trak gave the man a deadly look and he immediately swallowed and blushed.

"I dated that man and never once, even in his anger, heard a German accent. I trusted him." Her voice was so soft they barely heard her.

"What do you mean in his anger?" asked Tailor. His dark face seemed to suddenly get darker. Erin shrunk a little at the bass voice that seemed to rattle the plates and silverware on the table. Instead of Erin responding, Trak looked at the big man across from him. "We'll talk later." Tailor nodded and gave her a small smile, just enough to show his dimple.

Joe leaned over and whispered in her ear.

"Baby, maybe on second thought you shouldn't be here."

"No. No, I need to hear this. I have to know what's going on. I'm a woman of science, Joe. I need facts and data. I'm sorry. I won't react like that again. And Tailor deserves to know. All of you deserve to know. The man I knew as Chris or Christopher never hit me, but he wasn't exactly kind to me either. He wanted sex and I did not. At least not with him.

"Michael was different. It started out as verbal abuse. I was too fat. My hair was too short or too long. I didn't wear enough makeup or I wore too much. I was too stupid or too smart. It didn't matter what I did. He snapped one night. He punched me in the face and stomach. I immediately left. But my fath... the General told me it was most likely my fault. I'm smart enough to know it's never okay for a man to hit." The men all looked at her admiringly, noting the courage and fortitude it took for this woman to sit and tell her story, and then listen while her life was shredded for all to see and hear.

Tailor's face was dark and brooding and she looked up to give him the hint of a smile. He exhaled the breath he hadn't realized he was holding, but gave a small nod to her.

Bull looked up from his coffee.

"I like her." Joe and Trak grinned slightly, noting the familiar phrase. Joe nodded at Sly.

"Chris is a contract hitman slash cleaner. You want someone dead or gone or dead and gone, he's your guy. The General has hired him on numerous occasions for private contract work in Iraq, Afghanistan, Sarajevo, and Bulgaria, but no one can seem to figure out exactly what it was he was working on. The files are sealed tighter than a virgin in church." He winced and had the common sense to blush looking at Erin. "Sorry, ma'am." She graced him with a sweet smile and looked down at her hands.

"The second one, Michael Greenburg, was harder to find. We got facial recognition data from his last known whereabouts, old photos that we were able to bring down from Erin's phone." She looked up but decided it would be better not to ask how they got those. "It seems Michael Greenburg is dead. He died in 1987 at the age of sixty-three from lung cancer. This man, is not Michael Greenburg. He is Miguel Santos." They all looked at one another and Miller let out a slow whistle.

"As in the Santos cartel." Sly finished his thought. Joe frowned, nodding at the group.

"Ain't this some fucked up shit." Nods and murmurs of agreement followed.

"He has been on the FBI and ATF's most wanted lists for nearly ten years. I'm not sure how he is still in the country, but he's been spotted numerous places in the last few years. And," he looked around the table and pulled up a photo from his phone, "he was spotted with the General the last time he was in DC. I got this from a friend in the FBI who was happy to divulge information if we agreed to share. Seems they've been after the good General and Santos for quite some time. I think we have an ally in them."

"Jesus, Mary and Joseph," said Erin "what the hell is happening here?" Joe reached for her hand as she stood, but she moved away and stalked toward the kitchen. Her long auburn hair was shiny and the large waves were swept over her shoulder, covering her breast. She had no makeup on at all, yet her skin looked like peaches and cream and her green eyes sparkled, with the long thick black lashes fanning her cheeks. Her jeans hugged her curves beautifully and the cream-colored sweater made her pale skin almost translucent. He would have to thank Tailor and Angel for the shopping spree and then ask how the fuck they knew so much about women's clothes.

She turned around facing the group of men who all had pained expressions on their faces. They were trained for shit just like this. They were used to piss poor resources, cluster fuck operations, and shit that no human should have to endure. But this woman shouldn't have to put up with all of this.

She eyed the men, looking from one to the other. She didn't need their pity. She needed their intelligence and she knew in her heart, she needed their protection, and that was like a gut punch. She didn't want to depend on anyone. Ever. But she also knew she would die if she left this house without one of the men.

"For my own sanity, I just want to make sure that I have things straight in my head." There was a lot of sarcasm in Erin's tone and he knew that his girl was about to show her temper.

"General Murray, aka the man who pretended to by my father," her voice was thick with anger but they all just watched her warily. "General Murray is not my father. In fact, it appears he is the man who most likely killed my real father. He set me up to take the fall for not one, but two murders, which obviously did not take place because it appears both dead men are walking around living the good life, happy as pigs in shit.

"He placed me inside Dryden so that he could be sure I would either find something I shouldn't or help him to discover something we shouldn't. He then sends me on a mission he knows will kill me, except he wasn't counting on you guys. Then I find out he's after my money, wants my shares of Dryden, oh and let's not forget he most likely killed my mother, and oh yeah, fucking set me up with a drug lord. Is that about it? Do I have the situation about right?" She looked around the room.

"That's about it, baby," Joe half-smiled at her accurate assessment of this very fucked up situation and loved that she was angry about it. Anger would help to keep her alert and alive. The others still watched her warily, ready for her to crack.

"Well fuck that!" She yelled. "Fuck that and fuck him. The General thinks I'm naïve and stupid and weak. Well he won't think that when we're done. I'll tell you exactly what we're going to do. I'm going to make sure that he doesn't get a fucking red cent of my money or my shares of Dryden. If he doesn't know now, he will know by the end of the day that I'm not dead because I'm going to change my will and make sure that he sees nothing, do you hear me? NOTHING.

"I'm going to prove that the cocaine in my lab from DC Metro and the stuff we brought back is identical and that it's coming from him, designed to kill American military personnel.

I'm going to make him wish he'd never uttered my name." And with that she stalked down the hall and into the bedroom.

"I like her," said Bull and Trak simultaneously.

Joe let out a long breath and ran his hands over his hair, stopping midway. He grinned knowing that the approval of his men was not something he needed, but damn if he didn't love hearing it.

CHAPTER FIFTEEN

Wilson did not want to see Senator Alan Haley. He would have rather taken a beating from Tailor and Joe and Trak, all at the same time. He successfully avoided him for nearly thirteen years, although that brought him some feelings of guilt as well. It wasn't really intentional. Well, probably it was, but it had more to do with the fact that he didn't know what to say. How to explain things to him. He was also pretty damned sure Senator Haley had said to him, "If I ever fucking lay eyes on you again, I'll kill you myself." *Yep that was pretty close to accurate* thought Wilson. But this was different. He knew the one thing they might have in common was their hatred for the General. Well, that and the pain they both carried.

He walked along the marbled floors of the Senate building, glancing at the patterns of tile, and felt everyone turn to stare at him as he made his way along the corridor. He had the bearing of a military man, but no uniform, which probably confused people and most likely scared them. He also knew that part of why they all looked his way was his size and height. He was used to that and had learned to pretty much ignore it.

When you find yourself in eighth grade as the smallest person in the room, getting beat up every day and then suddenly by the start of your sophomore year of high school, you're nearly the biggest kid in school, things change quickly for you. He had been all legs, arms, and feet until he started playing basketball and volleyball. When his coach encouraged him to hit the gym and lift more weights, Wilson found that the muscles and weight packed on easily for him. That had changed everything for him, first with college scholarships for volleyball and then the military calling his name.

Finding the door he wanted almost at the end of the corridor on the left, he entered and saw the middle-aged woman behind the desk. Her gray hair pulled tight in a bun and her reading glasses were halfway down her nose. She was deep in thought staring at her computer screen when he cleared his throat.

She looked up and stared at the giant in front of her. Lucille Weaver was fifty-seven years old, but she wasn't dead. This was one tall drink of water. She swallowed and followed her eyes all the way up only to be greeted by a devilishly handsome smile. She cleared her throat and realized she had been caught in the act.

"Can I help you?"

"Yes, yes you can…" he picked up her nameplate on her desk, "Lucille is it? Can I call you Lucille?" She nodded and swallowed. Dear God her name sounded sexy coming from his lips. Down woman, you're a grandmother. *Yea but you're not dead.*

"Is Senator Haley available?"

"Who can I say is calling?"

Just then a large oak door to the left opened and a man was standing in the entryway.

"Lucille, I need you to call Senators George and Whitlow and… " he looked from Lucille to the large man in the center of the room. "What the fuck are you doing here? Lucille call security."

"No wait!" He grabbed the phone as gently as possible from Lucille's hands. "Please. Alan. Please. I need to speak to you about someone we have a mutual hatred for. It's a matter of life and death, and national security."

He eyed the man and nodded to Lucille to put the phone down.

"Does this hatred include you?" He winced but said nothing and Lucille let out a small gasp. She had never heard the Senator speak to anyone like this.

"Please." He said again with as much restraint as possible. Wilson didn't beg. Not ever. But he knew he needed help on this one. For Erin. For them all.

"Fine. Come in, Daniel." He said his first name with as much disdain as he thought any human could muster. He also knew that he hated that name. He'd never gone by Daniel. Occasionally Dan, but never Daniel.

Wilson passed by the man who strained to look up at him. The office wasn't big, but had two large leather chairs facing the massive oak desk piled high with folders and papers. Behind the desk was a wall of bookshelves, overloaded with everything from best sellers to legal books.

The Senator made his way around to his chair and sat down, regretting it immediately as it seemed he was now much lower than the big man across from him.

"Well?"

Wilson cleared his throat. He hadn't really expected that the Senator would be in and even if he was, he certainly hadn't expected that he would see him so quickly.

"How is Mrs. Haley, sir?" His attempt at polite conversation was nearly painful. He hadn't seen the Senator or his wife since that night thirteen years ago. He was trying to break into this gradually but when the Senator looked up at him with hate-filled eyes, he knew it wouldn't be so easy.

"How is Mrs. Haley? Mrs. Haley? Look you son-of-a-bitch, Mrs. Haley was so distraught after the accident she found her way to the deep end of a bottle and never came out. She killed herself almost a year to the day. So how is Mrs. Haley? She's dead you prick. That's how she is."

Punch the nuts. Check. Knock me down a peg. Check. Wilson didn't cry. Never. Well, almost never. But he was damn close to shedding a tear now. He knew he had done wrong by not visiting the Haleys and he had to correct that before anything else.

"Sir, I'm sorry. You have no idea how sorry I am and I know that I fucked up." The Senator started to speak but Wilson held up his hand and with pleading eyes, begged to continue.

"We were all drinking that night, sir. All of us. I just finished my final training with the SEALs and we were celebrating with the teams. It was supposed to be a happy time. We weren't hammered, but we certainly had a few. Julia... Julia and I were in love. You know that. I was going to ask her to marry me. When we all got a wild hair to go swimming no one thought the wiser of it. I mean we were fucking SEALs. That's what we do!"

His lip trembled and for just a moment, the old man looked as if he might reach for his hand.

"We were having a great time and then someone noticed that Julia had swam too far out. She was in dangerous water. We were calling her back and she was just waving at us like she didn't have a care in the world. She couldn't hear us and she must have thought we were just having fun. I could see her bobbing up and down. She seemed so relaxed. Then she started to go under. We knew the rip currents had her. My teammates and I all jumped in, but none of us could get to her. I tried. I swear to fucking Christ, I tried."

A tear slid down his face and he looked up at the man.

"My teammates had to drag me back to shore. My team leader sat on my chest to get me to settle down. By the time the Coast Guard arrived and found her, it was too late. I saw you both at the funeral but you were so distraught I knew there was nothing I could say to either of you. Then three days later, we were shipped out for a mission. By the time I got back five months later, it seemed pointless to come to you and put you through more pain. But now I know it wasn't and I'm sorry. With all my soul I'm sorry. But I wasn't much more than a fucking kid myself at the time – not making excuses – but Lord knows I didn't have my shit straight then. I'm sorry. I can never say that enough. But know that I loved her too. Still love her."

Silence filled the room and the only thing Wilson heard was the old man breathing softly across from him. It seemed like hours passed before either said anything. The old man finally nodded at Wilson.

Alan Haley looked at the man across from him and remembered the boy that had stolen his daughter's heart. She had been so excited that she had found the "one." When they met Dan, he and his wife knew that he was something special.

After the funeral when Dan hadn't come around, he got angry, really angry. But if truth be told, that anger fueled his work, but also made him blind to what was happening with his wife. He knew it wasn't Dan's fault. But he was a convenient person to blame. Now, seeing the young man ready to crack, he knew how wrong he had been.

"Thank you for that, Dan. That's the first time anyone has told me the whole story. I just wanted to hear it from you."

Wilson let out a ragged breath. The weight that his heart had been carrying seemed to lessen. The choked feeling that he walked around with always somehow loosened, just slightly.

"Now, who is this mutual enemy?" The senator asked.

"General Joseph Murray, sir."

"Fuck me blue balls. What has that son-of-a-bitch done now?"

Wilson was grateful to have confirmation of the Senator's feelings on the General. He relayed the information in every detail as best he could. Erin, her father, her mother and the alleged murders. When he began talking about the drugs and Orion, the Senator's eyes lit up. He knew he had him. The Senator had served on multiple armed forces committees and had been known to take a strong stance against drugs and particularly drugs in the military. He wanted no leeway. Only Wilson knew that Senator Haley's older brother had died of a drug overdose in Vietnam.

"Shit," said the Senator.

"Yes, sir. Indeed. Our main goal, sir, is to protect Erin at this point." He noticed the pained expression on the Senator's face and immediately added context. "She's also the girlfriend of my business partner and teammate."

He nodded realizing that his face must have given his thoughts.

"I'm sorry, son, you have every right to be happy. I didn't mean for that to look the way it did." Wilson only nodded, understanding the man's intent.

"So, what do you need from me?"

"Well sir, we can't fight him if he's there. We need him here; on U.S. soil if we plan to fight him and win. I'm not sure how we do that, but we have to get him back here and all the players in one place at one time."

Again, the Senator nodded.

"I have a select few of my colleagues that I trust and that have the same mission as I do. Give me a few days to speak with them. Leave me your number and I'll call you as soon as I know anything." Wilson nodded and rose to leave, feeling as though he had been dismissed.

"Dan? I will help you in this, and not just because I hate Murray. You were a good man. You are a good man. My hatred consumed me and I'm sorry we waited this long to speak.

Remember what I said, Dan. You deserve to be happy. I know you loved Julia, but you can't hold the love of a dead woman when it's cold outside. Find your happiness, son."

Wilson reached out his hand and the older man took it in his, holding his other hand on top of it. He walked into the reception area and saw Lucille refreshing her makeup. She immediately showed a soft blush and Wilson had an inward smile. She was an attractive older woman and he wondered if she and the Senator had something going on. He hoped they did.

"Thank you, Lucille." He held her hand in his for a moment, and gave it a gentle squeeze. "I appreciate your help and hope I see you again soon."

She let out a girlish giggle and he turned on his heels and out the door to make his way back to the compound and his team. His step was lighter, and he had to admit to himself, the weight that he had carried around his neck for so long, was gone and he could finally breathe.

When he left the building, he walked the two blocks to the parking garage where he left the Hummer. The wind was whipping off the Potomac and he pulled the collar of his jacket up, trying to block some of the cold. He loved the fall and winter months – he actually loved the cold weather. When you're a man his size, heat never seems to really be an issue.

Wilson enjoyed, and craved, the life he shared with his brothers, but knew that he would need to move fast on building his own home at the complex now that Erin was living with Joe. Although, he wasn't sure Erin knew she wouldn't leave. He chuckled to himself realizing his friend was not always the best at having conversations of the heart, so he seriously doubted that Joe had told Erin he had no intentions of letting her live anywhere, but right next to him.

The wind picked up again and he felt a chill, but it wasn't really from the wind. Wilson had that feeling again. The one that told him something was getting ready to go down.

He casually walked up the stairs to the second floor of the parking garage where he had left the vehicle. As he turned the corner, he looked in his periphery to see if someone was following him, but he saw no one.

When he neared the large vehicle, he heard it before he felt it. The familiar click of a weapon being prepared to fire. In rapid succession three bullets fired past him. *Pop, Pop, Pop.* Or so he thought. He looked at the tear in the left arm of his jacket and cursed to himself. There was a slight burn and he noticed the trickle of blood making its way down his arm.

He had left his weapon locked in the Hummer, knowing he would not have made it through security to see the Senator. Carefully unlocking the vehicle, he opened the gun case and pulled out the Glock he personally carried.

He crawled along the front of the cars closest to the concrete wall, making his way toward the area where he thought the shots had been fired. Peeking around each vehicle, his weapon drawn and ready – he was seriously pissed off. This fucker had gone too far. Shooting at people in public? What sort of shithead does that? It was one of the things that drove him crazy with terrorists. Be man enough to look me in the eyes and show your face!

Just as he was about to make his way back toward the Hummer, a dark older model Chevy Impala came barreling around the curve of the upper levels to the garage. With only the hand of the shooter and the weapon out the window, three more shots fired in succession. Whoever the shooter was, he either had no clue how to kill someone, or it wasn't his intent.

Wilson dropped to the floor, but not before getting the first three characters of the Virginia license plate. These bastards would stop at nothing. He knew that for a fact now and it made him even angrier. He would wait until he got back to the compound to speak to the others, but he immediately called the Senator and told him what happened, warning him to be extra cautious.

Now, I just have to protect my friend's woman. At all costs.

CHAPTER SIXTEEN

Erin gave the list of items to Code and Miller that she would need from Dryden. Pulling out the floor plans that Sly retrieved from the building codes archive, she carefully drew the corrections to the floor plan due to additions and remodeling that happened recently. She located her office and lab, circling them for the men. They viewed the floor plans but she knew the building better than anyone did and some of the office configurations had changed over the years.

Along the way, she pointed out the cameras that she knew were in the hallway. She also gave them the general entry code. They could get in the main doors, but the codes for the specific floors, they would need to create some magic sauce to break through those. Giving them her personal code, would tip off the company and the authorities that she had either been there, or helped someone. None of them could afford for that to happen.

"There will be a guard at the main reception area on the first floor. He may, or may not be awake." She grinned at the men. "But it won't matter, everything is on video and everything is recorded and fed to old man Dryden himself and the Arlington Police. I'm almost afraid to say it, but I bet the feed is viewed by our good friend as well. There will be four guards walking the floors and they are especially vigilant on the floors where the labs are located. The drugs are locked up. Even I don't have a key because they're locked in an evidence room similar to what a police station would have. Only more sophisticated."

She looked at both of them and noticed that neither of them was writing anything down.

"Don't you want to take notes?" she asked.

"Nope, baby sis," said Miller. "Got it all right up here." And he tapped his forehead. She smiled at him and he gave her a brotherly wink just as Joe entered the room.

"What did I fucking tell you about flirting with my girl?!" Joe bellowed, but was only half-serious.

"So possessive," teased Miller. Joe just grinned and kissed the top of her head.

"You guys about ready?" he asked.

"Always ready, boss," said Code standing and giving Erin a huge smile. They heard the commotion coming from the living room and moved to see what was happening. When Erin saw Wilson with his torn jacket and blood on his hand, she raced toward him.

"Good God, what happened? Sit. Take the jacket off. Code, get me the first aid kit." They all looked at her instantly taking charge of the situation and smiled, knowing that this was exactly what Joe had needed. And if they were honest with themselves, it was exactly what the team had needed.

"It's just a scratch, baby sis, I promise. Besides, I thought you weren't that kind of doctor." He smiled at Erin as her small hand pushed on his chest and forced him to sit on the stool at the granite bar. Code came in with the first aid kit and she immediately started to clean the wound.

"I'm not that kind of doctor, but I have enough knowledge to be dangerous. It does appear to be only a flesh wound, but I'm going to clean it and put some antibiotic ointment on it."

"What happened?" asked Joe.

"Fucker shot at me," said Wilson in a matter-of-fact tone. "I visited with Senator Haley and when I was walking back to the car, I had that feeling." Everyone nodded and Erin looked around wondering what they all knew that she didn't.

"As I was getting to the Hummer the prick fired three shots. Got lucky with this one. He fired three more before he sped away, but I did get a partial plate."

"Pigsty!" screamed Joe.

"Yes, sir," he came running up the stairs. Joe nodded to Wilson and the younger man's eyes grew wide seeing the big guy getting bandaged up.

"Virginia plate – first three letters EVG. Late-model Chevy Impala, dark blue, maybe black."

"On it," and with that he ran back down the stairs.

Erin taped the gauze around the big man's arm and patted his shoulder.

"Done." She looked around the room and drew a deep breath. "This has to end, guys. I can't let you all get shot at for me. Let the General know I'm alive. We can meet face-to-face and figure out what it is he really wants."

"No!" growled Joe. "Not a fucking chance. We finish this, but we finish this my way. Even if we met him face-to-face, Erin, he wouldn't tell you the truth. And more than that, he couldn't let you live knowing what you know." He pulled her tight into his arms and rubbed his chin on the top of her head.

"Wilson, what did Senator Haley say?"

"He's going to help us." All of the men knew Wilson's story and raised their eyebrows as one. "He was actually pretty nice. I mean he was pissed and spitting venom when I got there, but we talked. I mean really talked about it." He looked down, not wanting his teammates or Erin to see the pain in his eyes.

"Hey, I'm glad, man," said Bull. The rest nodded in agreement.

"He's going to talk to some of his like-minded senators and get back with us. But, Joe," he held his breath for a moment and looked around the room, "at some point we will have to let the General know she's alive. It's the only way."

Joe's face looked ready to explode.

"I won't fucking risk her life!"

"We may not have a choice, Nine," said Tailor. Joe continued to shake his head.

"Stop!" said Erin. "All of you stop talking as if I'm not here. I'm. Right. Here. I don't want to have to face General Murray. But Joe," she placed her hands on either side of his face and kissed him sweetly, looking into his eyes, "my sweet Joe. We both know that sooner or later I'm going to have to face that man.

"My suggestion is we get our plan together and be one step ahead of him for a change. If Wilson and his friend the Senator can arrange for him to be back here, we may have a chance. But we also need to make sure, somehow, that Chris and Michael are here as well. They have to all be caught or I'm still at risk for being thrown in jail." She kissed him again.

"All the kissing in the world isn't going to get me to change my mind, baby. I'm not putting you at risk." His hands rested on her hips and his fingers were kneading her ample ass.

"I won't be at risk. Billy Joe and Oscar will be with me." Both men let out a groan and she smiled at them. "Sorry, Trak and Tailor will be with me."

She let out a breath and continued.

"I've changed my will. I called my attorney's office today and told him I need everything made perfectly clear. He faxed the paperwork over and it's been signed, notarized, and filed. The General will know I'm alive. He will also know that if I die before my thirtieth birthday, everything goes to charity. The Dryden stock will go back to old man Dryden. He gets nothing."

"And if something happens after your thirtieth, Erin?" asked Code quietly.

"If something happens after thirty," she looked down not wanting to hear the responses she knew would come.

"Erin?" asked Joe.

"If something happens after thirty, everything, the money and the stocks go to REAPER." The men nearly gasped as she revealed her addition to the will.

"You what?? What the fuck, Erin?? What are you thinking? You can't do that! We don't need your money!" The words were flowing from all directions.

"STOP!" she screamed with her hand up. "For the love of all that is fucked up in this world, let me speak!" The men instantly quieted and waited for her to explain.

"If something happens after thirty it is clearly stated that REAPER will not only receive my liquid assets, all the money, but also the shares in Dryden. This way you control what happens at that point. He might try to kill one of you. But all of you? It's the right thing to do. You guys can give the money to charity if you want, if the worst happens, but the stocks, you hold onto those. It means you will control the majority in Dryden and the General will no longer be able to push his plans through. YOU. All of YOU will control him. Do you understand?"

They all nodded and Joe once again pulled her to him.

"You amaze me more every day," he whispered into her hair. "He will know, Erin. And he will be angry. But I know why you did it."

The sun had set and Erin knew everyone must be getting hungry if her own stomach was growling.

"I'm going to fix dinner. Trak will you help me?" The man nodded and moved toward her in the kitchen. The others, mouths open, only watched as Trak followed the woman like a lost puppy. Joe shook his head with a look of bewilderment and motioned for the guys to go into the living room and sit.

"Code. Miller. You better get your gear and be ready to move. Sly? Make sure you have them covered on systems. We leave no one behind, ever." They all nodded and moved to the door behind the stairs.

"We've got it, boss. The feed will get mysteriously disrupted once the guys enter the building. All cameras – traffic cams, ATM cams, everything – will be frozen within a two-mile radius for fifteen minutes before they enter and then fifteen minutes after." Sly nodded and backed away headed to the tech room, his favorite place in the world.

"Once we get the information from Dryden, we can get a better grip on this situation. Wilson? When did the Senator say he would call you?"

"He didn't. He just said it would be a few days." Joe nodded and looked at his friend again.

"Is it really just a scratch? Are you okay?"

"Yep." And Joe knew that was all he was going to get out of his friend.

Their heads down around the large table, the men walked through every possible variable and plan that would make this shit go away. Several times one of them would jump up and move to another room to retrieve the information and then back to the group.

But Joe's eyes were never far from Erin. He watched her move around the kitchen and a warmth gripped him so tightly he couldn't breathe. She had become his life and he wasn't ready for it to end.

Ever.

CHAPTER SEVENTEEN

Erin pulled the pasta and sauce from the pantry and set them on the counter. Without a word, Trak started pulling out pots, filling the largest one with water for the pasta. From the refrigerator, he pulled out tomatoes, lettuce, garlic, cucumbers, and the large block of parmesan cheese.

He easily maneuvered around Erin, taking out the chopping board and began prepping the salad. They moved in silence like the perfect dance team, and Erin thought this must be what it would have been like to have a brother.

Other than Joe, she felt closest and the most tied to Trak for some reason. When he was around, her anxiety dipped to nearly nothing. Joe calmed her. Made her feel safe, made her feel beautiful and sexy and needed. But Trak had a different effect on her, one she couldn't put her finger on completely. He made her feel safe and protected, but it was something else as well.

They worked efficiently and seamlessly. Erin would give him a small smile every now and then, and he would grace her with the same. But as always, the smile on his lips never quite reached his eyes. It made her sad and she wanted desperately to know her friend better.

Her friend. She marveled at the thought of that. She had never had many friends. A few girlfriends here and there, but no one she felt she could tell everything to. Trak felt like that kind of man – someone she could tell everything to and not feel self-conscious or worried that he would spew the information to the world. Hell, she didn't think the man knew how to spew anything.

"Tell me about yourself Osc... umm Trak."

"You can call me Joseph when it's just you and me, Erin." She didn't ask and he appreciated her ability to hold that secret close to her chest. The silence stretched between them and Erin decided she wouldn't push him; he would open up when and if he felt comfortable.

He looked as though he were working it out in his head. A way to tell his story, but she wasn't going to pressure him. She had learned with the General that you didn't push someone to get information. It never worked.

"I had a sister once. We used to cook together like this. She would be about your age now, had she lived."

Erin looked up at the man, sadness and regret filling his eyes. She stopped chopping the garlic and reached out to lay her fingers on his arm. She said nothing, but that small touch gave him the comfort he needed.

He spoke so softly, so quietly, even being right next to him, Erin barely heard him.

"I didn't have the best life, but I know others that had it worse. I was raised on the rez... reservation. Schools were for shit, the houses were falling apart, and poverty was prevalent... let's just say it wasn't Main Street USA. My father left right after my sister was born. I don't remember him and I never saw him again. Heard he died. But not really sure. The elders of our tribe and my grandfather sometimes were there for me when they could be, and when I could be.

"They did help me understand my role as the male in my family, how to be a man. They taught me our traditions, our culture and when I needed a place to escape or hide, they were there for me. My mom. Well my mom was an alcoholic and not a kissy, huggy kind of alcoholic. She was brutal. The kind of alcoholic most people think of from a male. She started hitting me when I was around six, I guess around the time my father left. My sister was only a baby at the time."

He took a shuddering breath.

"There was no pattern to what triggered her. It didn't matter what I did or didn't do, she took delight in beating me with anything she could get her hands on. A belt. A fireplace poker – hot or cold – a wire coat hanger. It just didn't matter. When I got smarter and bigger and would try to run, she would actually wait until I was asleep and tie me down. Then I started putting locks on my bedroom door to make sure she couldn't get in while I was asleep. But then I worried that I wouldn't be able to get out quick enough to protect my sister – so I just left it unlocked."

Erin had stilled completely, looking at the man beside her, silent tears falling down her cheeks.

"When my sister got older, she started moving on her and I put myself between her and Mom, which only made the beatings more frequent and more vicious. By the time I was sixteen I was tall enough and big enough that I could stop her. But if I turned my back, she was on top of me faster than you could shake a stick at. I learned to be quiet. Very quiet. I was seventeen when I left to join the Army. I was going to get established somewhere and come and get my sister. At seventeen I was going to be a soldier and a surrogate father to her."

Erin had long since stopped what she was doing, her eyes filled with tears, but she said nothing. The wetness freely flowed down her cheeks. But she dared not breathe, allowing him to finish his story.

"I came back from basic to get my sister. I had no plan; I just knew that I was going to get her away from there. Only I was too late. My mother was so desperate for her next bottle she decided she would sell my sister to make money – by the hour." He swallowed and turned looking at Erin. "You remind me so much of her Erin. Your face. Your eyes. She had our native black hair, but her eyes were so green. Her face so delicate. She was only thirteen."

"Oh God," she said in a whisper. She held her hand to her stomach trying to hold back the bile that rose.

"She couldn't take it. She didn't know how to reach me, so she figured it would be better to end her life than live it. I failed her."

Erin reached over and placed her hand on top of Trak's.

"Your mother?"

"Gone." Was all the big man said and Erin knew that she was gone for good.

"Joseph, you know that I'm here for you if you ever need anything, right?" He gave a slight nod. "But you do know that this was not your fault, don't you? Your mother's choices were her own. You weren't more than a child yourself. Protecting your sister wasn't your responsibility, it was your mother's. Her sickness wasn't your burden to carry. Your sister loved you and knew you would come for her. I think maybe she didn't want you to see what your mother had turned her into. Sometimes, sometimes we make choices in the moment that we have no idea how it will affect those around us or our futures. Know in your heart that your sister wanted you to remember the way she was. Not what your mother had made her into."

Trak nodded and Erin looked up at him again.

"What was her name? Your sister? May I know?"

He was quiet for what seemed like minutes and finally looked directly at her, his eyes were filled with tears and her heart nearly split in two for the pain this big man was experiencing sucked in a deep breath and in a barely audible voice, he spoke.

"Erin. Her name was Erin."

She let out a small gasp, squeezing his hand. He nodded at her and excused himself to the restroom.

Erin hadn't even noticed, but the men on the couches had turned at some point and were staring in her direction. They all saw the trail of tears that silently fell down her cheeks, but she shook her head as if to say, "don't ask." She had no idea if they knew his story, but she knew in her heart that they had heard at least part of it today. Their eyes filled with pain, and without question, she knew that these were the kind of men who would not only keep Trak's secret, but would have helped him make his mother "gone."

Several minutes later Trak returned and helped her finish the meal. As they all gathered around the table, Pigsty popped his head through the door.

"Dinner ready?"

"It is Pigsty... ummm do you have another name? Can I please call you something else?" She said with her nose scrunched up.

He shrugged and looked from Joe to her and back at Joe again. He nodded slightly.

"Wes," he said

"Wes. Much better." She smiled at him and handed him the two plates for Sly and himself.

"They're getting ready to enter Dryden. It won't be long now. All is going well."

The conversations around the table ranged from football to military bravado to women. Erin was drowning in testosterone and silently made a vow that she would find more women to fill this room. Although she had to admit being amidst the mountains of muscle and pure manliness was every woman's fantasy. She loved every one of these men like brothers, but they definitely needed a woman in each of their lives.

Pigsty popped his head through the door.

"They're out. No glitches to speak of."

Collectively they seemed to release a breath and all seemed more relaxed. Angel and Bull rose from the table to clear the plates.

"There's cake on the counter," said Erin.

All of the men turned to look into the kitchen and sure enough sitting on the counter was a large chocolate cake layered with strawberries.

"I think I want to marry you," said Grip.

"Get the fuck outta here, Grip, before I break your nose." Joe was half-kidding, but he knew what he had in this woman and he knew that soon he would need to let her know just how much he loved her.

Loved her? Yep that's what I said. Love her.

The groans all around the table filled her ears with pleasure and were almost erotic and sexual. She smiled inwardly, not wanting to show her satisfaction at their enjoyment. The cake was gone within minutes and once again, she made a note to herself to make two cakes next time or switch to a sheet cake, which would give more slices.

"Erin this reminds me so much of my grandmama's cake!" said Tailor. "We never have sweets around here. Angel is always watching his girly figure."

"Fuck you, asshole," said Angel. "Erin it's delicious really. Tailor is right we don't usually have sweets around here, but mostly because none of us bake. We all cook – we just don't bake."

"It's a great stress reliever for me," said Erin. "I love to try new things and seeing the pleasure you all get from it; I'll definitely make sure I add that to the list of things to do every day."

"Babe, no one expects you to cook every day," said Joe pulling her into his arms.

"I know, but I want to feel useful. I want to feel as though I'm making a difference here, helping. Let me do this. For now, anyway. I mean I saw the four dozen boxes of Pop-Tarts in the pantry. And sugar-coated cereal is not ideal. Do you guys have any idea what's in that stuff?" Joe laughed and just nodded his appreciation and approval.

"Thank fuck!" said Tommy. "These assholes say they cook, Erin, but I promise you pizza delivery and Chinese take-out is not cooking."

They all laughed and looked up as Code and Miller walked in carrying several boxes. They both wore black long-sleeved t-shirts, black BDUs and black combat boots. Their heads covered in black knit hats and watching the bulging muscles wrapped around the boxes, Erin thought she would definitely have fainted if she had run into them in a dark alley.

"Any problems?" asked Joe.

"A few," said Miller. "But nothing we couldn't handle. The offices were easy, but Erin was right, the labs and the sample or evidence locker had super sophisticated systems." Miller was quiet for a moment. "Like military-grade security systems." Joe nodded.

"But we're awesome," said Code with a huge smile on his boyish face.

Erin immediately jumped up to help lay out the items in the boxes. Seeing her files inside the box gave her a sudden wave of sadness. She knew that she would never set foot in Dryden again. Her career would be over and not knowing where she was headed or what she was going to do seemed to suddenly make her feel lonely in this room surrounded by a dozen large men. As if on cue, her "brother" Trak stepped up and stood behind her and she instantly felt better.

"Let me get the lab equipment set up and I want to start running the analysis of the two drugs. That will give us a solid place to start and then from there I can start to trace sources. It will take several hours, but I can start now and hopefully by morning it will be done."

"Okay, guys, let's recon at 0700. Get some rest."

Erin continued to set up the equipment carefully placing each piece in a logical way for her to work most efficiently. Once she had the analysis running, she felt Joe behind her, rubbing his hands up and down her arms, she leaned back into his warmth.

He kissed her temples.

"Do I need to be worried about you and Trak?"

She smiled to herself, finding his jealousy both flattering and annoying.

"You have nothing to worry about, Joe. Trak, well Trak and I have a connection but it's like a brother slash sister connection. I know it sounds weird, but even more than that, it's like a twin's connection. I can sense when he's around, whether he's anxious or sad or feeling joy, which is rare by the way. I can't explain it at all. I know it's crazy but he's very special to me. But you, you my dashing hero, you..." she chewed on her bottom lip and he took her chin between his thumb and forefinger.

"Tell me, baby, I'm what?"

"You, Joe 'Nine' Dougall, you I love with all my heart and soul. You don't have to say it back. I know it's too soon, but I needed you to know."

"Baby," he pulled her chin up again, "baby, look at me. I love you too, Erin. You're right, this is fast. But when things are right and you know deep down in your soul, well then there's no arguing. We're together you and me, for the long haul."

She nodded feeling the creeping heat make its way up her face.

"Is Trak okay?" he asked as an afterthought.

"I think he will be. He's as okay as someone would be in his circumstances. Did you hear our conversation?" she asked tentatively.

"Not all of it. But I know bits and pieces." He pulled her hand and moved toward the bedroom. "Come on. I want to make wild monkey sex with my woman."

She laughed and the sound carried through the entire house, enveloping it in warmth and love.

CHAPTER EIGHTEEN

Erin entered the bedroom and instantly smelled the scent of sex. She looked over her shoulder and saw Joe closing the door, turning the lock.

"I'm gonna shower, babe. Wanna join me?" she said seductively.

She pulled the sweater over her head and the plain white cotton bra, which shouldn't have been sexy at all, was sexy as hell. He swallowed hard, watching her slide her jeans down her curves, her hips moving from side to side, stepping out of them and moving toward the bathroom. She partially closed the door and he saw her hand flip her bra out onto the bedroom floor and next came her panties. He stood there suddenly gasping for air, his cock was so hard he thought he would burst inside his jeans.

When he heard the water start, he yanked his clothes off and stepped inside the glass enclosure behind her.

"I was worried I was going to have to shower alone," she said leaning back against his marble chest.

"Never, babe. Never. Let me cover the cast." He covered the cast with a plastic bag and taped it. Pulling her hair aside he kissed the back of her neck. She turned in his arms and moved their bodies so that he was under the showerhead. He grabbed her leg as if to lift her to his waist and she stopped him.

"Let me," she said shyly. "It's my turn." His eyes glazed over and the heat radiating from his body was so intense she thought she might actually burn.

She trailed kisses down his throat, the roughness of his beard scratching her tongue. She let her tongue glide down to the hollow, tasting his sweat, his cologne, him... just the taste of Joe. Her Joe. Her nipples were aching and her pussy clenched with need. She wanted to do this, wanted to show him how happy she was. She continued down his body, sucking on his nipples.

His reaction didn't disappoint. He sucked in a breath and jammed his hands in her hair holding her to him. She took small bites, taking his nipples with her teeth and teasing with her tongue. Her hands slid down his sides, feeling the muscles rippling at his abdomen. She kissed the trail of hair at the center of his vee and moving further down, until she found what she was looking for.

His cock was bobbing up and down, ready for her to take as her own. Kneeling before him, his hands still grasping her hair, she slid his cock in her mouth, taking the head first, teasing his tip with her tongue. Erin grabbed the base and squeezed and his sharp intake of breath told her what she needed to know.

"Fuck, baby, fuck! Squeeze my balls, Erin, fucking squeeze my balls, baby." He was hurting in the most excruciatingly good way.

She reached for his balls and rolled them in her hand, gently squeezing and sliding his cock further into her mouth. Her tongue rolled over the long rigid shaft and she pushed further, taking him deeper into her mouth. She sucked hard and pulled away letting his cock bob in the air and wetness of the shower. From her kneeling position, she looked up at him, through her dark lashes, her green eyes glowing with desire and heat.

"I want you to cum in my mouth, Joe. Please. I want to taste you. I want all of you."

He didn't want to cum this way. He wanted to cum inside her, but he would do anything for her and he knew he would be hard again instantly. He nodded, not able to let the words flow.

She began sucking again, harder this time. She pulled at the base of his cock and squeezed his balls, running her finger along the smooth ridge to his anus. He sucked in a breath and she smiled inside, knowing she had found his weakness. Finally, she reached around and grabbed the cheeks of his ass, she pulled him closer and felt his cock hit the back of her throat. She tried to relax, forcing the gag reflex away. Joe groaned, leaning his head back and arched into her further, pumping harder.

She knew he was close, she could hear his breathing become rapid and labored, so she sucked harder. The rumble in his chest let her know that he was letting go. She felt the warm, saltiness that was Joe flow down her throat and she swallowed, relishing in his flavor, in his manliness.

Leaning against the tile wall on shaky legs, he pulled her to him kissing her hard.

"Fuck, Erin, baby. That was the most beautiful thing ever." He kissed her face, her neck, then back to her lips taking her mouth hard.

She grabbed the loofah and body wash and started to wash his body, but he stilled her hand, holding her wrist. He took the sponge from her.

"No, baby, it's my turn."

She turned and he massaged the soap into her back, her bruises fading to nothingness.

"Fuck baby, do you know how beautiful you are?" She didn't reply and he turned her, holding her chin between his thumb and finger. "Answer me, Erin. Do you know how fucking beautiful you are?"

"I'm not beautiful, Joe. I'm curvy and my breasts are too big and my hair is somewhere between red and brown..."

He stopped her with a hard kiss and then stood back.

"Listen to me, baby. You. Are. Fucking. Beautiful. Everything about you. Jesus Erin, even when you were filthy in that hut, bruised and cut, I couldn't breathe when I found you, baby – I could not breathe. You have to know I've NEVER and I do mean never crossed the line on a mission of any sort. God Erin, your fucking tits make me hard no matter where we are or what we're doing. That ass of yours? That ass made my dick stand straight up watching it wiggle up that fucking mountain. You were fucking hurt and I got hard looking at you? Your hair? Baby, I think about that hair laying across my body every day." He kissed her softly, his hands resting at her hips, slowly making their way to her hard nipples. "These nipples? By all that is holy, Erin, these fucking nipples make my day."

She giggled and threw her head back as he squeezed and pinched her nipples.

"You my baby girl, are everything I have ever wanted. You are mine, Erin. Mine and mine alone. You and I? You and I are a permanent thing. I know this is fast and I know you deserve flowers, and chocolates, and date nights, and wine, and I promise I'll try to give you all of that. But know this, baby, we will get married one day, but for now, have no doubt you are mine."

She let out a breath of desire and happiness and brought her leg up around his thigh, pulling him closer.

"I love you, Joe."

"I love you too, baby, but now I have to get busy and make my woman cum for me." She giggled again and he kneeled pulling her leg over his shoulder. Joe's tongue was sliding up the slit to her pussy, tasting her, sucking on her. He slid one finger inside her and then another. In and out. In and out. His thumb was rubbing the hard nub at her clit and she moaned in a way that made his dick jump again. Her moans of pleasure made him work fast. He loved this woman so much, her responsiveness to him, her willingness to do things she had never done before.

Her hands held his short hair, holding his head to her pussy.

"Oh God, Joe... Joe please I need to cum, baby." It was all the sign he needed. He moved his fingers faster and sucked on her clit – rubbing and sucking – rubbing and sucking and then reached up and tweaked her nipple hard and she gasped bucking against his lips.

With one final thrust she screamed his name and he felt her juices warm his lips and he smiled. Soft kisses moved up and down her pussy and her knees shook so badly she knew she would have fallen if he hadn't held her leg over his shoulder still.

He slid her leg down, kissing up her thighs. Holding her hips, kneading his fingers into her flesh, and he felt himself harden again.

He stood and framed her face in his hands, kissing her deeply, long and hard.

"I love you, Erin. Don't ever doubt me in that."

She nodded and lay her head against his chest, the beating of the shower reminding them they hadn't even gotten clean yet. He finished first and made his way to the bed.

When she was done, she dried off and combed her long mass of hair, loosely tying it in a braid. She started to pull on one of his t-shirts and he shook his head.

"Not in our bed, baby. I want you naked in my bed. Always."

She blushed but made her way to his side and slid in between the sheets. He pulled her close and she draped a leg over his, feeling his erection grow with the touch of their flesh. She ran her hand down his abdomen and the deep rumble in his chest was so erotic she launched herself on top of him, straddling his body.

"Oh, seconds for my baby tonight?" He joked, grabbing her tits in his hands, kneading them.

"Mmmm I need you again, Joe. I'm greedy. I've been deprived. I need that big cock of yours inside me." She blushed at her sudden aggressiveness and boldness. He let out a loud laugh.

"My girl has a dirty mouth? Well, baby, let me just tell you..." he sat up grasping her waist and thrusting her down hard on his cock, "that fucking turns me on."

She rolled her hips against him and knew it would be fast for her. His cock and her clit were rubbing perfectly and the fact that his hands and mouth were all over her tits, made her crazy. But when his hand slid around and one finger moved down the crack of her ass, electricity shot through her and she arched her back with excitement.

He smiled at her and knew that their adventure would wait until another day, but he was pleased that she didn't recoil at the idea. Wrapping her braid around his fisted hand, he drilled his cock harder inside her and as if on cue, they both reached climax and spilled into and all over one another. She fell against his chest and lay there, their heavy breathing loud in the stillness of the night.

Joe pushed her hair aside and kissed her sweetly, softly. His thumb ran along her jaw and she rolled to his side. He pulled her into his tight embrace and ran his lips across her forehead.

"Love you, Joe."

He smiled in the darkness and just as she was falling asleep.

"Love you more, baby."

"What?" who the fuck was disturbing him on his personal line.

"General Murray, nice to speak to you too." He hated this man. Despised him with everything that he had.

"Congressman, what a pleasant surprise. What can I do for? Some fucked-up country needs to be saved by my special services?" He was dripping with sarcasm and hatred.

"Actually General, you'll be receiving orders by the Commandant of the Army to return to Washington, DC on the next flight out. You're to appear before a senate committee on funding for your little projects. It seems things aren't quite matching." Senator Haley could hear the man's blood pressure rising on the other end of the phone. He didn't like to be inconvenienced and he knew that without funding he couldn't continue with all the side missions he was performing.

He held his temper in check and chuckled, a vile sound, "In case you haven't kept up with the news, Senator, I'm a bit busy. We're fighting a war here. I can't be bothered with the nonsense from politicians."

"Well then, I'll just let the committee know that funding can cease immediately and I will let the Joint Chiefs know that you're probably ready for that retirement party. After all, you know how important it is to keep the system of checks and balances." He could sense the steam and anger coming on the other end of the line.

Fucking politician.

"Fine. Have it your way, Senator. I'll be there within forty-eight hours. Besides I have some things to take care of stateside anyway."

Senator Haley hung up the phone and immediately sent a text message to Dan. He set his phone down and smiled. This was going to be worth the wait.

"Fucking asshole!" He threw his phone across the room and it shattered in pieces.

"Sir? Is there something you need?" The big German stood beside his desk.

"Yes. You need to finish the fucking job you started. But I want to see her first."

"Sir, I have no idea where she is."

"Well, fucking find her then you moron! Find the men and you'll find her. I'd bet my left nut on it. I will expect to see you and her at my cabin tomorrow night – midnight."

CHAPTER NINETEEN

"They match!" Erin's excitement couldn't be contained. "The drugs are a match. I think we can be sure that they came from the same source. They're both laced with arsenic and a nice variety of other nasty chemicals."

The men sitting in the living room all looked at the woman who acted as if she had discovered the vaccination for smallpox. Well, in reality, she may have found something equally important. Keeping the deadly drugs off the streets might save thousands of lives, and certainly the lives of military men and women.

"Okay, we need to call DC Metro, get them involved in this as well. Wilson? The Senator is certain that General Murray will be here by tomorrow evening?" Joe looked at Wilson across the room.

"Positive. He's not happy but he'll be here," said Wilson.

Erin's face paled and she edged herself closer to a stool at the bar. Instantly Trak was behind her, pulling the seat closer to her so she wouldn't fall. He placed an assuring, protective hand on her shoulder and she let out a long breath.

"Nothing will happen to you, sister."

"But he'll come for me. You all know that right? He doesn't like to lose."

Joe rose from the sofa and moved in front of his woman, kissing her softly on the forehead.

"He'll have to get through us to get to you, baby. No can do." He smiled at her and she nodded softly.

"Trak. Tailor. You don't leave her side." Both men nodded and immediately took position near her, despite the room filled with their teammates.

"Code, you and Miller will have eyes on the General from the time he gets off the plane until he arrives in the senate chambers. Make sure you watch him every moment. He doesn't enter or leave without you notifying me. We're all wired from the moment we leave this house."

"On it, brother," said Miller.

"Wilson, you and I will talk with the DC Metro and get into the Joint Chiefs to discuss what we've found." Wilson nodded. "Tommy, Bull, and Grip we need to find Christopher and Miguel Santos, aka Michael. Miguel will probably be more difficult. But I want that prick Christopher found. Find his last known whereabouts, is he still working with the General, where the fuck is he? I want to know when he takes a dump." Again, the men nodded.

"Sly and Pigsty, we need view on all street, ATM, and business cameras, possible in and out routes of the General when he lands. Do not lose his vehicle."

"Understood, sir," said Pigsty. He took off towards the communications room knowing that he had his orders and knew what he was supposed to do.

Erin looked around the room at the men who were risking not only their lives, but their careers and reputations for her.

"What about me?" she asked quietly.

They all turned to stare at the brave young woman behind them. The admiration in their eyes and the battle-hardened faces, suddenly softened.

"You, baby girl," said Joe "you stay here. Don't leave the house. Don't even go into the yard. Don't answer the door. Trak and Tailor are responsible for your safety. They know what to do." She started to protest and he held his hand up.

"Non-negotiable, babe. Sorry. Your safety is number one priority. Trak and Tailor will be your shadow and if for some reason they have to step outside and check the perimeter or anything going on, Sly and Pigsty are capable as back-ups. Remember that you can head to the basement and lock yourself down there as well."

She gave a resigned nod and Tailor and Trak, still standing beside her, stood a bit taller casting a shadow over her body.

"Erin," said Wilson, "if you can give us all copies of your findings on the drugs, we can take everything with us to the senate and command." She nodded again, moving towards her work and gathering the files together.

Joe's phone let out a shrill ring and he looked at the caller ID. His face twisted into a look of disgust and he looked around the room. Pushing the button and pressing the speaker.

"Good morning General or should I say good afternoon?"

"Listen you prick, I know that you're behind me having to take this highly inconvenient trip. I know that you know I will be in DC soon. I want to see my daughter." He said the word 'daughter' with a hint of disgust and disdain.

"General, we both know that this is a lovely time to be in DC. And as for your daughter, well we both know that's not happening."

"You son-of-a-bitch, you have no idea who you're dealing with. I can end you now. I can end all of you now. One word and you'll be history. I will erase you from the fucking books you insignificant piece of shit."

"Oooh such language, General." Joe feigned his disapproval. "Really, I expected more from you. Actually, that's not true, you're giving me exactly what I expected. You won't see Erin. Not now, not ever. End of story. And just so you know, General, I will end you. You will be erased from history. You have a great fucking trip." He ended the call and held in his anger. He heard Trak's voice.

"Nine."

Joe looked to where Trak and Tailor were standing on either side of Erin. Her face was completely devoid of color and tears were silently falling down her cheeks.

"Hey, hey my little warrior. It's okay." He rushed to her and held her tight against his chest.

"I can't let you all do this, Joe. He's right. He'll ruin you all. He'll kill you if he gets the chance. Please, just let me go to him. Maybe I can make him see what a mistake this is. I can try to reason with him. Hell, I don't care. I'll give him the money if that's what he wants. I just want to be left alone."

"NO!" A dozen men chorused the response and she jumped slightly at the deep tones.

"He cannot be reasoned with, baby sis," said Tailor. "You have to trust us."

"Erin, Tailor is right. You have to trust us. He won't stop until he erases everything and everyone that knows about this. We have the upper hand right now. We can't let him get to you or get to our data." Joe held her hand in his, kissing the back of her fingers.

"Nine!" they turned to see Pigsty at the door of the comm room. "You're not going to fucking believe this, but I have Miguel Santos on the business line."

They all looked at one another and moved to the large conference room. Pigsty nodded that the call was transferred and Joe pressed the speaker button.

"Mr. Santos, this is Joe Dougall of REAPER. How can we be of service to you?"

"Actually, Senor Dougall, I believe I can be of service to you." He spoke with a slight accent and Erin's hands started shaking. Trak tried to lead her from the room, but she stood steadfast and refused to move. Santos began speaking and wove his tale and history of his partnership with the General. He told them of his plans and why the General was no longer of use for him. His story was interesting but they all waited for the other foot to drop.

Joe sighed running his hand over his head, looking at the phone, a deep frown on his face, the lines and wrinkles more prominent.

"I see. And what do you get out of this, Mr. Santos?"

"Simple, Mr. Dougall, I get my business back on track. And you, all of you, stay away from me."

There was silence in the room and they looked from one man to the other, all nodding silently. Sleeping with vermin was something you had to do on occasion to get to the end result. He knew it. The team knew it. But it didn't mean they had to like it.

"Alright. We agree."

"Spectacular, Senor Dougall. Oh, and can I assume my little bird Erin is in the room?" She gasped and stood closer to Joe, linking her fingers with his.

"I'm not your fucking little bird. I'm not your anything you bastard." The men all hid smiles at her tenacity. This man was not someone you wanted to piss off, but she was determined not to be a victim again. They admired that in her. Hell, they admired everything about Erin.

"Oh my, I see your military friends have become a bad influence on you, Erin. Well, no matter, just know that this was not about you. It was about money, it's always about money. I'm truly sorry. Your father... "

"He's not my father," she said resolutely.

"Yes, well the General then, is a man I needed. He set you and me up, Erin. My little tirade, well, let's just say I was in a particularly painful period of my life and that is not the man I am. As for the General, I've discovered I no longer need him, so we both win. You have my word that I will never approach Erin again. I will have no contact with her or your organization." There was a silence so thick they could have cut it with a knife. "Alright, gentleman. Erin. I hope we never meet but I believe our partnership will be a fruitful one for all of us."

The line went dead and Erin plopped into the closest seat.

"I think we just a made a deal with the devil himself."

"Maybe, baby sis," said Wilson, "but at least we know who we're getting into bed with, and the added bonus is he will stay away from you. He won't mess with us. He doesn't want anything messing with his operations."

"But what about all of those drugs?" Erin said in a beautifully innocent voice.

"We're picking our battles, sis," said Tailor. His dark face was suddenly full of features she would have found disturbing and frightening in another room. "We let someone else fight that cause."

She nodded and they all sat for a few moments in silence.

"I'm going to fix lunch." Erin rose from her seat headed to the kitchen; her mindful bodyguards close behind. She slowed as she started to exit the room. The burden, the weight of what had happened was suffocating her.

"I know you all have things to prepare for, but…" she stopped and turned looking at the room full of men. So brave. So willing to lay their life on the line for her. How could she ever repay them? God, she thought, please let them all be safe.

"What baby? But what?" said Joe coming to her.

"Please, please don't get hurt on my account. Be safe. Come home. I'll be seriously pissed if any of you has so much as a scratch." The single tear fell down her cheek and she turned and walked out of the room.

And as Joe had anticipated, in unison he heard Tommy, Grip, Trak and Tailor all say the same thing.

"I like her."

CHAPTER TWENTY

Code and Miller watched as the General's plane taxied to a halt. Each was prepared for the job they had to do. Their earpiece comms had been checked and double-checked; both carried weapons, multiple weapons; and both knew that they could not fail at this mission.

As the plane's door opened and the steps lowered, both men tensed, readying themselves. They immediately noticed the man they knew as Christopher, exit the plane. He walked toward the waiting black SUV and threw his gear near the back hatch and the driver tossed it into the rear of the vehicle. He then slid into the back seat. The General sauntered down the stairs as if he were the fucking King of Siberia. The arrogance of the man oozed off him like sick, cheap cologne. They could feel it even from their hidden location five hundred yards away.

"I hate that fucker," said Code sitting in the seat next to Miller.

"Me too, brother. Me too. I'm telling you right now if he touches a hair on Erin's head, I will kill that motherfucker personally."

Code turned and saw the hint of purple color in Miller's face and the large vein throbbing in his neck. His thick, corded muscles were bulging from his black long-sleeved tee. Code smiled to himself and thought he wouldn't want to be on the end of this man's anger.

They all knew that Erin was Nine's woman, but each man had fallen in love with her in a brotherly way. Her presence around the team had changed their dynamic and their vibe. It had many of the men wondering if there would be an 'Erin' out there for them. Code wasn't too concerned with that, but he knew for a fact some of the brothers wanted women in their lives, they just wouldn't admit it out loud.

"We're moving," said Miller into the receiver.

"Show time, gentlemen," they heard Nine's voice in their earpiece and they slowly moved the black Dodge Charger into traffic a few cars behind the General's car. They wove their way through DC traffic staying far enough behind not to draw attention.

This wasn't their first rodeo, both men were well aware that the General and his staff would be watching for following cars. They also knew that he would be even more alert considering his paranoia at being called back stateside. As they neared the Senate, Miller pulled over and parked the car, watching the SUV pull up to the front of the building.

The General left the back seat of the car, with Christopher closely following. As they watched the two men enter the building, Code sent a quick text to Senator Haley. Once the two men had entered the building, Code and Miller left the parked car and followed. Senator Haley had arranged for them to be seated in a private room, just off the chamber floor where they could access the chamber if needed, but they could hear everything that was happening via closed circuit television and listening devices.

"Let's see this prick get out of this," said Miller.

Entering the chamber, the General swaggered over to the table. His uniform appeared freshly starched. Every ribbon, every medal, every button absolutely perfect as if the bastard expected a parade in his honor. His eyes scanned the dais and he recognized only a few of the men, but no matter he thought, I will win the day.

He sat with frustration and a look of inconvenience on his face, indicating to everyone in the room what he thought of this hearing. The man known as Christopher was seated in the rear of the room, careful not to be too close to the General and definitely trying to blend into the crowd that had gathered.

"General, thank you for attending this meeting today," said Senator Haley in a sickly-sweet voice.

"I didn't really have a choice now did I, *Alan*? In case all of you have forgotten I'm doing a damn job over there. I'm not on vacation. Now ask me your stupid ass questions and let me get back to my war."

"It's SENATOR Haley in this room, General. Please use the proper decorum." Again, Senator Haley smiled at the man like they were golf buddies.

"Your war, General?" The junior Senator from Ohio raised his eyebrows at the man sitting across from him. "I don't believe it's 'your' war, General. It's a war. Period. And you will sit here and answer our questions until we're satisfied or you're in jail. Or perhaps both."

The General glared at the young man noting his appearance. His perfectly cut blue suit, crisp white shirt, and red tie suggested Ivy League and silver spoon fed. This little prick probably has no idea what dirt even looks like, let alone a battlefield. *I've got combat boots older than this asshole and he's going to try and intimidate me.*

"I can see your wheels turning, General. And before you make a fool of yourself let me just tell you that I have twenty years in the Navy. I spent four tours in 'your' war. I know my way around the military and I damn sure know right from wrong. So, don't look at me like you think you have something on me. Because you don't."

The General gave a half-smirk at the man. He had guts; he'd give him that. Men like him, well their morals tended to be too high and mighty and most didn't want to get their boots dirty the way he was willing to do in the name of freedom. Freedom. Who was he kidding? It wasn't about freedom anymore, not for him. For him it was about money. Plain and simple. He wanted to own his kingdom and by damn he would. The General glanced at the placard with the Senator's name and raised an eyebrow.

Code and Miller smiled behind the door. They knew the junior Senator well; they had served with him and he was more than just a guy from the Navy – a former SEAL. Special Forces and one bad-ass dude. Senator Haley had really come through with the right team on this one.

"Very well, Senators, I'm ready when you are." He casually sat back in his chair, folding his hands loosely on the table. Whatever they threw at him he could deflect it. Always.

"General, please tell us about the drug manufacturing facilities that are under your control?"

Well, no punches pulled 'ey asshole. Alright then.

"I have no idea what you're referring to." His face was void of any emotion and his breathing was even and controlled. *I can do this shit in my sleep you little fuck.*

"Perhaps these photos will help you to remember, General. Three, in total, in the Middle East. Two here stateside, which by the way as of..." the Senator looked at the clock on the wall "twenty minutes ago are now under the control of the FBI and DEA. Ringing any bells, General?"

His breath quickened and he felt an invisible gut punch as a light sweat broke out on his face.

"I have no idea what you're referring to. If you've shut down drug manufacturing sites, well then, I suppose Americans should thank you. But I can assure you I have no investment with these sites." He needed to leave. He needed to get out of this building and get to that bitch.

"So, you're unfamiliar with the name Orion?" The General gave no response. Not even a blink at the name.

"No?" asked the Senator. "It seems that a number of individuals have indicated that you, in fact, are Orion, General."

"This is preposterous! You are accusing a General in the United States Army of being a drug lord? You little shit! You have absolutely no idea who you're speaking to." His voice was raised, his face red and the anger in the room was palpable.

"Actually, General, are you familiar with this gentleman?" The screen on the wall flashed a picture of Ajib, and the slight flinch in the General's face told them what they needed to know.

"No? Well then perhaps this gentleman?" Another photo flashed, this time of Miguel Santos. "Both of these men claim that you are in fact Orion."

"I highly doubt that the American public will take the word of a probable terrorist and a drug lord against a decorated American General." His confidence was waning. Ajib was supposed to be dead. And Santos? That miserable fuck would be dead soon enough!

"Alright then, perhaps you could tell us where more than 4.8 billion dollars in funding in the last eight years has gone? Funding that was supposed to be used to help the Afghan and Iraqi people rebuild their country. Funding that was supposed to be delegated, by you General, to construction teams to help build villages, safe water systems, schools, and hospitals. Care to tell us where that is?"

"Senator..." he stopped with a grin, "I'm sorry you didn't tell me your name."

"Senator Michael Bodwick." The dark-haired man smiled at the General's face. He knew this man well. He had placed his team into a definite death trap. But what he didn't expect was that Michael would save his team and live to exact his own revenge.

The General's face dropped. He wasn't often shocked. He knew this man's history, and once again he knew that he should be dead. *What the fuck do you have to do to keep someone dead?* He thought to himself, next time I'll do it myself. He knew that Bodwick had taken down nearly an entire division of Iraqi soldiers by himself, saving every man in his command. But he thought the man had died from his sustained wounds. He was not someone to fuck around with.

"That's right, General, *that* Michael Bodwick," he grinned to himself.

"Well, *Senator* Bodwick," he put emphasis on Senator trying to show that his military career was no longer a concern for him. But he knew in his gut that this man would not give up until he was satisfied with blood on his hands. "Well, Senator, I don't have all of the spreadsheets with the financials in front of me. Clearly, I have analysts and financial assistants who handle those things for me. I assure you that if there is any wrongdoing, I will personally form a team to investigate." He gave a smile of satisfaction. By the time they got any of those reports he would be long gone.

"I see," said Senator Haley. He hated this son-of-a-bitch. He knew that he was responsible for the death of dozens of men and women serving their country, and he would be damned if this man left the country again without punishment.

"I believe we have those financials right here. It took us a while, but we were able to pull those for you in advance. Interesting though, we had to really dig and get some help from an encryption team to find this. Why do you suppose that is, General?"

He felt his face become heated and he waited for his signal. On cue, the fire alarms sounded and people stood staring at the dais of men. The security team in the room nodded, and began moving the people to the exits in the room.

"Fuck," said Code under his breath. "I don't have a good feeling about this, brother."

"Nine, the building is being evacuated due to the fire alarm. Seems a bit convenient to us."

"Roger that. Follow them and make sure they get back in that building once it's cleared."

Code and Miller stood outside the building in the cold wind with the other office workers and staff. They watched the General out of the corner of their eyes, Christopher milling around him about five feet away.

Senators Haley and Bodwick stood near Code and Miller.

"Mike, good to see you, brother," said Miller offering his hand. "Been a long time. You clean up good."

Michael Bodwick flashed a megawatt smile and shook the other man's hand.

"Well, we all gotta do something when we get out right? I mean politics? How hard could this be?" He laughed and Senator Haley smiled at the young man who had become his protégé.

"Well, if you ever get antsy for a little action, just let Nine know. We'll put you to work." He winked at the man.

"Brother, I would love nothing more, but Melanie would have my balls in a pot of soup before the night was over. And with this," he raised his pant leg and showed the prosthetic limb, "not sure I'd be much help." Miller and Code both nodded and smiled, but Miller's smile belied something else and Code knew it was a bit of envy for their brother. Not about his leg, but that he had a woman at home that worried about him.

"That leg wouldn't stop you, brother, you and I both know a sniper doesn't need both his legs to kill from a mile away." The men laughed and nodded, but said nothing more on the subject.

The all clear was given twenty minutes later and people started working their way back into the chambers. Since they had stayed in the building until the last moment, Code and Miller were forced to enter first and find their place once again.

"Man, I just want this fucking shit to be over with," said Miller.

"Imagine how Erin must feel, dude." Code looked around at the oak paneling, placing his headset back on. They waited for what seemed an eternity the sounds of people moving around the room. Suddenly the door to their office space opened and Senators Haley and Bodwick entered.

"They're gone."

"What?!" screamed Miller. "What the fuck do you mean they're gone?"

"Son, we're on your side," Senator Haley placed a hand on Miller's shoulder.

"Sorry sir, no disrespect intended." The senator gave a slight grin and nod.

"When we all reconvened after the fire alarms, they didn't come back in. They're gone."

"Shit!" Miller pushed the earpiece. "Sly? Pigsty? The General and Christopher are both gone. There was a fire alarm and they left and didn't return. We need eyes on the cameras."

"On it," said Sly from his ear.

"Nine?" said Code.

"Yea, Code," came the quick reply.

"Nine, they're gone. There was an alarm and they left and didn't come back in. We lost them, man. We're sorry."

Code winced as he heard the man cuss at the other end of his earpiece and even he blushed a bit at the words flying from his leader's mouth.

"Find them! Find them now! I'm calling Trak and Tailor," he said gruffly. "Fuck! Fuck! Fuck!"

That was enough f-bombs to last him the day, but somehow, they all knew it wouldn't.

Erin pulled the cookies from the oven, the smell of vanilla, sugar and chocolate filling the downstairs. Both Trak and Tailor watched as she placed them on the racks to cool, their mouths watering and their eyes taking in the sweet treats.

"Don't even think about it!" she said eyeing both men. "They need to cool first and I want to make sure there are enough for everyone."

Both men nodded, but when she turned to put the cookie sheet in the sink, they each grabbed a piping hot cookie and shoved it in their mouth. She turned to see the two missing cookies and smiled to herself.

"I saw that."

Sensors started to buzz all over the house. From the basement Sly flew up the stairs.

"We have multiple breaches! Two in the southwest corner of the property, one at the front gate and one down by the pond. We don't have visuals but the sensors are going off like crazy."

"Stay here," said Trak pushing Erin down the hallway. "Lock yourself in the bedroom and don't come out until either Tailor or I come." She nodded.

"Promise me, sister."

"I promise, Trak." Her voice was shaky and he placed a chaste kiss on her forehead.

Weapons drawn Tailor and Trak headed out the backdoor, while Sly went to the front gate. Erin held her breath watching the men leave the house.

"God please, please let them be safe."

Trak motioned for Tailor to head toward the pond and he moved toward the southwest corner of the property. They were close enough that they could see one another moving through the tall grass, but far enough away that they knew they would be on their own if something happened.

As he neared the pond, Tailor caught sight of two men, both in black cargo pants and dark shirts, both carrying heavy firearms. He knelt low and belly crawled closer as they stood near the dock. They weren't doing anything. Neither appeared to be military or even close. One was short and heavy around the middle. The other was medium height and so thin, he looked like a drug user. What the fuck? He thought to himself. Raising his weapon, he fired two shots, hitting both men in the knees. They dropped immediately screaming. He raised his weapon again.

"Drop the fucking guns now!" The men eyed one another and threw their weapons into the pond. "The knife too you prick." The man on the left eyed the giant in front of him and immediately regretted his decision to take this job. Up close, Tailor could tell he wasn't military at all. His long hair was half in his eyes, he was too thin, and he clearly had no idea what the hell he would do with any of the weapons strapped to him.

"Man, we don't know anything! I swear!"

"Shut the fuck up!" screamed the shorter man next to him. "We talk, we don't get paid."

"You don't get paid if you're dead either you son-of-a-bitch. Now who sent you?" Tailor was angry.

"We don't know," said the frightened one.

"Shut up!" his partner was getting panicked and Tailor walked closer, his weapon trained on both men.

He knelt down grabbing the man's knee, pressing his thumb against the bullet wound, the pain making him scream in agony.

"Now you listen you miserable fuck, you will tell me right now. Who? Sent. You?"

The man passed out from the pain and Tailor shook his head. He moved toward the weaker man.

"Please, please don't hurt me. I don't know who it was. We were just hanging out and this big blonde dude said we could have these clothes and the guns if we just played a prank on someone. He said all we had to do was walk on the property to scare somebody. We came in over the fences over there, and we were supposed to run to this spot."

Fuck! Tailor thought, its' a fucking diversion. He grabbed the zip ties from his waist and secured both men at the ankles and wrists.

"Stay! Do not fucking move and if you do, I will hunt you down and kill your sorry ass."

"Trak?" He spoke into the communications device.

"Yea. I know. I'm moving back toward the house." Trak's voice was barely audible, but Tailor knew he was running.

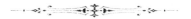

Erin heard the shuffling of feet on the front porch and without thinking ran to open the door, knowing that it would be Sly or Joe. Flinging the door open her blood froze, her feet stopped moving and everything spun around her head.

"Hello, sweetheart," Christopher had a sick, twisted look in his eyes. "Unless you want your little buddy's head blown off, you're going to come with me."

Her stomach dropped and she laid her hand flat against her belly, trying to hold back the bile and vomit that she knew would come. She looked at Sly, a gash across his forehead indicated that someone had already taken a shot at him. His eyes were staring directly at her.

"Don't Erin. Go back in, lock the doors..." he was cut off as Christopher squeezed his arm tighter around the man's throat.

"Stop! Stop it!" she pleaded for the man's life. "Let him go. I'll... I'll go with you. Just please don't hurt him anymore." Her voice was so weak, her knees felt as though they would buckle sending her collapsing to the floor.

The wind picked up and her hair flying across her face and she shivered from both the cold and fear. God how she wished Joe were here. Or Trak. Anyone. Where were they? Were they injured as well? Surely not. These men were too good.

She willed herself to take the step that she knew would endanger her life but save the life of Sly. As she moved closer, she watched Christopher shove Sly to the ground. Sly attempted to stand, he hit him again on the back of the head, and the man went down. She rushed to his side, laying her hands on his bleeding head wounds.

"Stop it! I told you I would go with you!" She cradled his head in her hands. "Sly? Sly, please wake up." She was sobbing now, uncontrollable sobs.

"Stupid fuckers. They didn't think we'd come right to the front door, did they?" He looked at Erin with a mixture of lust and disdain, "Oh Erin, you always were so compliant. Just a meek, weak little mouse. Of course, I never got to fuck you, but rest assured we will remedy that before I kill you."

She glared at him and swore that she would show him just how strong she was. This man would not break her. He grabbed her by the upper arm, squeezing to ensure she felt the pain. Dragging her to the waiting vehicle he shoved her inside and just as he was about to close the door, he turned and fired a shot, hitting Sly in the back.

"NO!!" she tried to crawl over Christopher and get out of the car. As he slammed the car door, Pigsty stood in the doorway and fired two shots at the tires of the vehicle, missing as they drove through the gates.

Erin looked back, tears freely streaming down her face. Her hands were covered in Sly's blood and she wiped them up and down on her blue jeans.

"Why? You didn't have to kill him. Why?"

"Because," she jumped at the sound of the General's voice, "because dear *daughter,* I want them all dead."

CHAPTER TWENTY-ONE

Joe flung the front door open and saw his team standing in the living room. He searched the faces of each man hoping that his woman would be in the center of them or that they had word of where she was.

"Nine," Tailor whispered, "brother we're sorry. They got her and they shot Sly while they escaped. It was all a fucking diversion. The police took the two I got near the pond and the two Trak got in the pasture. All four hired by Christopher from what we can gather. They had no shot at stopping any of us. Their only task was to make sure we were distracted."

Joe sat on the sofa and all the men took a seat watching the defeat on the man's face. But it was just a flash of defeat. Joe didn't give up on anything and he certainly wouldn't give up on the woman he loved.

"How is Sly?" he asked in a low voice.

"He'll live," said Trak. "Bullet wound to the back, two large gashes on his head, but the bullet missed anything important."

They all nodded. Silence consumed the room for a moment. They knew Joe was thinking.

"Nine," said Pigsty, "I have the tracking device on. She's about twenty miles from here in an empty field from what I can see. I'm bringing up satellite imaging right now and sending the GPS coordinates to all of you. NVGs and heat sensors are all ready and charged. Our asset is at the ready."

He looked up at the confused faces of the men. Their eyes scanned from him, to Pigsty, to one another.

"You had a tracking device placed on her?" said Tailor.

"I couldn't lose her." He said in a whisper. "I can't lose her." The men all nodded.

"Gear up." He pulled up the map of the area where her device was pinging. As they started to talk, Code and Miller ran through the door.

"Nine," Miller swallowed, "fuck brother, we're sorry. Senator Haley and Senator Bodwick have sped up the process for us. There's a BOLO for the General and his staff members. They've also got the MPs involved and an order for the General's arrest should be signed within the hour."

Joe nodded at the two men, and he looked at Wilson who had a pained expression on his face.

"It's no one's fault, Nine. Any of us would have done exactly the same thing all over again. Who would have thought they'd grab her right in the front of the fucking house? We will find her. Alive. No other options." His voice was clipped and heavy with emotion.

The men gathered around the map once more looking at entry points. Pigsty threw some photos of satellite imaging on the table showing a crumbling cabin in the middle of a field. Nothing else was seen for miles around.

"This has to be the holding point. There's one way in," he pointed to the dirt road. "But they could get out through the woods. Personally, I don't think our friends will get their feet dirty. But there is a space in the back of the cabin, between it and the woods, large enough for a chopper to land."

Joe nodded again.

"Okay, teams of two we move on the cabin. I want heat sensors, I want infrared, I want everything we have. They're not going to kill Erin. They want what she has. Bull and Grip, you two head to the hospital." They both nodded. "I don't want Sly waking up alone and we certainly don't want anyone fucking with him." The men turned and headed out the door.

"Wilson, you and I in one team, Code and Miller, Trak and Tailor, and Angel and Tommy." They all nodded. "Pigsty, I need your geekiness, brother. I need you to keep eyes on that cabin and on the tracker. Make sure my woman is safe."

Pigsty nodded at his leader. This man had given him a chance when his only other option might have been prison. In hindsight, hacking into the CIA databases to try and find his mother probably wasn't his finest hour, but it did grab the attention of every hacker organization in the world. His skills were unparalleled and when Joe saved his ass, telling everyone that he had been on a mission at the time, he knew he had found a home with these men. They taught him how to fight, how to shoot and the ins and outs of what a brotherhood and successful mission look like. He wouldn't let him down.

"Alright, we leave in five."

The men scattered and the sounds of weapons being loaded, checked, and rechecked echoed in the house. No one said a word. No one spoke. They didn't need to. Their movements were precise and calculated, just as they would be in the field. They knew that getting Erin back was not something they would fail at.

They loaded their equipment into the two waiting black Hummers and headed in the direction of Erin's tracking device.

Trak drove the first vehicle with Joe, Wilson, and Tailor. Miller drove the second with Code, Angel, and Tommy.

"When did you place the device?" asked Trak quietly to his leader next to him.

Joe let out a long sigh and ran his fingers through his hair. It nearly brought a fucking tear to his eye. He wanted to hear Erin fuss at him about pulling on his hair. He needed to smell her scent again. To hold her. To make love to her. He knew that Erin wouldn't have allowed him to place a tracking device on her, but he just couldn't take the chance that something exactly like this wouldn't happen. Without it, he would have no clue of the direction that she had been taken. He would deal with her anger later, at least he would know that if she was pissed, she would be alive.

"I can't lose her, Trak," he said so softly that only Trak in the front seat next to him could hear. Trak nodded looking at the big man again. "It's inside the air cast on her hand." Again, Trak just nodded and continued driving down the long road. Joe looked at the device in his hand, following the guidance on screen.

"Make a right on Route 608, then we drive about three miles and should see the dirt road."

"You know that this area was a big civil war battle ground, right? This bastard is obsessed with war. Past and present." Joe nodded looking into the darkness.

Trak took the hard right and the vehicle behind him followed.

"We're about a half-mile out; we stop here and walk in."

They moved so quickly and silently Joe knew that these men were treating this mission with the same importance as any other mission they had ever been on. He signaled for Trak and Tailor to head east and around the back of the structure. Angel and Tommy moved west to meet them in the same space. Using their own version of sign language, Joe indicated for the men to proceed.

Stepping cautiously, each step wary of what could be under their feet, they moved closer to the cabin. In his earpiece he heard Trak's low voice.

"Three warm bodies. One seated. Two standing."

He heard her whimpers and he stilled, listening to the sounds that were breaking his heart, knowing he couldn't make a move yet. The loud crack of a slap across her face had him nearly running to the cabin, but Wilson grabbed his wrist and pulled him back. He shook his head and sent his large friend a sign that the cabin could be rigged. They had no idea what was happening inside, nor what had happened prior to them bringing Erin out here.

Joe waited outside the cabin, the weathered wood porch was nearly falling apart, and he knew that as soon as he stepped on it, that it would creak, giving his position away. He signaled to his men to move back into the shadows. Wilson, Code and Miller all moved near the tree line, positioning their weapons on the front door.

"You're going to sign this new will, Erin, or I will fucking kill you myself. Then you're going to sign over your shares of Dryden. After that? Well, after that you and I are taking a nice long vacation where no one will ever find you." He heard the General's gravelly voice and his insides curdled. His fists clenched so hard he felt his short nails drawing blood in the palm of his hand.

"Why? Why are you doing this? You don't need my money. You don't need any of this." Erin was sobbing, pleading with the man she had once tried so hard to impress.

"Why? I'll tell you why you sniveling little bitch. You think you're so smart. Just like your daddy." His evil grin made her suddenly stop crying and she jerked her head up, staring straight at him.

"What about my father?"

"Oh, so you know then." He laughed an evil sound that coated her body like a sickness. "You see I tried to get your mother to marry me while she was dating your father. I knew who she was. Who her family was. Your stupid father had no fucking clue how much money that bitch had in the bank."

He smiled and Erin threw her leg out kicking him so hard in the shin he nearly doubled over. He stood with fury etched on his face but made no move toward her. Taking a deep breath, he continued.

Good girl thought Joe watching the heat patterns from the cabin.

"But no, she didn't want anything to do with me. So, she ran off one weekend and married that fucking asshole. Well that wasn't hard to fix, but I needed leverage and thanks to your parents fucking like rabbits, you were the perfect tool."

She held his gaze as her breath hitched in her chest.

"Your father had no clue what I was doing. I made sure that he had a little training accident one weekend. It was so fucking easy! I couldn't believe my good fortune. Rain can be a nasty thing when you're so close to a river with a rapid current. No one even thought to question it. I was the only one who knew that he would have never drowned; he was a great swimmer. Of course, I did my job and consoled your mother to no end. I held her hand at the funeral. I even played nicey with you and your running snot nose. You were so young, barely a year old at the time. I tried to convince that stupid cunt to marry me, but she wouldn't have any part of it. I think she always knew about me."

"Why. Did. You. Kill. Them."

"Simple, sweetheart. Dryden." She peered through her now swollen eyes, watching as Christopher paced around the room.

"Dryden has the ability to make my distribution of drugs and weapons easy. Dryden has been a favorite government contractor for nearly forty years. He's their golden boy. Can do no wrong. Problem is the golden boy has a nasty little secret; he likes little boys."

Christopher let out a loud snort and Erin couldn't believe what she was hearing. Old man Dryden had always been so nice to her, so sweet. But then again, what did a pedophile look like? What did he act like? She hadn't seen the evil in this man, so apparently her judgment wasn't as great as she thought.

"So, you see, it was easy. Dryden didn't want his dirty little secret told and I could get all of my shipments in and out. Then you received some of my drugs from DC Metro and you couldn't leave it alone. Dryden got a bleeding heart and couldn't let you just die in the fucking desert. Instead, he called in that asshole team. I needed you out of the way, and I needed your shares of Dryden. If it was completely within my control then you were no longer needed. Pity really. Such a waste of a brain."

She couldn't believe what she was hearing. All the years of trying so desperately to get his approval. All the times she wished he would just tell her 'job well done.' This man had been who she wanted to please and look up to and now she discovered the horrid monster he really was.

"When your bitch of a mother refused to marry me, well the easy choice was to get rid of her. I never expected her to hold on for so long. Of course, I also didn't expect her to change her will without my knowledge. That put a fucking monkey wrench in my plans. But there was still you. Sweet, always willing to please Erin. I just had to bide my time. I mean you dying so close to your mother and father might have cast a shadow in my direction."

The two men looked at one another with sly grins. She held her breath recognizing the leering look.

"I'm going to get you to sign these fucking papers and then Christopher is finally going to get to fuck your ass like he's been begging to do. I will be rid of you, rid of this country, and finally ruling as a king of mischief should." His cackling laugh sent shivers up her spine.

"You're insane," she whispered in the room. His face darkened and he moved toward her. A loud creak from the front door sounded and both men pulled their weapons.

"I know you're in there you son-of-a-bitch. All I want is Erin back. You can leave if you send her out." Joe's voice was so loud, she felt the rumble of the floorboards beneath her feet, and the breath she hadn't known she was holding was suddenly released.

The General laughed,

"Boy, you don't get to make the decisions here. You move and I fucking blow her head off."

Christopher moved between her chair and the back wall with the weapon pointed directly at her temple. He wrapped his hand around her ponytail and she let out a small whimper as she felt the sharp pain in her head.

"I know you have men out there, but I also know you don't have the balls to risk her life. So why don't you come in and join the party." The General smiled knowing that Joe would never enter the room without his weapon or his men.

"Alright," said Joe calmly, "I'm coming in, unarmed."

Christopher looked from the General to the door, his questioning, nervous gaze moving from one to the other. The General's face fell, realizing that they might not leave here, but come hell or high water, he would kill Erin, just because.

The door to the cabin opened and Joe stepped just inside the doorway, hands raised. The blackness of the night was behind him. No lights, no noise. Nothingness enveloped them all as if they were in a black hole.

"Stop there," said the General pointing his weapon at Joe's chest. "You've really fucked up my plans, son. I don't like it when someone fucks up my plans. No matter. I'm going to kill you and Erin before I leave here. But I think I'll let you watch my friend here have a little fun with her before we go."

A flash of anger crossed Joe's eyes, but he held onto his temper, waiting. Then Joe smiled a knowing smile as he saw the flash of light through the boards of the crumbling back wall. A large crunch sounded as Tailor crashed through the brittle wood, taking Christopher down with him, and Erin's chair flew across the room.

The large dark warrior's fist raised as Christopher raised his weapon to shoot. He wasn't quick enough. Erin heard a sickening crunch as Tailor's hand connected to the other man's face. He didn't stop though, he continued to pummel the man until there was no life left in him. His face was a bloody mess of smashed meat and bone.

Erin's face remained frozen as she watched the scene play out. As Tailor crashed through the wall, Joe rolled on the floor bringing her, still tied to the chair, close to his own body, protecting her from the line of sight of the General.

As Joe placed his body in a protective stance for Erin, through the hole that Tailor created, moving in the stillness, Trak silently used the darkness as his friend, until he was positioned behind the General, the curved blade of his Bowie knife held firmly against the older man's throat.

He didn't want Erin to see what he was going to do. He knew there would never be any punishment for this man. He would remain free until he died. The judicial system would stretch this out until no one was left to talk. He wasn't taking that chance. He would protect this sister.

"You touched my sister," he whispered in the man's ear. The General's eyes grew wide as the cold blade touched his skin. Joe rolled to conceal Erin from the view that was surely about to occur. And without thought or remorse, Trak laid the blade across the old man's throat and sliced from one ear to the other, shoving him to the ground. His blood flowed freely against the dark wood, his eyes still wide with terror and surprise, and the sickening gurgling last breaths leaving his body filled the room.

Without a word, Trak left the same way he entered, through the rear of the cabin and walked into the night.

CHAPTER TWENTY-TWO

"Are you okay, baby?" Joe pushed her hair from her face, kissing her lips softly, her forehead, touching her arms and shoulders, rubbing a hand up both her legs.

"I'm fine, Joe. I promise I'm fine." She kissed him back and he gave a weak smile. "How did you find me?"

The creaking of wood behind them saved him from having to tell her about the tracking device. Wilson, Code, Miller and Tailor all stood at the doorway. She smiled at her knights and they all graced her with a smile back.

"You doing okay, baby sis?" asked Miller. She nodded her head slowly.

"Where's Joseph?" They all looked at her confused. "Trak. Where is Trak?"

"He left, baby. I'm sure he'll be back at the house by the time we get there."

Wilson looked behind him as headlights appeared in the driveway. The other men raised their weapons, but he raised his hand to stop them.

"Our friend is here. We need to go." Joe nodded at Wilson lifting Erin from the floor, cradling her against his chest. As they stepped off the rickety porch, Joe turned and nodded at Miguel Santos.

"Goodbye, Senor Dougall. I hope we never meet again." His flash of white teeth in the darkness made Erin curl into Joe's shoulder more tightly. The other men surrounded her and she knew she was safe. But this was still the man that had hit her more than once and she didn't want to get near him again. The memories of him would be erased by the love of Joe, but she had no desire to relive any of those memories tonight.

"Count on it, Santos. Fucking count on it." Joe and the team walked to the Hummers and loaded up with Erin. Joe held her tightly on his lap, stroking her hair, trailing soft kisses on her forehead. Wilson was driving and looked in the rear-view mirror and smiled at the big man melting into a puddle. He was happy for Joe and Erin. They deserved happiness and they deserved to live in peace.

As they neared the main road, Erin looked back towards the dirt road that led to the cabin, a huge ball of light coming from that direction. The flames licked the sky and she knew that she was finally free. She let her eyes shut and within moments she was awakened by Joe moving her from the vehicle.

"You can put me down," she whispered to Joe.

"Not on your life, baby." He kissed her forehead and walked through the front doors.

Reality finally slapped her in the face and she gasped.

"Where is Sly? Where is he? Is he... is he..." She sobbed against his chest.

"No baby sis," said Code. "We just heard from Bull and Grip. He's doing fine. The bullet was removed and he'll make a full recovery. He's got a nasty concussion but that's all."

She nodded looking at all of them.

"He tried to save me," she said with sniffle. "He wanted me to go back inside even though they were going to kill him. Christopher had the gun to his head," her hands were shaking and she stared at the front door. "Sly told me to go back inside. He was willing to get

shot for me. I couldn't let them do that. When I said I would go willingly, he hit Sly on the side

of the head again with the pistol and then when we drove off; that's when he shot him. The

General said he wanted all of you dead." She shook her head again, wrapping her arms around

her middle, a chill ran down her arms.

"We all would do the same, sis. It's how we operate. But you did good."

She looked around the room at her fierce warriors. Had they been dressed in armor, or

kilts with claymores, or any other uniform, they would have been the same as they were in

their black pants, black shirts, vests, and modern-day weapons – unstoppable.

Joe looked at her as her eyes moved from one man to the next, each of his brothers

nodding and smiling at his woman. Her clothes were dirty, her hair matted, she had bruises on

her face again, but she was still the most fucking beautiful woman he had ever seen in his life.

"Where is Trak?" She said looking around the room.

"I think he needs some time, Erin," said Tailor in his booming voice, looking down at his

feet. "He'll be okay. He'll come back when he's settled down."

She looked at the big man, his dark face, dark eyes seemingly melting with her gaze.

Her intense stare made him nervous, and she knew there was more to the story, but wouldn't

press. If Joseph needed time, she would give it to him. She looked around the room and

nodded again at all of them.

"How did you find me?"

Joe shuffled his feet nervously, looking at his team, all with shit eating grins on their faces.

"Well, now don't get mad, baby, but well, I put a tracking device in your air cast." He waited for her anger to surface, the telltale sign of her fury, the redness of her face. But it never came.

She opened her mouth to yell at him, to rant about her freedom, about how she couldn't believe he would dare put a tracking device on her. But in that split second, she realized that his decision had saved her life and she leaped forward and hugged him, kissing his face.

Chuckles of the men behind her started softly and then became booming voices of nervous laughter.

"Is it over?" she asked looking at all the men.

"Done," said Angel, his mop of blonde curls hanging around his head.

"By the way, Angel, I've been meaning to ask how you became such an expert on women's clothes," said Joe smirking.

"Four sisters, dude. Four crazy-ass sisters." Erin smiled at the big blonde and then turned.

"Okay, I'm going to take a shower," she smiled at Joe and kissed his cheek. She moved down the hallway and then turned and walked back to the group of men.

"Thank you all," she said softly. She moved from one man to the next, taking their faces in her hands, she pulled them down to her and kissed their cheek or their forehead, moving around the room. They all blushed profusely, even Tailor's mocha skin turned a darker shade. "Goodnight, big brothers." Her sing-songy words made them all laugh again.

As Joe heard the door to the bedroom shut, he looked at his teammates. Thank you wasn't enough for what they had all done for him. It would never be enough. How would he ever repay them?

"I..." he couldn't seem to find the words and then Wilson slapped him on the back.

"Shut the fuck up. I'm tired and going to bed. We can discuss all of this in the morning."

The men silently made their way to their own homes. Well as silently as a group of men their size could move. Joe turned off the lights and made his way down the hall. He heard the shower stop and Erin came out wrapped in a towel, her wet hair hanging down her back. She gave him a light smile and he looked at her as she placed the air cast back on. She looked down at her wrist and back up at him.

"So, where are we going to place this device once I lose the cast?" She grinned wide at him and his heart melted.

"I'm sorry I didn't tell you, Erin. Really. I just..." She placed her fingers on his lips then kissed him softly.

"You don't have to explain your love to me. That was one of the most romantic things anyone has ever done for me." She kissed him sweetly, softly, her body aching, her muscles suddenly weak.

"Sleep, baby, we have forever now." He kissed her forehead and she climbed between the sheets, naked just like he wanted.

Joe closed the door to the bathroom and stripped, turning the water as hot as his body could stand it. As he let the warmth take over his body, he crouched on his heels, holding his head in his hands and silently sobbed with relief. This woman had taken over his soul and when he had left in a panic to get her back, he knew he would succeed. The thought of possibly losing her had nearly crippled and paralyzed him. He had nearly pulled himself out of the mission worried he wouldn't be able to focus.

Then when he made the decision to go, he was worried he wouldn't be able to hold back. But he knew that Trak, Joseph, would be the one to take the General down. Joseph. His tears stopped and he smiled. The big man had told her his real name, something only Joe and Tailor knew. Their friendship was something special. All his concerns initially swept away when he saw their sibling affection for one another.

As with any mission, there had been a niggling thought that they might fail. Had he failed; he wasn't sure how he would have gone on. Hell, had he failed, he wasn't sure how his own men would have gone on. He worried about Trak. His disappearance wasn't unusual. Trak was a loner. But he knew that the big man took the responsibility of guarding Erin very personally and that he would blame himself.

He stood and rinsed the suds from his body and turned off the water. The steam on the mirror didn't allow for him to even look at himself, so he simply dried off and climbed between the sheets. He could hear Erin's soft, even breathing and knew that she was asleep. He turned and curled his body next to hers, pulling her close, kissing the back of her neck. He would never let her go. Never.

⸱ ⸱⸱⸱ ⸱⸱⸱⸱⸱⸱ ⸱⸱⸱ ⸱⸱

Joe woke to the sound of his phone. As he glanced at the bedside clock, he realized that he had slept way past his normal wake-up time. Hell, to him 8:00 a.m. was half-way through the day. He looked at Erin still sleeping and slipped his boxers on and moved into the hallway.

"Hello."

"Joe. Senator Haley here with Michael Bodwick." Joe walked into the living room and sitting in sweats was Wilson and Miller.

"Good morning, Senator, Mike, how are you? I'll be damned if I'll insult you by calling you *senator*." Mike laughed and Alan Haley gave a nervous laugh. "Sorry, sir, I was just teasing Mike."

"No problem, son. How is Dan?" Joe looked up from the phone and saw Wilson's knowing gaze.

"I'll put you on speaker, sir. Two of my top team members are here with me."

"Senator, how are you, sir?" Dan was nervous. Joe could tell and he suddenly knew the depths that this man had to go to in order to call in this favor for him.

"I'm well, Dan. I understand you boys had a little drama yesterday after the hearing was stalled."

"Yes, sir. But Erin's safe. We're all fine."

"Good, good, that's good," said Senator Haley. "We heard from the Virginia State Police and then the DEA this morning that there was a pretty nasty fire not far from you boys. Seems it might have been a drug deal gone badly for our friend the General. State Police found two bodies, badly burned, but one was definitely in uniform. There was drug paraphernalia found and other evidence that suggests there was a big deal happening. They also found 150 kilos of prime heroine in the trunk of the General's car."

Joe smiled to the other men in relief, knowing that Santos had done what was promised.

"Is that so? Well, I can't say we're sorry to hear that. We do have the evidence that Erin collected on the two drugs that we'll be sending to you, sir."

"Fine, fine. In fact, Dan, why don't you bring it on down one day next week and have lunch with Lucy and me at the office?"

Dan was stone cold silent. He never in a million years foresaw him seeing, let alone having lunch, with Alan Haley again.

"You don't have to, son, I just..."

"NO! No, sir. I'd love that, really I would," he said smiling at his friends. "Besides, I think I should ask Lucille to dinner." The Senator knew when he was being baited and Wilson had a mile-wide grin on his face. Joe was happy for his friend. This chapter of his life would finally end well.

"Don't get stupid, son," the Senator laughed. "I'll see you next week."

They all said their goodbyes and collectively let out a loud sigh. Miller looked at Joe and Wilson.

"What now, boys? What excitement awaits us next?"

"Actually, I need your help?" said Joe with a serious tone in his voice. Miller and Wilson looked at one another and knew instantly what he was asking.

"You lucky son-of-a-bitch!" said Miller.

Erin walked into the room and they immediately fell silent which made her still instantly, a ghostly white face peering at them.

"What? Oh God, what happened?" Joe jumped up to grab her hands.

"Nothing, baby, honestly. Everything is perfect. We're all perfect and safe."

Joe explained that they had spoken to the Senator. The relief on Erin's face brought the men such happiness.

Wilson smiled to himself and suddenly realized he wanted this again. What Joe and Erin had, was what he and Julia had. He wanted that again. The problem was, there weren't a lot of Erins or Julias in the world. They didn't grow on trees and they certainly didn't just fall into your lap during a mission.

As the next few days passed, they all found their rhythm again. Joe and the men continued to train and work smaller jobs that they were given for cybersecurity, personal protection, and research. Erin was trying to find her place, and Joe knew that she would want to return to work soon. Her career had been important to her and she worked hard to find her place at Dryden.

He should feel bad that he didn't want her to leave, but he didn't. She had gone back to her condo and retrieved her remaining clothes, of course Angel was tagging closely behind. A few times she had gone out shopping, always with one of the guys or him tagging along, but she didn't seem too anxious to test the waters alone yet.

She was a brilliant woman and could do whatever she wanted to do, but he definitely didn't want her going back to Dryden or for that matter, anywhere near DC. He wanted her here, tucked safely next to him. A woman like Erin wouldn't be happy cooking and baking for a dozen men every day. He knew she would want something else.

There had still been no sign of Trak. Erin walked to his home twice a day knocking on the door, leaving notes, bags of cookies and treats. She needed to see him. She needed the man that was most like a brother to her, among all of them. If this were the *Wizard of Oz*, Trak was her Scarecrow – *I think I'll miss you most of all.*

The team came in and out of the house at will, as they had always done. Although it was still the home of Joe and Wilson, and now Erin, it was also their main office, conference room, tech room, and general all around get together spot.

Joe and Miller had been whispering and planning something, but she didn't know, nor was she sure she wanted to know, what it was. She was just happy to see everyone back to a relative normal. Except her. She felt that she was in the right place, but not sure if it was *her* place. She loved Joe so much it hurt. And she couldn't imagine her life without all the guys in it on a daily basis. She had craved family growing up and now she had a dozen hunky men hovering over her every day.

CHAPTER TWENTY-THREE

By Sunday, the house was like a normal male-dominated household and the guys were all spread out in front of the huge television watching the football games. Erin busied herself in the kitchen. She made a big pot of turkey chili for the guys, homemade cornbread, and pumpkin cupcakes. She made sure she had several types of chips and dips as they snacked throughout the game.

"Halftime!" shouted Code. They all stretched and started to stand, when Erin rushed into the middle of the room.

"Wait!" she looked at all the men as they slowly sat back down.

"What's up, babe?" Joe was unsure if he really wanted to know the answer to his question. He worried that Erin had finally decided to return to her life. He couldn't let her; he just couldn't let her leave. *Mine.* His heart would break. *Mine.* But if that's what she wanted; he would do it. He would track her. But he would do it.

"So, this affects all of you. Just let me get it all out or I don't think I can." They all nodded and waited. A large crease covered Tailor's forehead. He cared for his friend's woman and he worried that something was wrong.

"I've been doing a lot of thinking. I need to make some changes in my life." Joe let out a loud sigh and she looked at him. Her loving eyes swallowed him and watched her with water gathering in her green pools. "My sweet Joe. I'm not going anywhere. You said you wanted me here, well I'm here to stay if you all agree with my whole plan."

Joe let out a long breath and smiled at her. Okay. That was one good step.

"I've decided to sell the majority of my Dryden stock. I am giving each of you equal shares." They all looked shocked, mouths open, gasps. Great effect she thought smiling, I wanted them to look like this.

"No, Erin, no you can't do that!" said Miller.

"No way, baby sis," chimed in Angel.

She held up her hand and surprisingly they all stopped talking.

"It's not up for discussion. It's done." She handed each man an envelope, with only Trak's still left in her hand.

"This is smart don't you see. This way I don't have so many shares that it becomes dangerous to me again, or that I hold all the risk of the company. Now, you can sell your shares if you want to, or you can keep them, I don't care. But they will be evenly distributed to all." She glared in the direction of Sly and he shifted uncomfortably. His face had guilt written on it and she knew he felt he didn't deserve the stocks.

"Sly, sweet, geeky, nerdy Sly. You saved my life. Don't you see that? Some woman will come along one day and she will get a man unlike any other." Sly blushed and she smiled at them all. "Don't you all see that? You all saved my life. Twice!" She gave a nervous laugh and they all smiled.

"Your shares will equal approximately $12.6 million each. Do as you wish with them. Donate it, invest with it, or simply be a majority shareholder." The gasps could be heard around the room and Erin smiled at them.

"I'm not done. I've sold my condo and I'd like to move in here if it's okay with all of you." She blushed looking at Joe and then around the room. "Ummm, if it's not okay, I can find something else." *Oh God, what have I done?*

"Baby sis, it's not up to us," said Miller.

"Yes, it is. You're a family. All of you. What happens to one happens to all. Letting me move in here means changes for you all. Family. All of us. I'm asking to be part of this family, don't you see?"

"Erin, you are family. Don't you know that? You've been family since the day they picked you up in that shithole." Tommy smiled at her and the guys all nodded.

"What kind of changes, baby?" asked Joe

"Well for one, you all start putting the toilet seat down." The collective laugh released all the built-up tension. "But you know there will be other things. I don't want Wilson to leave the house. This is your home too and it's big enough for all of us." Wilson nodded at her and smiled.

"You know I want that, baby girl. You know that we all want that." His big hand swept around the room and all the men nodded in her direction.

"Great! Then the last thing is, I want to work for REAPER." The silence was so startling you could have heard a pin drop. Each man stared at her, and then at their teammates, and then at Joe.

"I think I can be of value here. My skills with science and technology, my computer skills, and even my shooting skills with a little practice, could be valuable." Joe started to say something and again she held up her hand.

"Joe, I know what you're going to say. I won't go on any dangerous missions, nothing you don't approve of. I promise. Look, I love you all, dearly, truly, deep in my heart love you all. But I can't just cook and clean and be happy. I want to feel as though I'm contributing to the business. To the finances."

"Baby, you are contributing," said Joe pulling her onto his lap.

"I know, Joe. I know you think that, but I need to *feel* that. Please let me do this, Joe. All of you. It's all or nothing. That's my offer."

Joe looked at his men and knew what their vote would be.

"Okay, a vote then. All those in favor of Erin as our newest *Junior* teammate say aye." The ayes were resounding and she kissed Joe's cheek.

"Junior huh? Well, I can live with that."

She saw the men's eyes travel across the large windows at the rear of the house and as she looked up, she saw Trak's large frame walking slowly from the direction of his home. The wind was blowing his shoulder-length hair; his head was down, his hands in his pockets. He looked like a man lost.

She leapt off Joe's lap and ran to the door. The men all started to stand, but Joe signaled for them to be seated.

"Let her go," he said softly. "She needs to see him. They have a brother-sister bond like I've never seen. She's been having nightmares that are more like his nightmares. She says she can see what he went through as a child. She sees his sister." Joe shrugged. "I think they both need this."

Erin ran across the patio, her running shoes slapping against the pavement first and then the gravel path. Her black leggings and long sweater blocked some of the cold but not all of it. She needed to know he was okay. She needed to know that Joseph knew how much she cared for him.

He stopped, watching her fly across the path. The smile didn't reach his lips, but his heart skipped a beat at the little woman running towards him. It wasn't passion or lust in her run. It wasn't sex in his heart. Their bond was something so unique, the Navajo word would be *nizhoni*… beautiful.

She stopped in front of him, unsure what to do and when he looked down at her smiling face, he returned her smile and she flung her arms around his waist and laid her head on his chest.

"Where were you? I was so worried about you, Joseph! Please don't leave me like that again. Please!" Her words came out so quickly she felt, rather than heard, his soft rumbling chuckle from his chest.

"Easy little one. I had to think." She pulled back and looked up at him. "I killed your father, Erin. Without remorse. Without thought."

She looked up at her *brother* and saw his dark eyes swirling with pain.

"He wasn't my father, Joseph. You know that. I know you had to kill the General. Someone had to. I saw. And I was glad you did it." He looked shocked and pulled back from her staring into her familiar green eyes. "I knew that you would do it. I knew you would protect me. That's what big brothers do."

"But I didn't protect you. I failed. I let them lead me away from you. My job was to be here."

"No, it was not your fault and we will not go there. I know that you will always be there for me. He would have found a way, Joseph, one way or another. He was crazy, certifiable and I think Christopher was as well."

He nodded, his arm around her shoulder now.

"You've been busy, sister. I have three dozen cookies at my door." She blushed and smiled at him.

"I was worried about you. Please don't leave like that again. I can't explain, Joseph. I love Joe. I'm in love with the Joe. But I need you to be near. Does that make sense?"

He looked at her and looked up toward the house, where crowded around the large windows were all of his brothers. He smiled and looked back down at the tiny woman beside him.

"I know what you mean, sister. I need to be near you as well. It makes me feel human again. It's as if we are blood in some way. I don't know how, but somewhere in our history, we are connected, little one."

She nodded and looked toward the house where he was staring. She waved at the brothers and they all knew they had been caught, only Code and Pigsty in their childish way waved back.

"Come to the house. I have food," she smiled.

He laughed a genuine laugh. One she had never heard from him, and it actually reached his eyes. His large white teeth shone and he grabbed her hand pulling her toward the house.

"With you around, little sister, there is always food." She half pulled, half skipped with Trak to the house and opening the back doors shouted.

"Look who I found!" Still holding his hand, she pulled him inside the house.

Tailor met his old friend and drew him into a man-hug, slapping the smaller man on the back.

"Trak! I'm glad you're back, brother." The other men nodded and Miller, breaking the tension in the room.

"What the fuck, dude!? He's holding her hand and I can't even wink at her."

The men all laughed and Trak quickly let go of her hand, but smiled at her as she sat on the arm of the chair with Joe. She kissed Joe soundly on the lips and the man felt no jealousy at all for his woman and his friend.

Trak looked at the room full of men he considered only his team at one time, suddenly feeling a warmth in his gut knowing they were his brothers.

"It's Joseph." They all looked at him, stillness in the room so overwhelming, so quiet. "My real name is Joseph Redhawk. Oscar Smith doesn't exist."

The men just stood silent until Tailor came forward and reached out a hand.

"Nice to meet you, brother. Billy Joe Bongard, they call me Tailor." Joseph felt the water in his eye and reached for his friend's hand, as he pulled him into a man-hug.

"Fuck, get a room you two!" yelled Bull. The men all laughed and started talking again, the volume escalating considerably.

As the second half started, Erin put out the food and everyone immersed themselves in the game. Although the Redskins lost, a good time was had by all. As she started clearing the plates, Joe stood.

"How about a few beers and some pool at Malones?" Wilson immediately jumped up.

"Damn fine idea! We haven't been there in ages." The group agreed and they all stood. Erin watched the men gather and head toward the door.

"Hey, babe, why don't you freshen up and Trak can bring you. We'll get a few tables and order some appetizers."

She looked at him suspiciously and smiled.

"Oookay. Just give me about thirty minutes."

She looked at Trak and he shrugged his shoulders, continuing to help her clear the food. She knew Joe and he would never want to go to a bar or pool hall without her next to him. Something was definitely up. If they were going off to plan a mission without her, she was going to be seriously pissed off. She placed the last of the dishes in the dishwasher and walked toward the bedroom.

"I'll be ready in a minute," she hollered back. He only nodded and sat patiently on the stool at the bar. His face with its typical void of expression.

When she reappeared about twenty minutes later, she was dressed in worn blue jeans, a soft yellow sweater that accentuated her curves, and worn brown cowboy boots. Her face was clean and fresh with just a little mascara to enhance her eyes and a soft pink lip gloss.

Trak stood and just gave her an approving nod. They left the house and headed toward Malones in Trak's pick-up truck.

"I've only been here once," she said looking at Trak. "It seems like a nice place."

He nodded.

"The team likes to unwind there." He offered no other words and she knew that their ride would be in an understanding silence. Erin saw the familiar Hummers and SUVs parked in Malones lot and she exited the truck with Trak. He held open the door for her and gave her a slight nod and pushed at her lower back. When she looked up at him, he had a half-grin that was genuine and warm.

She eyed him curiously, but continued through the front doors of Malones. Inside the small enclosed coat room, were six dozen roses in a variety of colors. She turned to look at Trak and he shrugged his shoulders as if to say 'I have no clue,' but he nodded for her to continue through the next door.

Opening to the main room of the pub, she came face-to-face with the entire team. On each table were more flowers, dozens of heart-shaped balloons were hanging from the rafters. Plates of chocolates were left on every table. The men all stood, their big frames leaning against the bar and Erin, still open-mouthed, stared at their gleaming smiles. Other patrons had been moved to tables further back. A few people were at the opposite end of the bar, but Erin's eyes were only on Joe.

From the backroom, Joe walked forward with a single rose in his hand. When he reached her, she started to speak.

"Joe, what..." he held a finger to her lips and kissed her sweetly.

"My turn," he said softly. He looked at his brothers for strength. He could walk into a firefight or a shitstorm and not bat an eye. But standing in front of this woman, he felt as though he would collapse.

"Erin, you stole my heart in a cave in Afghanistan. How many men could ever say that?"

The men leaning against the bar all raised their hands.

"We could."

"Yep, me too."

"Me three." He gave them a loving dirty look and they all quieted. Erin let out a small girly giggle and felt her cheeks flush.

"As I was saying. I fell in love with you from that moment in the cave and I haven't looked back. You are the light to my darkness. You are my heart and soul and I know that I cannot live another day without knowing that you are mine. Mine. Do you understand?" She nodded, still trying to breathe without passing out. Joe knelt before her and reached inside his pocket for a small blue box.

"I love you, Erin. Will you do me the honor of becoming my wife?" he stopped and looked back at the bar, "and their sister?" The men all stood straight, each holding their breath, waiting for the answer.

She let out a laugh that filled their hearts with joy.

"Yes, Yes, Yes! I will be your wife and their sister. All of them!" Joe slipped the ring on her finger and picked her up in his arms and kissed her soundly.

The men all clapped behind them and as Joe let her slide from his arms, each man came forward and hugged her, kissing her forehead or cheek. As they all grabbed their drinks, Trak stood at the end of the bar with his iced tea. She walked toward him and gave him her loving, sister hug around his waist. He kissed the top of her head and smiled.

"Joseph," she said softly, "will you do me the honor of walking me down the aisle?"

The men in the room stilled and they all turned to look at the dark man standing straight and the curvy auburn-haired warrior. His eyes filled with water, but all he could do was nod to her, and he pulled her close again.

Breaking the silence once again, Miller shouted.

"What the fuck, dude! He gets another hug!"

The men all laughed and in unison, raising their glasses, they shouted.

"We like her!"

EPILOGUE

For a Sunday night the pub was a happening place and everyone gave congratulations to the couple. People were eating, drinking and generally having a great time. Erin excused herself and retreated to the restroom. Standing at the sink, she washed her hands and checked her hair and face. She noticed the pink in her cheeks glowing against the porcelain of the rest of her face, her eyes were bright and shining, and on her left hand, the huge diamond with sapphire accents on either side glimmered in the light. She was so content and happy she let a small giggle escape her lips.

"Congratulations," said a small voice beside her.

She jumped slightly, startled that she hadn't seen the woman.

"Thank you. It's a bit overwhelming."

The woman behind Erin was leaning against the tiled wall as if she might fall down. Her long blonde hair braided to one side and fell over one shoulder, falling nearly to her waist. It was so beautiful, Erin wanted to touch it. Her startling eyes are what caught Erin's attention. The bright amethyst color was so stunning. Her full red lips were cracked and dry, as though she were dehydrated. Erin noticed her tattered jeans that hugged her small frame. She was tall, taller than Erin's five-foot-eight, but she was thin, other than the curve of her full breasts. But it was the sad look on the woman's face that made Erin concerned and then she saw the marks at her throat, her eyes instantly jumped.

"Are you okay?" she asked. "The men I work with can help if you're in trouble. Believe me, they're experts."

She looked at Erin and bit her lower lip, water filling her eyes.

"No, no thank you. I don't think… I'm fine. Really. Well, congratulations again."

She started to leave the room and Erin reached for her hand.

"Please, take our card. Call me if you need anything. My name is Erin. I promise you we can help you. You have to trust someone sometime." Erin lifted her ring finger on her left hand and wiggled it. "I did and I got more than I could have ever dreamed of in return."

The woman took the card and reached out her hand to Erin's waiting one.

"Lauren. Nice to meet you, Erin. I'll think about it. But, well, I'll think about it."

She nodded and the women walked out together. The men all looked in Erin's direction, smiling and then something more, something predatory. The tall blonde standing next to Erin, half slid behind her, almost hiding. Erin noticed immediately and gave a warning glare to the men. She could feel Lauren's shudder and the fear was coming off of her so fast Erin could sense it down to her very soul. This woman was in serious trouble and she definitely was afraid of men. Judging by the marks at her throat, Erin knew exactly what type of trouble she was in.

"Don't worry, they would never hurt a woman. Ever. I promise you. They're all like my brothers." The girl doubted that all of these men were her brothers. The only thing they had in common was their size, but other than that, nothing. "Really, why don't you let us help you? I know you're in trouble, I can feel it.

Lauren looked around the room again and shook her head. Then her eyes moved to the end of the bar and noticed the tall, muscled, dark-haired man. His forearms were massive peeking out from his long-sleeved shirt, the sleeves had been pushed up just enough for her to see the ridges of muscle. His hand wrapped around a glass of tea, his fingers long, beautifully strong-looking, and she swallowed hard.

His eyes bore into hers and she felt herself blush. He hadn't said anything, he had only looked at her and her face heated. She didn't need this now. She didn't want this now. His gaze continued to burn into her, but he made no move at all. He just stood there staring at her.

He couldn't believe the vision standing next to Erin. She was taller than baby sis. Probably close to five-feet-ten. He liked that. Her long blonde hair looked like spun gold and her eyes; her eyes were unlike anything he had ever seen. They weren't blue. He could tell that from where he was standing on the other side of the damn room. They were violet. Purple. Purple eyes.

She will have eyes of amethyst my son.

He felt her fear in his soul and he yearned to grasp her hand and pull her to him. The glimpse of the dark marks on her neck made his fingers squeeze tighter on his glass, nearly cracking it beneath his grip.

"I have to leave. I need to leave. I'm sorry, Erin, but thank you for being so nice. I hope you're happy." And without another word she left the pub, no jacket, no bag, into the cold November wind, and headed into the street.

Erin's gaze rose and watched as Trak followed the slender woman out of the building. Interesting, she thought, very interesting. Joe came up from behind her, kissing her neck.

"Who was that, baby?"

"Someone who needs our help, but won't take it yet," she said softly.

Joe looked back at the door watching Trak's retreating back.

"Should we follow?" he asked. Erin shook her head and turned in his arms.

"No, I think she needs to think. But she had marks on her neck, Joe. She was scared and thin and dirty. She had no coat, no bag, nothing. I know that fear. I've felt it." She could barely get the words out of her mouth.

Joe kissed her head and squeezed her tight against him.

"Everything alright, sis?" asked Miller. She gave a huge sigh and looked up at the big man.

"Yes! Everything is wonderful! Alright boys – we have a wedding to plan!" There were groans and grunts and she slapped a few of them on the arms, but in her heart, she knew that this wedding would be what she had always wanted. Her family and the man of her dreams.

EXCERPT for LAUREN'S WARRIOR

The beatings started almost immediately after refusing to have sex with Trent. They only dated for a few weeks, what would make a man think that a woman would just jump into bed with him? Raised to love herself and her body, Lauren wasn't going to just give it to anyone. Her grandmother always said that saving yourself wasn't old-fashioned, it was respectful of yourself and the man that you would spend the rest of your life with. God, she missed her grandmother right now.

Her father died when she was only twelve, killed by a drunk driver, but she and her grandmother became a team. Her mother was there physically, but not really. Life had taken her too soon as well, breast cancer in Lauren's junior year of college.

It attacked her body without remorse and took her mother far too soon. Perhaps that's why she started dating Trent, she needed something to distract her from her pain.

She should have known after the first incident. She should have left then, but she hadn't. He had been very possessive and overbearing during their dates. Even on the first date, he held her tightly around the waist, too tightly. She had been so uncomfortable at one point, she literally extricated herself from him and asked for some space. He looked as though he was going to hit her then, but he didn't, he just sweetly replied, "Of course." She wasn't sure why she had agreed on a second date. Boredom? Maybe, but that didn't excuse taking him back after that.

He made the decisions on their dates – about dinner, what she could wear, where she could go and with whom, which was usually nowhere and with no one. He was from one of the most influential families in the country – money, means, and an expectation of their men. When she refused to give up her virginity until marriage, he had become beyond angry.

He broke the lamps that her grandmother had given her for her first apartment and stormed out of the room calling her a cocktease and a bitch. He threw curses at her that made her sick to her stomach, and in fact had made her vomit.

When he returned, of course, as usual he was kind, sweet and apologized over and over again. She always took him back. Why had she always taken him back? *Because you're stupid, that's why, Lauren. Because you're not loveable and no man will ever want you.* That's what she had told herself. That's what he made her believe.

"*You should be grateful that I do come back, Lauren. I mean I'm not even sure why the fuck I do it! You're not putting out. That little pussy of yours is so tight no one will want it. It's not like you're something I want to take home to my family. I mean look at you! You're fucking eyes give me the creeps, you're so tall you look like Big Bird, and other than your tits you have no shape at all.*"

She cried for hours after that tirade. She wanted to scream out, "Then STOP coming around!" She had been scared that he actually might stop coming around, and where would that leave her? She really was like Big Bird – yellow hair and all legs.

With both of her parents dead and her grandmother now in an assisted living center, Lauren had no one she could turn to for help. She had finished her master's program on political science at the University of Georgia and had wanted to get a job in Washington DC, but Trent would not allow it. He was Atlanta born and bred and that's where they would be going.

When she tried to leave, he hit her again, but this time when he returned it wasn't to apologize, it was to beat her again and again until she begged him to stop. Except he didn't, he took delight in kicking her, punching her face, pulling her hair, he didn't care.

He left her for a few hours, screaming at her to clean up and take a shower. She had smelled the other woman on him that time. The cheap perfume, the lipstick marks on his chest and the bile rose so quickly she thought she would vomit on him.

When he returned, her bruised and battered body was curled in a ball on the bed, barely able to breathe for the damage done to her ribs. He was drunk or high, she couldn't tell which, and when he tried to rape her, she grabbed her bedside clock and smashed it against his head. He rolled to the floor moaning and bleeding, slurring curse words at her.

She didn't hesitate. She pulled on her jeans and sweatshirt, threw what little clothes she had in her duffel bag and grabbed her keys. She didn't even bother to shut the door. She just drove and drove, until she couldn't drive any more.

When she finally felt like she was far enough away, she pulled into the closest ATM and withdrew as much money as allowed. She would find a branch of her own bank when she was able to. She didn't have much, a few thousand dollars, but it would be good enough until she could find work.

Unfortunately, her bad luck didn't seem to stop. While eating in a fast-food restaurant outside of a small town in South Carolina her wallet had been stolen from the seat of her car. The only thing she had done right, was to put $200 in the armrest of her older model Honda Civic. That's all she had. $200 to her name. No job. No ID. No credit cards.

She found herself in a small town north of DC when she was so hungry and tired, she could barely see the road any longer. She had been sleeping in her car and desperately needed a shower. When she had pushed her way through the door of the pub, it had been relatively quiet. The pub was warm and inviting and the bartender looked her up and down and must have taken pity on her.

"You need something, hun?" he had said.

"Can I just get a glass of water and maybe some crackers?" she asked quietly.

"Why don't you have a seat at one of our back tables. I've got a private event happening up here in a little while, but I'll grab you some of Martha's soup. It'll really stick to your ribs."

Her eyes grew wide, and the man could see the panic in her face. He held his hand up,

"No worries, it's on the house." She simply nodded and shuffled to the back of the pub, where thankfully there was only one other table with an older man and woman, just finishing their dinner.

When the bartender brought her the hearty white bean soup, she nearly shook with the need for nourishment. He placed a basket full of crackers and warm bread in front of her, along with a glass of water and a steaming cup of coffee.

"You enjoy and let me know if you need anything."

"Sir, you wouldn't happen to need any help around here would you? I'm a good waitress, I have experience."

He looked her up and down carefully.

"Are you on drugs? High?"

Her big eyes looked shocked and her mouth formed an "O".

"Oh my gosh, no sir! I've just had some bad luck. My wallet was stolen, so I won't have any ID until I can get to a bank or something tomorrow. But no – never done any drugs or alcohol."

He looked at her again, seeing exactly what he thought. A scared, abused woman who needed a chance.

"I could use some help on my three to eleven shift. Let's see how you do for a week and if things work out, I have a room upstairs where you can stay."

Her eyes filled with tears and she smiled up at him and nodded as he walked away. She ate in silence thinking about her situation and she was so lost in her own misery, she hadn't realized how full the pub had become until she almost felt boxed in by people. She needed to leave. One more night in her car and tomorrow was Monday. She could go to the bank and get the rest of her money out and hopefully they could access her safe deposit box in Georgia and get her other things that she would need to get her ID. Once she had that, she would try and get a new license. She couldn't get replacement credit cards because she had no home yet, but she definitely wasn't worried about that right now.

She would call Miss Greta at the diner she had worked at and let her know she wouldn't be returning. It wasn't that great of a job anyway. Drunken college kids wanting late-night food and lecherous old men wanting to cop a feel. She hated the job. She jumped at the loud round of applause and cheers and decided that now might be a good time to exit. She headed toward the restroom to wash up and relieve herself one last time for the night.

As she reached the door, she looked to her right and saw the front room of the pub was filled with huge, muscled men, and one small woman. It scared her to no end for herself and for the woman. What could she be thinking being out there with all those men?

Lauren finished and stood in front of the mirror washing her face and hands. She took her matted, dirty hair, and braided it over her shoulder, leaning against the wall, closing her eyes for just a moment.

The woman who had gone into the stall behind her came out and was lost in thought at the sink. She had been the one in the middle of all those men. She looked nice, she looked happy. Happy. Would Lauren ever be happy again?

"Congratulations," she said in a small voice.

The woman jumped slightly, startled that she hadn't seen the woman.

"Thank you. It's a bit overwhelming."

Erin looked at the woman behind her, leaning against the tiled wall as if she might fall down. Her long blonde hair braided to one side fell over one shoulder, falling just below her breast. Her startling eyes are what caught Erin's attention. The bright amethyst color was so beautiful. Her full red lips were cracked and dry, as though she were dehydrated. Erin noticed her tattered jeans that hugged her small frame. She was tall, taller than Erin's five-foot-eight, but she was thin, other than the curve of her full breasts. But it was the sad look on the woman's face that made Erin concerned and then she saw the marks at her throat.

"Are you okay?" she asked. "The men I work with can help if you're in trouble. Believe me, they're experts."

She looked at Erin and bit her lower lip, water filling her eyes.

"No, no thank you. I don't think, no, I'm fine. Really. Well, congratulations again."

She started to leave the room and Erin reached for her hand.

"Please, take our card. Call me if you need anything. My name is Erin. I promise you we can help you. You have to trust someone sometime." Erin lifted her ring finger on her left hand and wiggled it. "I did and I got more than I could have ever dreamed of in return."

The woman took the card and reached out her hand to Erin's waiting one.

"Lauren. Nice to meet you, Erin. I'll think about it. But... well, I'll think about it." She nodded and the women walked out together. The men all looked in Erin's direction, smiling and then something more, something predatory. The tall blonde standing next to Erin, half slid behind her, almost as if she were trying to hide. Erin noticed immediately and gave a warning glare to the men. She could feel Lauren's shudder and the fear was coming off of her so fast Erin sensed it down to her very soul. This woman was in serious trouble and she definitely was afraid of men. Judging by the marks at her throat, Erin knew exactly what type of trouble she was in.

"Don't worry, they would never hurt a woman. Ever. I promise you. They're all like my brothers." The girl doubted that all of these men were her brothers. The only thing they had in common was their size, but other than that, nothing. "Really, why don't you let us help you? I know you're in trouble, I can feel it."

Lauren looked around the room again and shook her head. Then her eyes moved to the end of the bar and noticed the tall, muscled, dark-haired man. His forearms were massive peeking out from his long-sleeved shirt, the sleeves had been pushed up just enough for her to see the ridges of muscle. His hand wrapped around a glass of tea, his fingers long, beautifully strong-looking, and she swallowed hard.

His eyes bore into hers and she felt herself blush. He hadn't said anything, he had only looked at her and her face heated. She didn't need this now. She didn't want this now. His gaze continued to burn into her, but he made no move at all. He just stood there staring at her.

He couldn't believe the vision standing next to Erin. She was taller than baby sis. Probably close to five feet ten. He liked that. She would fit well with his six-foot-two.

Her long blonde hair looked like spun gold and her eyes; her eyes were unlike anything he had ever seen. They weren't blue. He could tell that from where he was standing on the other side of the damn room. They were violet. Purple. Purple eyes. *She will have eyes of amethyst my hatsóí ashkiígíí*. He felt her fear in his soul and he yearned to grasp her hand and pull her to him. The glimpse of the dark marks on her neck made him squeeze tighter on his glass, nearly cracking it beneath his grip.

"I have to leave. I need to leave. I'm sorry, Erin, but thank you for being so nice. I hope you're happy." And without another word she left the pub, no jacket, no bag, into the cold November wind, and headed into the street.

ABOUT THE AUTHOR

Mary Kennedy is the mother of two adult children and grandmother to two. She works full-time at a job she loves, and writing is her outlet. She lives in north Dallas and enjoys traveling, reading, and cooking. Her passion for assisting veteran and veteran causes comes from a strong military family.

Dear Readers,

I love hearing from you and encourage you to visit my website http://insatiableink.squarespace.com. Leave me your thoughts and ideas on new books or expanding on characters. It's also a safe space to give your own feelings, similar to those of the characters. I look forward to hearing from you and hope you enjoy other books in my collections.

Explore... and enjoy!